STARS

of

TWILIGHT FAIR

a sweet Victorian romance

K. LYN SMITH

Paperback ISBN: 978-1-7376579-9-6
Davenwood Press, USA

"Her eyes as stars of twilight fair"

- William Wordsworth,
Perfect Woman

CHAPTER ONE

The trouble with perfection is that it requires tending.
And a careful attention to one's loops.
—From the private journal of Miss Amelia Thorne

SUMMERFIELD COTTAGE
LAKE WINDERMERE, 1852

MISS AMELIA THORNE leaned against a plush velvet cushion in her cousin's window seat, stockinged feet tucked beneath her and a volume of poetry tucked before her. Arthur's *Advice to Young Ladies on the Exercise of Proper Behavior* was secured against the emerald-green cushion, a precautionary measure if not an earnest one. With Aunt Mary, one never knew when the appearance of decorous intent might be required.

Across the room, her cousin was at her dressing table while her maid pinned another loop into place. Dipping a finger into a small pot, Octavia dabbed the merest bit of color onto her lips. "Do you think Mama will notice?" she said before pressing her lips together.

Amelia snorted but refrained from comment. None was necessary, and Octavia wiped at the cosmetic with a cloth as another loop went up. Though Amelia enjoyed her solitude at Summerfield, she was pleased to have her cousin returned from London these past weeks, if only for the entertainment she provided.

"Are you certain you won't join us on our calls?" Octavia said. "You know the cook at Stonecroft makes a fine almond cake."

A pair of warblers flew past the open window, their distinctive *chiff-chaff* song cheerful in the sun-warmed air. Amelia returned her attention to her book. "There's no need," she replied.

"You will never regain Society's good opinion if you keep yourself tucked away," Octavia said. "How do you mean to go on during Mama's house party? Certainly, you won't forgo Lady Staveley's ball. You know she looks forward to Mama's guests filling out her numbers."

Amelia lowered her book, marking her place with one finger, and eyed her cousin's waiting expression in the mirror. "Octavia," she said with what felt like heroic patience. "There are so many false assumptions in that pile of nonsense, I'm uncertain which to address first."

Octavia had a rare talent for speaking complete sentences with only an elegant motion of her finely-shaped brow. *Give it a go anyway*, her brow suggested.

"Firstly," Amelia said, "I take exception to the phrase, 'tucked away.' You know very well that Lord Byron and I walk the fells every day, often two or three times." Lord Byron lifted his head from where he'd been napping in a spot of sun. Seeing his attendance wasn't required for a crumb of biscuit, he lowered it again with a sigh. "And," Amelia added, "I go into Emerson's on the regular."

Octavia's brows shifted. *Hmm, yes, the bookshop. A veritable* hive *of Society. Pray, continue.*

"Secondly," Amelia said, "you and I both know neither your mother's heart nor her house party would survive my scandalous presence, and I've no wish to make you an orphan."

"I'd still have Papa," Octavia said reasonably. "But do go on. I suppose there's to be a thirdly?"

"*Thirdly,* my thoughts haven't changed. I still find I've no use for Society's opinion, good or otherwise. It's too self-serving by half and not the least inclined to original thought."

Octavia released her brows as Jane fastened a final loop. "Well, of course it's unoriginal, dearest. It's *Society*."

Amelia suppressed a shudder at the word. She and Society had no liking for one another. Indeed, whenever Amelia thought she might finally emerge from the shadow of The Great Disgrace, the news sheets resurrected the story of the Poisoned Thorne to entertain their readers all over again. Her father had been wrong years before, to think it would blow over in a fortnight. It was a bittersweet truth that he'd not lived to know it.

Octavia, oblivious of Amelia's thoughts, continued her campaign. "As much as I value my own conversation, surely, you must desire better company than mine."

"If I desire company, I've only to go as far as the Vicarage's library." (That statement was not as pious as it sounded, the Vicarage being the name given to her father's cozy old hunting lodge at the edge of the property.)

"Never say you're still reading that dreadful poetry," Octavia said with a frown for her mirror.

"Dreadful! Mr. Keats' verse is transcendent, and it's a cold heart that doesn't feel anything on reading Percy Shelley. And Mr. Wordsworth..." Amelia paused, as there were no words adequate to the task of describing Mr. Wordsworth's poetry.

She and her father had spent long hours debating their poet laureate's choice of phrase here, or his meter there. Indeed, if ever she could procure a copy of *The Prelude*, she might consider her life complete. But alas, the tourists bought up every printing faster than Mr. Emerson could receive them. It was *de rigueur* to read Wordsworth while on holiday in the Lake District.

"You know how Mama feels about poetry," her cousin reminded her.

"Which I should think is its own recommendation."

"A persuasive point. But your poets are all dead, and their verse is so *old*."

"Just listen to this," Amelia said, turning to Shelley's *Mont Blanc*. "'The everlasting universe of things flows through the mind, and rolls its rapid waves, now dark, now glittering, now reflecting gloom'—"

"Everlasting universe… gloom, yes," Octavia said with a wave of one hand. And then, with single-minded persistence, she pressed, "But if your hesitation to join Mama's party is on account of your wardrobe, you need only say the word. Jane's ever so clever with a needle and thread. She can take in some of my gowns for you. Heaven knows I've plenty enough as it is."

Amelia cast a frowning glance at her own plain-but-perfectly-serviceable grey skirts as Jane nodded in agreement.

"Or you could allow Sir Frederick to have his way with you. He'd have you outfitted with a proper wardrobe in no time." Octavia's tone was bright, as if the idea had only just occurred to her, but Amelia knew her cousin's tricks better than that.

She sniffed. "I cannot see myself frequenting a male dressmaker, and I'm surprised your mother allows it."

"One does what one must in the name of fashion," Octavia said in perfect imitation of Amelia's Aunt Mary. Then, squaring her shoulders, she added, "For a Scandalous Female, Cousin, you are depressingly prudish."

"I am not." Amelia's protest came easily, but it lacked heat. It was little more than a reflex, left over from a time when she'd had a care for what others thought of her. But that time had passed. Her irritation with the news sheets notwithstanding, her exile from Society had had a rather liberating effect, like a corset unlaced. With no husband to catch or calls to make, she did what she wanted and said what she thought—within reason, of course. Amelia wondered that more ladies didn't think to create scandals for themselves.

"Then you'll do it?" Octavia said. "You'll allow Sir Frederick to outfit you?"

Amelia cast a derisive glance at the yards of linen frothing about Octavia's form. *Four* petticoats by Amelia's count. "And be obliged to wear piles and piles of underpinnings again? No, thank you. Besides, I've enough gowns of my own."

"Your gowns are five years out of fashion. Much can happen with a sleeve in five years."

There was no time to respond to that as the distinctive swish of silk could be heard in the hall, and Octavia's mother soon glided in. Lady Worth's wide *au courant* skirts must have required *five* petticoats, at the very least, to achieve such fullness.

"Octavia," Aunt Mary said briskly, "we must hurry if we're to visit with the Crenshaws and the Archers before we call at Stonecroft." Then, spying Amelia in the window, she added, "Oh, you're here as well." She drew the words out, her lips flattening into a narrow ribbon of displeasure.

Amelia tucked her stockinged feet more securely beneath her skirts and away from her aunt's censure. Diplomatic relations between Amelia and the sovereign nation of Aunt Mary were tenuous at best, and there was no sense tipping the balance with unshod feet. She might be liberated, but that didn't mean she'd lost all reason.

Uncle George still held the purse strings of her inheritance. He would continue to manage Summerfield for her until she married (an unlikely event) or reached the age of five and twenty (a much more probable occurrence in a year's time).

It was an unusual arrangement as Amelia had passed her legal majority some years before, but it was the arrangement her father had made and one to which she was resigned.

"Mama," Octavia said, "why don't we simply begin at Stonecroft, if that is your objective?"

"We can't *begin* at Stonecroft." Aunt Mary lifted a hand to her temple as if warding off a headache brought on by one too many explanations. "One doesn't *begin* at Stonecroft if one wishes to leave a lasting impression."

Lord Byron's ears twitched, his little white head resting on his paws, dark eyes flicking from Octavia to her mother and back again.

"I've just been trying to coax Amelia to visit Sir Frederick so she might have some new things to wear for the house party," Octavia said, to which her mother gave a strangled, choking sound. Amelia was tempted to let Sir Frederick outfit her to his heart's content, if only so she might hear her aunt's reaction again.

"Amelia will do no such thing," Aunt Mary said when she'd recovered. Then, recalling who owned the house in which her family resided, she tempered this with, "Perhaps, once the scandal has had a chance to lose its potency…"

"Mama, it's been five *years*."

"Don't be impertinent, Octavia. It serves no one. No, Amelia knows it's best this way."

Amelia returned her attention to her book. "I would rather read anyway."

Aunt Mary looked more sharply in Amelia's direction. "You are *not* reading that dreadful poetry again, are you? It's nothing but immoral tripe meant to subvert decent values and lead the weak astray."

Amelia lifted her poetry, now tucked securely behind Arthur's improving tract.

Her aunt read the cover aloud. "'Advice to Young Ladies on the Exercise of Proper Behavior.'" Disapproval creased her forehead. How could she object to such an improving title? It was precisely the sort of tract Aunt Mary was always shoving at her.

"I can't like the presumption of the Americans," Aunt Mary said finally, "to go about offering advice to young ladies as if *they* have all the answers."

Arthur was an American? Amelia made a note to be more diligent in choosing her schemes going forward.

"But," her aunt continued with a sigh, "I suppose Arthur is better than nothing. Certainly, what he writes must be preferable to the drivel these poets have the audacity to pen. *That's* what puts such scandalous notions as duels and elopements into the heads of young people."

Amelia opened her mouth then closed it again. Correcting her aunt would serve no purpose.

With a pinch of her lips, Aunt Mary challenged, "Well? What lesson have you taken from your reading today?"

Amelia lowered her gaze to the volume behind her poetry. By some bit of random fortune, it was opened to a chapter entitled "Improvement of the Mind," but Arthur's first sentence did not inspire confidence in her strategy.

For a young lady to indulge overmuch in poetry and novel-reading is a very serious evil.

Amelia checked her frown. She'd meant to appease her aunt with something unobjectionable, but that was too much.

"Come now," Aunt Mary said briskly. "Surely, Arthur has some advice of value."

"Yes, Cousin," Octavia tossed out with a grin. "Do tell us what guidance you've found in your little book."

Amelia slid her poetry lower. Resignation dulled her voice as she read aloud from the middle of Arthur's page. "'The worthy maiden does not attempt cleverness, but exercises reserve in all things.'"

Aunt Mary sucked in her cheek, considering.

"Yes," she said finally. "I suppose that's a point to the Americans. A young lady can't be too reserved. You'd do well to heed Arthur's words." Then she consulted the pendant watch hanging round her neck and warned Amelia's cousin, "Five minutes, Octavia."

And with that, Aunt Mary sailed from the room. Amelia swung her stockinged feet to the floor and reached beneath the cushion for her slippers as Lord Byron stirred himself.

"A worthy maiden?" Octavia said as Amelia slid her feet into her shoes. "At least now, Cousin, we know what you are not."

Amelia collected Shelley and Arnold, tucking the former into the latter. "Though I do try," she said. Lord Byron's nails tap-tapped on the wooden floor as they left Octavia's room, and Amelia thought they made a rather nice, theatrical exit.

———

AMELIA'S UNCLE, SIR George Worth, summoned her to his study later that day. Or rather, he summoned her to Amelia's study, which he'd taken as his own for the duration of his guardianship. That the irony wasn't lost on either of them was of little comfort.

Amelia greeted him from across her father's old desk. "Uncle George."

"Amelia," he said in his gruff manner. Then, indicating the chair before the desk, he added, "Please, sit."

She sat. He eyed her for a moment, hands steepled before him. "Mr. Cowell tells me you've inquired about planting German cabbages in place of turnips in the north field."

Robert Cowell, and his father before him, had overseen Summerfield's farm for longer than Amelia's family had owned the property. The land was profitable under his management, and the younger Mr. Cowell wasn't so set in his father's ways that he wasn't willing to entertain Amelia's suggestions, so long as those suggestions were presented as "inquiries."

"I have," she said. "The cabbage is called kohlrabi. The Royal Agricultural Society reports success with the variety and that it produces a firmer bulb and fatter sheep than the Swedish turnips. But if it's to be done to good effect in the spring, the fallows must be cleared now."

Sir George rubbed his shiny forehead, buffing it with his sleeve and closing his eyes on a sigh. Finally, he looked up. "Do you have the Society's report?" he asked, as if Amelia walked about with agricultural journals tucked in her pockets instead of poetry.

She went to a shelf across the room and plucked a volume from it. "I've marked the page," she said.

Her uncle thumbed to the article and read in silence while she waited. Finally, he looked up. "I can't deny it has promise. Do you think this... this kohl-rabi... would serve for my fields in Surrey?"

"I believe it could do well there." It wasn't the first time he'd sought her advice for the management of his own crops back at Ambervale. Though crop rotations weren't half as romantic as sonnets, Amelia liked to think she had a fair grasp of the fundamentals. She must if she would have the management of Summerfield one day.

Sir George rubbed his forehead once more. "Sometimes, I wonder who, precisely, is overseeing whom in this arrangement."

———

AUNT MARY WAS consulting with a fresh-faced maid at the base of the stairs when Amelia left her uncle. On seeing her niece's approach, she dismissed the girl. "Amelia," she hissed.

"Yes, Aunt?"

"As my house party approaches, I wish to ensure we are of the same mind."

"I've no intention of joining your guests," Amelia reassured her. This was the only topic on which she and her aunt would ever agree. The very idea of making polite conversation with her aunt's guests, of suffering their judgment and whispered speculations, caused a lump to settle in her stomach. Why anyone would willingly endure such a trial was beyond her.

Aunt Mary eyed her with suspicion for a long beat before saying, "Octavia will make a splendid match soon. It's only a matter of time, and I've no wish for any… unpleasantness… from the past to impede her success."

"Nor do I."

"Then we are agreed? You will remain out of sight for the duration?"

"We are agreed."

Her aunt gave a single, rigid nod of acceptance before adding, "We've had a late addition to the guest list—a London gentleman. It's fortuitous, really, as Mrs. Lawson means to bring her niece with them, and now our numbers are even again. But I'll need you to prepare another invitation. I wish to send it straightaway."

Amelia held her snort of irritation. While her presence would sully her aunt's party, Amelia's penmanship was fine enough to write out the invitations on her aunt's best paper. But she'd do it, if only for her cousin's benefit, and then she and Lord Byron would escape to the Vicarage for an afternoon with Keats and Shelley.

"Give me the direction," she said.

Her aunt took a paper from her pocket and passed it to her. "And mind your loops, Amelia. They've grown a bit too spirited of late."

"Mind my loops. Of course."

CHAPTER TWO

Babies, like science, can be rather messy.
Less explosive one might hope, but messy, nonetheless.
—From the scientific journals of Mr. Edmund Corbyn

REDSTONE HALL, KENT

EDMUND CORBYN COULDN'T say his grandfather's summons had come as a surprise, but he should have been better prepared. He should have affianced himself by now, or at the very least, made firm strides in that direction. He ought to have had a short list of eligible young ladies, all of whom were properly turned out and beyond their Queen's reproach. As it was, he'd arrived at Redstone Hall in the dark of night, a bachelor still and without a single name to his list.

Now, he stood in the quiet of the breakfast room and watched the dawn break over the eastern corner of the estate. He'd dismissed the lone footman from his post near the sideboard, and the only sounds to be heard were the distant goings-on of the household staff below stairs.

Blue, his elderly wolfhound, nudged Edmund's thigh with her large head. He gave her ears a stroke and she angled her gaze toward him, one eye dark as pitch and the other light blue.

"What do you make of that view?" Edmund asked her. He'd always enjoyed the spectacle of a new day pulling into Kent. It came from far off, like a distant train, huffing and chugging along its track, vibrant blues and purples and pinks stretching along the horizon like steam clouds until the day screamed into the station in a blaze of golden warmth and light.

What he wouldn't give to capture the colors with his camera, but the science hadn't caught up with his aspirations. And anyway, today's view lacked much of the vibrancy he was accustomed to seeing. He had his grim mood to thank, he was certain, for the day's pale, muted appearance.

Odd though it was to admit, emotions came to him in degrees of light and color. Boredom cast everything in a dim grey shroud, and grief shadowed the very air. When his heart was full, there was a sharp vibrancy to his surroundings, and when it was heavy, as it was today, colors had a pale, watery quality to them. It made the business of photography, which relied on an accurate accounting of light, rather tricky.

He set his cup on the breakfast table with more force than he'd intended, and coffee sloshed into the saucer. Blue, sensing his mood, nudged him more firmly. When her heavy tail threatened a porcelain bust on a nearby pedestal, he guided her to a place at the hearth where she could lounge with less danger to his grandmother's fine things. As he turned, he caught the eye of the first Earl of Ashford, looking down grandly from his gilt-framed perch above the sideboard.

Eadmund St. James, with his sable-trimmed cloak and jeweled scabbard, had been a large man with thick black brows in proportion to his impressive bulk. The first earl had received his title during King John's time, and an unbroken course of Ashford earls—over six hundred years of them—had followed to line the upper gallery of Redstone Hall. A gallery that ended with Edmund's grandfather, now the fourteenth Earl of Ashford.

Edmund rubbed his jaw as the weight of the first earl's stare bore down on him. He'd spent many a youthful holiday at Redstone Hall, laughing and teasing his sisters and being teased in return. Debating matters of physics with his father and grandfather. Sharing tales of his school successes with his parents and explaining his failures. Thankfully, as he disliked disappointing either of them, there had been more of the former than the latter. And Eadmund St. James had watched it all with his inscrutable gaze.

Edmund's grandfather, who was also christened Edmund, had once explained the meaning of their shared name. It derived from "ead," meaning wealth, and "mond," protector. Edmund thought that could only mean they were meant to be wealthy protectors, but his grandfather explained they were also protectors of wealth. Of the first earl's legacy.

But Edmund's grandfather had only Edmund's mother for his child and no sons. The earldom's letters patent stipulated the title and entailed properties must pass "from the holder of the first creation to heirs male of the body lawfully begotten." Though lawfully begotten, Edmund's mother was not an "heir male of the body," and therefore, neither was Edmund.

The fourteenth earl had long comforted himself with the knowledge that the earldom would continue through his younger brother and his brother's sons. He'd set his daughter up with property and accounts of her own, and none of them had worried overmuch about the succession. But then, nearly four years ago, all the heirs had died within a depressingly short span of months, plunging the earldom into dangerous territory.

Since then, his grandfather's solicitor had, at great expense, endeavored to find another heir. When that produced no results, and as his grandfather's age advanced, the fourteenth earl petitioned Queen Victoria to make Edmund his heir. Such an amendment to the letters patent could only be accomplished at the pleasure of their monarch, and she had taken the position that Edmund must marry first, and marry well, to set the title up for the future. Barring that, the earldom, and all its entailments, would revert to the crown upon Ashford's death.

One need not stretch the imagination to its limits to conjure Queen Victoria's notion of a suitable bride, as their Queen had been very explicit in that regard. A young lady of genteel breeding, Church of England morals and good family lines. A spotless reputation without any hint of scandal. Wealth was not a requirement as the earldom was flush, but certainly, no actresses or enterprising widows need apply.

The significance of Edmund's new, elevated role as potential heir was not lost on him. He felt a high measure of pride that his family would rely on him in such a way, but also some private degree of alarm, as he knew nothing about being an earl. He would learn, though. He would not allow the legacy of six centuries to crumble to dust.

The sounds of a fussy baby came from the corridor beyond the breakfast room, and Edmund turned away from Eadmund St. James with more relief than such a noise warranted. Seconds later, his oldest sister appeared in the arched doorway with her infant son Harry in her arms. His nephew's face was flushed and tear-stained, and Aster's own eyes were red-rimmed. It was a fair debate as to which of them appeared the most done in.

"Edmund," Aster said with mild surprise. "I didn't know you'd arrived. Welcome."

Edmund crossed the room and bent to place a dutiful kiss on his sister's cheek. As he did so, she took the opportunity to divest herself of the squirming infant. Edmund held Harry with one hand beneath his padded hindquarters and another behind his head and neck as his sisters had taught him. "What's all this fuss about, young Harry?"

"His teeth are coming in," Aster explained as she leaned wearily against the door frame. "I've been awake most of the night walking with him. Though I dislike comparing my children, I don't mind telling you that John never complained half so much."

Harry's chin shone with drool, and he clutched a wet cloth-covered rattle in one fist. He jerked in Edmund's arms, displeased with life in general and with Edmund in particular, and squeezed his eyes shut on a long wail.

"He looks like you," Edmund said as he tucked the infant more securely against his chest. "I didn't see it before, but it's clear now."

"Oh, wit, thy name is Edmund," Aster said without inflection.

Edmund paced the perimeter of the room, murmuring to the lad as he went. "I've no doubt you'll grow to be a man of great wisdom and charm like your uncle, but I dare say fits like this will only give the ladies the wrong impression."

Harry sniffed and shook his head in vehement denial. Blue watched from her place at the hearth, curious and a little alarmed at the turn the morning had taken.

"He favors a man's voice," Aster said, "but I suppose yours will do."

Edmund smiled. Even in her exhaustion, his sister's jests had a fine point to them. He gave Harry a finger to chew, and eventually the lad's sobs eased to stuttering hiccoughs. Blue lowered her head back to the rug, but she kept one eye on them as Edmund paced.

"Where is Sir Andrew?" Edmund said. "Dare I

ask how your husband has escaped this duty?"

"He's gone to meet a man about a new contract." His sister's husband, who'd recently been knighted for his military service in India, now operated a successful trading business in London.

Harry released a watery sigh and shifted sleepily in Edmund's arms. A bubble bloomed from his nose, expanding and contracting with each breath. Edmund wiped it away with a napkin from the sideboard just as an expression crossed the lad's face that, in Edmund's experience, preceded a full wardrobe change.

He quickly handed Harry off to his sister. She cradled the now-drowsing infant against her breast while Edmund used the other side of the napkin to dab a lake-sized puddle of drool from his waistcoat.

Aster leaned up to kiss his cheek. "Thank you," she whispered. "Despite the crying, and the puddles, babies are the best. I hope you find your Cinderella soon so you might have one of your own."

Like a splash of cold water, her words brought him back to his purpose in Kent. Marriage. Heirs. Rescuing the earldom from the brink.

"I don't require a fairy tale," he assured her. "Only a bride."

"We all require a fairy tale," Aster said gently.

CHAPTER THREE

The pressure to find the right reaction mounts.
—From the scientific journals of Mr. Edmund Corbyn

ASTER HADN'T BEEN gone more than minutes when Edmund's grandfather appeared in his wheeled chair. Cranston, who'd been his grandfather's valet for longer than Edmund had been alive, pushed from behind, and Edmund was uncertain as to which of them required the chair more. He hurried forward to relieve the man of his task.

"Edmund, my boy," his grandfather said before a low cough shook his frame. Once he'd recovered, he added in a hoarse voice, "Cranston, I'll have a moment with my grandson. Go rest your knees."

Cranston bent slowly at the waist in imitation of a bow then left them.

"Grandfather," Edmund said. He was struck by how much his grandfather's form had diminished since he'd last seen him mere weeks before. The years showed themselves in his bent shoulders and frail hands.

Edmund wheeled his grandfather toward his place at the table. The chair was a great, leather-tufted affair with brass nails and steel wheels that rolled easily—the carpets having long since been taken up in the earl's residences. The carved oak armrests slid neatly beneath the tabletop as Edmund eased the chair into position.

"I'm surprised you haven't pensioned Cranston off by now," Edmund said. "He must be nearing… what, eighty?"

"I have pensioned him off. Thrice, in fact, but the fool keeps returning. Claims no one can maintain my coats like he does. Though I don't mind telling you," Ashford added with a stroke of his side whiskers, "I've given over my razor to one of the footmen. Cranston's hand shakes like an old crone's."

Edmund laughed and moved to the polished sideboard to fix them each a plate. "It's good to see you, Grandfather."

"The feeling is mutual, my boy."

"Sausage?" Edmund asked as he filled their plates.

"Of course. And since your grandmother's not down yet, make it two. No, three."

"Three sausages," Edmund agreed, adding the requested meat to his grandfather's plate of eggs and kippers. To his own plate, he added eggs, a rasher of bacon and two Bath buns. He had his mother to thank for his preference for the sweet treats.

"Now," his grandfather said once they had their plates before them. "Tell me about your latest experiments. Have you made any progress on your dilemma with color?"

Edmund had expected their conversation to take a different path, but he shouldn't have been surprised his grandfather would lead with an academic discussion. As an astronomer of some standing, Ashford had always had a passion for science and innovation.

"Progress, yes," Edmund said, "but there's no solution as of yet. I've tested a number of theories—different glass and filters, varying exposures, new chemical solutions—but none have been successful in rendering the colors accurately on the plate."

"Ah, but at least now you know what *doesn't* work. And that is the true effort of innovation."

"I have plenty of notes on what doesn't work," Edmund conceded ruefully. "But I do believe the answer will be in the emulsions used. I just need to find the correct combination and layering needed to capture the light's various wavelengths."

"Consider all the variables and challenge your assumptions. That's the surest way to a solution."

As they discussed light refraction and color spectrums, Edmund's mother arrived. Her appearance in the breakfast room was a surprise to both gentlemen, as Lady Celeste Corbyn was not one given to early mornings.

Edmund rose to greet her. "Mother, you've risen early."

"I knew you would be here, darling, and I wished to see you." She leaned up to place a kiss on his cheek. Edmund held a chair for her, but before she sat, his mother leaned toward his grandfather's plate and speared his last bite of sausage with a fork.

"Sausage, Papa? You know Dr. Grey has advised against it."

A good-natured growl came from Ashford for her interference. "What is the point of living if a man can't enjoy a good breakfast sausage?"

"I think *living* is precisely the point." Her blue-green eyes, mirrors to Edmund's own, sparkled with humor as she poured herself a cup of chocolate from the warm pot on the table.

Edmund crossed to the sideboard and fixed her a plate. When he set it before her, she thanked him then frowned. "Edmund, would you mind adding one of Cook's Bath buns?"

She was his mother, so he felt a trifle guilty when he said over the rim of his cup, "I can't think Dr. Grey would approve, Mother."

"Oh, ho!" his grandfather chortled. *Chortled.* The sound was jolly and impish, and Edmund knew they'd not hear it for many more years. His grandfather was nearing eighty, after all. "Serves you right, Daughter." Ashford's grin was gleeful, though Edmund had already returned to the sideboard for his mother's requested bun.

They ate in easy accord for a time, exchanging idle talk of the fading summer in Kent and Edmund's latest research. Eventually, though, his grandfather's smile fell away and worry creased his forehead. When the forks had been laid aside and the coffee had cooled, Ashford cleared his throat.

Edmund's reckoning had arrived.

"Grandfather," he began before either of them could pose the question uppermost in their minds. "I know you wish to hear news of my betrothal, but I'm afraid I can't oblige you. Not just yet at any rate."

Ashford nodded, tucking his chin and closing his eyes for the briefest of moments. Then, clearing his throat with a low cough, he said finally, "Marriage is a weighty decision that requires thoughtful consideration, and this marriage more than most. But I don't think I need to remind you what's at stake."

"No," Edmund replied earnestly. "I'm well aware what we stand to lose if we—that is, if *I*—don't take our Queen's mandate to heart."

He looked up and his mother's eye caught his. Her expression was soft and sympathetic, which only increased Edmund's discomfort. It was the same look she'd worn whenever he'd been called before his father to account for some youthful prank. Not that there had been so many such occasions, but a respectable number, nonetheless. He'd been a boy with three sisters, which should have been enough of a defense but rarely was.

Now, as then, he resisted the urge to shift in his chair. Perhaps his family would withhold his pudding until he presented them with an acceptable bride. Or, horror of horrors, they might forbid him his laboratory. But no, he wasn't a lad who'd left a frog in his sister's bed. He was a man grown, who risked bringing the centuries-old Ashford earldom to a whimpering end.

His grandfather waited, and he realized further explanation was in order. "I understand what's at stake," he reiterated. "It's only that I haven't yet found a lady worthy of the title of countess." Even as he said the words, he felt their inadequacy. He'd made the acquaintance of any number of ladies who'd been brought up just for that purpose, buffed and polished to a high sheen and well prepared to take on the role of nobleman's wife.

He just hadn't met a lady for whom he felt any… vibrancy. Edmund neither required nor expected love, but he hoped to have a bit of color in his days. Certainly, he'd seen from his own parents and sisters that much enjoyment could be had from a well-matched union. Companionship and enlivening conversation. A warm hand to hold on cold nights and a pleasing countenance to gaze on over breakfast. Contentment and —

"What about Miss Gladstone?" his mother suggested gently. "She comes from a fine family with ties to the Duke of Northumberland. And, if I didn't misread the situation, she seemed amenable to your suit."

Edmund shifted his jaw to one side. "She's a pleasant lady, but I suspect she carries an affection for Lord Boutwell."

His grandfather harrumphed, and the sound turned into a series of low coughs. When he'd recovered, he prompted, "And Miss Drumbury?"

"I overheard her to say she's holding out for a marquess. Even if we had the presumption to make our hopes known, an earl's heir would not meet her requirements."

His mother released a delicate snort. "A fine, mannerly gentleman is not good enough for her?"

Edmund hid a smile for his mother's loyalty. "It would seem her aspirations stretch a bit higher than that."

"Well, then," she said, thinking. "What about Lady Anne Chesterwood? You took her in to supper at her mother's ball, and the pair of you seemed to have quite a bit to say to one another."

"I, that is—" The truth of it was, Lady Anne would have made a proper countess. She would have met with Queen Victoria's approval and their Queen would have consented to amend the earldom's letters patent, but Edmund had dragged his feet. "She's newly betrothed to Lord Emberson," he admitted. "The announcement was made in yesterday's paper."

Another cough shook his grandfather's frame and rattled deep in his chest. Soon though, one cough became many. Sweat gathered at Ashford's hairline. His face reddened as he wheezed with the force of the attack. Alarmed, Edmund stood while his mother reached for a silver pitcher of water.

Cranston returned. By the valet's prompt arrival, it was clear he'd been waiting just beyond the doors. The elderly retainer went to Ashford's side as fast as his shuffling gait allowed. When the coughing subsided, Ashford drew several slow, shallow breaths, mopping his face with a linen handkerchief.

"Here, Papa," Edmund's mother said as she extended a cup to him. His grandfather took it with a shaking hand.

"To your rooms, my lord?" Cranston asked, to which Ashford only nodded.

Edmund swallowed. "Grandfather, can I get you anything?"

Cranston maneuvered the chair away from the table, and Edmund's mother followed. As they went, Ashford said weakly, "A bride, Edmund. That is all I require."

CHAPTER FOUR

A multitude of viable hypotheses
demands careful consideration.
—From the scientific journals of Mr. Edmund Corbyn

EDMUND RETREATED TO his favorite place in the garden—a stone bench that captured the best view of the ancient woods beyond the garden wall. Tidy hedges lined the paths and a nearby apple tree offered fragrant blossoms in the spring and bountiful sun-ripened fruit in the autumn. Some of Edmund's most inspired inventions had come to him while he'd contemplated physics and mechanics in this precise spot, but no solutions were making themselves known today. If only his challenge were one of simple mechanics.

Blue sat next to him, her large body warming the side of his leg as he stroked her soft head. Light steps sounded on the gravel behind them, and Edmund was unsurprised when his mother appeared around the hedge. She carried a stack of cards—invitations by the look of them—and she wore no bonnet. Her russet hair with its fine threads of silver shone warmly in the sun. He stood and made room for her skirts on the bench.

"Grandfather's grown frailer since last I saw him," Edmund said.

"Time spares none of us," she agreed.

"Is he very ill?"

"The cough is intermittent, but it grows worse in the mornings. Dr. Grey has arranged for him to consult with another physician in London, if only he would follow his advice. I think sometimes he chooses to forget that he's aging."

"He's always been stubborn," Edmund said.

His mother smiled ruefully. "That is a sure fact. I think it must be an inherited trait, for I have it, and you as well, though I choose to blame your father for our children's most irksome qualities."

"Mother," Edmund said earnestly, "I don't mean to be irksome, and it's not stubbornness that keeps me from finding a wife." Indeed, he'd hoped to have the bride hunting well behind him by now so he might return his attention to his photography experiments.

"I know, darling. It was a poor attempt to lighten

the moment. None of us, Ashford included, would wish for you to sacrifice your happiness. As your mother, and someone who has been very happy in her own marriage, it is my greatest hope for you to find a lady who matches your heart like no other. You deserve all the brightest colors." His mother, who shared his affliction, understood him like no other in his family could ever do.

He shook his head slowly. "Though it's a fine and loyal sentiment, our family's legacy must come first."

She eyed him with equal parts warmth and motherly concern. "Have you not met *anyone* in London for whom you might come to feel an affection? Has no lady caught your eye?"

Edmund leaned forward, elbows on his thighs and head between his shoulders as he considered the question. He'd enjoyed the company of Sophia Richmond the previous season and then there was Eliza Dumond, with whom he'd most recently spent several companionable evenings. But Sophia was a widow of some repute, Eliza an actress, and neither of them acceptable matches for the heir to an earldom.

"And," his mother continued, "I don't mean fast widows and actresses and opera singers."

Edmund sucked in a harsh breath and nearly choked on it. "Mother," he said sternly.

"I may be your mother, but I'm not blind."

He felt a blush start at the roots of his hair that she would speak so plainly. Gentlemen did not discuss such things with their mothers. He sought to turn the conversation. Motioning to the thick creamy papers she held, he asked, "What have you there?"

She hesitated, and when she spoke it wasn't to answer him directly. "Darling, if you're certain you remain set on this course…"

If he remained set? What other choice was there? His family needed him, and he would not let them down. The earldom and Queen Victoria's mandate went beyond Ashford's wish to see his legacy settled before he moved on from this earth. There were tenants to consider, and servants, all of whom would be affected if the earldom reverted to the Crown.

And Edmund thought of his unborn children… and of little Harry and his other nieces and nephews. They were all too young to have known the unbounded pleasure of holidays spent at Redstone Hall, or the comforting weight, like a wool cloak on a cold night, of the earldom's steady history. If it was within his power to preserve this for them, then he would do it. Of course he would.

"I'm set," he affirmed.

She smiled, but it was a bit shadowed as she lifted the stack of cards. "Then I've brought invitations," she said, confirming his suspicion. "With the season nearing an end, Ashford thought a house party might be just the thing to further your search. Something away from London where you can get to know young ladies in a more convivial setting."

"Very well." House parties could be diverting, he supposed, if one enjoyed lawn games and scavenger hunts. Generally speaking, he did not. "What are my choices? Or rather, who?"

His mother searched his gaze for a long, uncomfortable moment before turning her attention to the cards in her hand. Her voice became brisk as she read the first invitation. "A week in Hampshire with the Dunmores. I understand the Miss Burkes and Miss Stratton are to make up the party as well. They are all of them very charming young ladies with irreproachable manners. Her Majesty will find no fault were you to select one of them. The Burke girls are very accomplished on the pianoforte, and Miss Stratton has an exceptional singing voice. And an interest in lepidopterology, I'm told."

"Lepi… I beg your pardon?"

His mother waved a negligent hand. "Butterflies and moths. I'm certain it must be a fascinating area of study. Perhaps you might find you've a shared interest in photographing specimens."

"Perhaps." Though Edmund strove to conceal

the doubt in his voice, his mother was no fool. She wrinkled her nose and moved on to the next invitation in her stack. It was printed with precise lines on thick, gilt-edged paper.

"Yes, well, here we've an invitation from Briarcliffe. Lady Vale always plans the most enjoyable activities, and she writes that there's plenty of room in her stables for Blue to share with Vale's hounds."

Edmund pulled his head back at that. No matter how large the Briarcliffe stables were, he didn't think Blue would take comfort in being separated from him. He pressed his lips and motioned for her to continue.

She read off the details of the next three invitations and finally reached the last card in her stack. She angled it so he could read the script. It was finely done, though perhaps a bit more lively than the others, with arching loops and flourishes that bordered on indulgent. Edmund was intrigued.

"A fortnight at Windermere," he said, taking the card from his mother's fingers.

"The invitations went out some weeks ago. Lady Worth writes that although her rooms at Summerfield are already spoken for, there's a small hunting lodge at the edge of the property. She would be pleased to have you enjoy it for the duration of the house party."

"Lady Worth... How are we acquainted with the

family?"

"Let me think," his mother said, tapping her chin with one finger. "Your grandfather is friends with Lord Marbury, who is cousin—or perhaps grand-uncle—to Sir George Worth's stepbrother."

"That's a rather… oblique… connection."

"We made their acquaintance last year at some to-do of Marbury's. They've a comely daughter, Miss Octavia Worth, who made her come-out in Surrey. I believe it was only with the family's im-proved circumstances some years ago that she was able to join the season in London."

"Years?" he said doubtfully.

"She's a bit older than the Burke and Stratton girls, it's true—two and twenty, I imagine by now. But perhaps a lady with a bit more polish would suit you better."

Edmund couldn't disagree. He found little in common with twittering debutantes. Searching his memory, he recalled Miss Worth as a classical English beauty. "I recall the daughter," he said slowly, "though I don't believe I spent much time in her company beyond an introduction."

"I understand from Lady Worth that she's a charming conversationalist."

"So says her mother?"

His own mother gave him a rueful smile before adding, "I'll grant the lady's opinion may be biased, but I don't think you can go wrong with anyone Lady Worth has included. She's made a very respectable guest list."

His mother named a few more families of Edmund's acquaintance, though none of the young ladies were known to him beyond a dance or two. All were of fine breeding and above reproach, though.

He was unfamiliar with the gentlemen guests, save Valentine Temple. Temple had been at Oxford while Edmund was at Cambridge. They'd often rowed or bowled against one another, exchanging barbs and insults within the confines of genteel competition.

Something about his mother's pile of stationery seemed suspect, though. His family was well regarded in Society and rarely lacked for invitations. But the fact that they'd received such a quantity now, and clearly after the original invitations had gone out, gave him pause. "How did we come by these?" he asked.

His mother wrinkled her nose in reply.

"Never tell me Grandfather has posted an advertisement in the *Times*," he said. "'Prospective earl seeks lady of refinement.'" The words were spoken in jest, but at his mother's sudden interest in the fringe of her shawl, Edmund's breath caught. "Mother, tell me he's done no such thing."

"No, no, it's nothing like that." At Edmund's silence, she continued. "It's only that he might have hinted to others that you're seeking a match with some urgency."

Edmund narrowed his eyes, knowing there must be more to it than that. Every season, there were any number of gentlemen and ladies seeking a match with some degree of haste. He rolled his hand to prompt her. "And?"

"And… he may have been overly forthcoming in describing your… income."

"My income?" Edmund received a respectable allowance from his grandfather's holdings, of course, but few knew the greater part of his funds came from his inventions and patents.

"Well, it's not as if he can put it about that you're to be the next earl," she said.

Edmund couldn't disagree. Certainly, the business of finding a bride would have been easier if Edmund's potential title were known, but it would be the height of presumption to suggest he was heir to an earldom before the letters patent were signed and sealed.

But titled or not, he had respectability. An easy manner and a countenance that ladies seemed to find pleasing. Surely, there was no need to dangle his income about.

And yet, the thick stack of invitations in his

mother's hand couldn't be denied. He took them from her and shuffled them about. Perhaps he ought to simply choose one at random—pull a card from the deck and hope for an ace.

But when he considered his choices, it truly wasn't much of a dilemma. The singing lepidopterist or a holiday in the Lake District? A private lodge for his use versus Blue in the stables? Perhaps, with his own accommodations, he'd even find time between the planned entertainments to continue his photography experiments.

He traced the Worth invitation's lively script. "Windermere it is then."

"Perhaps I should accompany you. We could make a holiday of it, and I could provide insight into the young ladies if one should catch your—"

"Mother," Edmund said hurriedly. No gentleman wished to arrive at a house party with his mother in tow, especially if he meant to be serious about finding a bride. But he said only, "I am perfectly capable of making a match on my own. And besides, don't you have an exhibition at the National Gallery?"

"Oh, that. This is far more important than any exhibition. And while I'm certain you're very capable of winning the lady of your choice, I also know your heart can be a bit... impulsive. It won't do for you to become distracted by the wrong sort of female."

"I can manage my heart," Edmund assured her.

She gave him a look that could only be described as motherly indulgence.

"Regardless," Edmund pressed, "you said your-self Lady Worth's guest list is very respectable. What could go wrong?"

"Yes, well, I suppose you're right."

"I know what's at stake," Edmund assured her. "I won't let our family down."

"And that, my darling, is what I'm afraid of."

CHAPTER FIVE

Oh, the trials I have suffered in the pursuit of books.
—From the private journal of Miss Amelia Thorne

A KNOCK SOUNDED at the door of the Vicarage, and Amelia stirred from the sunny chaise in the library where she'd been writing in her journal. It was Davy, a boy who ran messages along the shore. He thrust a folded note toward her then waited while she collected a coin.

The note was from Octavia, not more than two hundred yards away at Summerfield. Her cousin wrote that she would be traveling into Birthwaite for the final adjustments to her gowns for the house party, and would Amelia provide her company for the short carriage ride?

Amelia considered her cousin's hastily scratched

plea with suspicion. She'd made it quite clear that she had no intention of visiting Sir Frederick for herself, but it had been some time since she'd explored Birthwaite's bookshop.

The Laurel Leaf Emporium was no match for Emerson's in Bowness. In fact, there was much to be desired about the place. It was a carriage ride away, for one thing—clear over to Birthwaite—whereas Emerson's could be gained by a short walk on a lovely day.

To add to that unfortunate circumstance, the Emporium's mahogany shelves were deceptive in their abundance, for they held twice as many guidebooks for the London tourists as they did novels and volumes of poetry. And the Emporium's guidebooks weren't the lovely sort of prose like Mr. Wordsworth's *Guide to the Lakes*, but dull accounts of train tables and lodging expenses and precisely planned walking itineraries. Amelia didn't have any need for a *schedule* to find the most sublime spots along Windermere's shores.

But perhaps the most egregious of the Emporium's offenses was its proprietor. Mr. Tidwell was a stern, dour individual who wasn't the least inclined to overlook a lady's long-ago scandal. He wore his disapproval like a cloak—and a ratty, moth-eaten cloak at that.

Despite these marks against the place, though, a

bookshop was still a bookshop, and the beckoning aroma of ink and paper and leather couldn't be denied. And so, Amelia replaced the lid on her ink bottle and collected hat, gloves and reticule.

In short order, she was taking her seat next to Jane as Octavia settled across from them. Before the coach could depart, though, the strident sounds of her aunt's voice came through the open door.

Amelia tossed her cousin a narrow-eyed glance. "You neglected to mention your mother would be joining us," she whispered.

"Did I?" Octavia said as she made room for her mother's voluminous skirts on the seat next to her.

"Make haste, William," Aunt Mary said to their coachman. To Octavia and Amelia, she added, "We mustn't tarry in Birthwaite. We're getting a much later start than I would like"—here she cast a frown at Octavia who never displayed urgency for anything—"and our guests will begin arriving before supper."

As the carriage bowled along the road to Birthwaite, Amelia cursed herself that she'd not thought to tuck Keats into her reticule. She attended the passing scenery while Aunt Mary recited the guest list for her house party, unconcerned that they'd heard it all before.

"Lord Hargreave, along with Misters Pearson and Temple have all accepted. I hear Mr. Pearson's uncle does very poorly—an inflammation of the lungs, I believe—so that gentleman should realize his expectations sooner rather than later, I should say. And Mr. Temple... well, his family's estates are said to be the epitome of refinement, and I understand his father has lately expanded his stables."

She didn't pause to allow for comment but continued ticking guests off her fingers. "The Lawsons bring Mrs. Lawson's niece with them. Then we have Lord and Lady Foxgate, of course, with their youngest, Miss Rebecca Newton. She's very well mannered, Miss Newton is, though not as accomplished on the pianoforte as her mother might wish. Which is all to the better for us, Octavia, as none can deny your beauty when you play."

"Do not forget that Amelia is quite talented on her violin," Octavia put in.

Aunt Mary acknowledged this with a long indrawn breath before continuing. "To round out our numbers, we have the late but fortuitous addition of Mr. Edmund Corbyn, who has ties to the Earl of Ashford. Certainly, it would be better if the gentleman himself were in line for the title, but I understand he's nearly *six thousand* a year. You will charm him, Octavia."

As Amelia wondered where her aunt planned to put all of her guests, Octavia asked the equally reasonable question, "What if this Mr. Corbyn is odorous and gone to fat?"

"Then you will find him easily charmed."

"What if he's horse-mad or takes an unnatural interest in..." Octavia paused and Amelia stepped into the breach.

"Taxidermy?" she suggested.

"Taxidermy," Octavia agreed.

"Then you will ask him to regale you with his favorite specimens."

Octavia gave a visible shudder, but her mother had already turned her attention to the scavenger hunt she'd been planning these two weeks past.

"I will, of course, see you paired advantageously, Octavia, but you must pretend ignorance of the answers and not solve the riddles too swiftly. Allow the gentleman his victory. Of course, if it appears he will not be victorious, you may guide him to the correct conclusion, but gently. He must feel he's impressed you with his wit."

"I understand, Mama. I will play the insipid deb."

"Not insipid, Octavia. Reserved."

Amelia snorted softly, uncertain which was more ludicrous—that her aunt would cheat her guests by providing Octavia with the answers or that Octavia's unsuspecting partner would be so easily gulled by her cousin's reserved insipidity.

Insipidity... insipidness? Both words sounded

right, neither sounded wrong. Her first order of business when she reached the Emporium: consult Mr. Johnson's dictionary.

Aunt Mary turned them next to a discussion of costume. Namely, which ensemble Octavia would wear for each activity. Aunt Mary had planned for her guests a number of diversions, including not only the dubious scavenger hunt, but also charades and cards. Lawn bowling and a picnic outing to the ruins on St. Mary Holme, one of Windermere's many islands. Then, to put a fine period to the festivities, there was Lady Staveley's ball, to which all of Aunt Mary's guests were invited.

Each event had a very precise wardrobe assigned to it, all with the aim of showing her cousin to greatest advantage. Octavia tucked her tongue in her cheek and bore it all in her unflappable way, but it was enough to give a body cause to regret the lure of books.

As if a person could ever regret books! What madness was this? She would persevere. She would watch the scenery roll past and recite Mr. Wordsworth's *Daffodils* to herself.

Reprieve, if it could be called such, came two miles outside of Birthwaite when the sharp snap of a carriage wheel interrupted Aunt Mary's dissertation. "Oh!" she exclaimed as she braced one hand on the wall of the carriage and the other on Octavia.

The vehicle lurched and veered to one side as the coachman shouted to the horses. The carriage rolled to a stop and a half-minute of stunned silence passed before the ladies stirred themselves. Aunt Mary's bonnet sat askew and Amelia's gloves had slid from her lap, but they were otherwise unharmed.

"William!" Aunt Mary called. "William!"

The carriage dipped as William let himself down from his seat. His hurried movements were visible through the window as he assessed the damage. When he stepped up to the carriage, Amelia slid the window open. Adjusting his cap, William nodded and addressed Aunt Mary. "We've a broken spoke, m'leddy. I kin sort it, but 'twill tek an hour, mebbe longer if t'axle's cracked."

Aunt Mary blinked as she deciphered the coachman's strong Cumbrian accent. And then, eyes widening, she gasped. "An hour! We can't spare an hour!" She lifted her pendant watch to check the time. "No, you must see to it more swiftly."

William tugged his cap and pulled open the door. "I'll do what I kin. Tha'll wish t'step doon from t'carriage while I repair't."

Amelia collected her gloves and moved to the door, Aunt Mary's put-upon sigh following her from the carriage.

As William set to removing the damaged wheel,

her aunt began formulating a brisk battle plan. "As soon as William has finished with his repairs—surely, it can't be more than a few moments' work to do whatever it is that needs doing—we shall continue on. We haven't a single moment to tarry in Birthwaite."

"Mama," Octavia said reasonably, "I do think it must take more than a few moments to repair the wheel."

Aunt Mary sucked in her cheek for a long beat then shook her head. "There's nothing for it then. An hour's delay will be cutting things much too close. We'll simply have to return to Summerfield" —Amelia drew in a sharp breath of disappointment at this—"and Sir Frederick can come to us. We'll send for him to attend you directly, Octavia. I'll not miss the arrival of my guests."

Octavia nodded and clasped her hands before her. "It's a wise course, Mama. I can always wear my plum muslin for your picnic if Sir Frederick is unable to finish the blue poplin in time."

Aunt Mary's mouth gathered into a pursed frown. "The plum... no, that won't do at all. The blue will be much more flattering in the sunlight." Aunt Mary tapped her chin, thinking. "No, you and Jane will carry on to Sir Frederick's by foot. Hire a carriage in Birthwaite when you've finished, and Amelia and I will return to Summerfield with

William."

Amelia's head came up. What? Oh, no.

"Oh, no, Aunt," she said. She'd not sacrifice an afternoon in a bookshop if it could be helped, and certainly not to suffer her aunt's company without Octavia's buffering presence. "Why don't I accompany Octavia into Birthwaite?"

It was an undisputed fact that the Poisoned Thorne was hardly a suitable chaperone for anyone, much less Miss Octavia Worth, and her aunt's response was an immediate, "No."

"Excellent," Octavia said with a decisive clap of her hands. "Amelia can be on hand then to help you greet our guests."

Aunt Mary's indrawn breath was audible, and she released it with a long sigh. "No, that will not be necessary. Very well, Amelia. You and Jane will *both* accompany Octavia. But you are to go only to Sir Frederick and return straightaway."

"Yes, Aunt."

"Of course, Mama."

"And for heaven's sake, Amelia, do not speak to anyone. Do not even look at anyone. You are to be the Silent Companion."

"Silent," Amelia repeated.

She maintained her dignity until she and Octavia had walked some distance along the road, Jane trailing them. Then, unable to keep her relief to herself any longer, she chanced a glance at her cousin, whose grin rivaled her own.

———

EDMUND RETURNED TO London after securing his mother's promise to keep him apprised of any change in his grandfather's health. The journey was a somber one as the weight of his task pressed on him. He collected his things then reserved a private car on the train to the Lake District.

It was an extravagance, to be sure, but a necessary luxury. His photography equipment—the camera and stand and cases of lenses, plates, solutions, and developing trays—wouldn't withstand being tossed about like common baggage. And neither Blue nor Finch, Edmund's valet-turned-assistant, offered complaint at having a car to themselves.

With the assistance of a pair of porters, they boarded at Euston and soon left the sooty air of London behind. By the time the train neared Stoke-on-Trent, Edmund had regained some of his equanimity, and at Lancaster he was cautiously optimistic. His was a cheerful nature, and it wasn't in him to remain morose for long. He was resolved to his situation and determined to make the most of his time at Windermere. He would find a bride worthy of Queen Victoria's approval.

He counted the fact that the trains were ahead of schedule as a portent, a good omen of success to come. They'd even managed to catch the early connection to Birthwaite. From there, it would be but a short carriage ride to Summerfield Cottage. They'd arrive earlier than planned, but perhaps the extra time would allow him to settle his equipment before Lady Worth's entertainments began.

Edmund had never had occasion to visit the Lakes before, but he'd acquired a volume of Mr. Wordsworth's poems about the area. He hoped the verse might put him in a proper frame of mind for the journey. Though he wasn't much for poetry, one piece in particular—a verse about fluttering daffodils—had struck him with its cheerful optimism.

Blue snored at his feet as the train steamed toward Birthwaite. Edmund retrieved his Wordsworth and leaned back in the car's velvet-upholstered seat. With one booted foot crossed over his knee, he began to read. He didn't get far before Finch interrupted.

"*The Prelude*," Finch said.

Edmund cast his valet a questioning glance over the rim of his spectacles. "I beg your pardon?"

"Once we arrive, you'll want to find a copy of *The Prelude* instead of that," Finch repeated with a nod toward Edmund's book. "As I understand it, Mr. Wordsworth's widow published the piece a few months after his death. Weatherby's valet says it's all anyone reads when traveling in the Lake District. Although," Finch added apologetically, "I'm sure what you have there is perfectly suitable."

"I'm sure," Edmund replied dryly.

He returned his attention to the book and attempted to read a few more pages, but he could practically hear his valet's disapproval. Or perhaps that was merely Finch's impatient tapping on the table. Setting the book aside, Edmund turned them toward a more practical topic. Namely, his latest experiments. Finch leaned forward with enthusiasm, leaving Edmund to assume his valet wasn't much for poetry, either.

"Let's say for the sake of argument," Edmund said, "that Maxwell's theory on color perception is sound, and that any color can be achieved with the appropriate combination of blue, green and red light. The question then becomes how to accurately capture those wavelengths on the plate."

"Your recent trials with silver chloride-based emulsions are promising, my lord."

Edmund sighed and pushed his spectacles up with one finger. "I've told you to cease with the 'my lording.'"

"I'm merely practicing."

Edmund's jaw tightened, but he knew what a feather it would be for Finch's cap to find himself in service to an earl's bona fide heir. He let the argument go. Uncrossing his legs, he picked up the thread of their debate. "What if we could combine the emulsions with the filter screen on the same plate?"

And so it went.

Miles Finch was absolute rubbish when it came to stocks and cravats—the man couldn't tie a proper knot to save his life. Years before, Edmund had been on the verge of suggesting Finch seek another vocation, but then a photographic exhibition had changed his mind.

While preparing a portfolio of landscapes for submission to the Geological Society, Edmund had struggled to achieve the proper exposure. Nearly every image he captured was dim and shadowed by the time he finished the developing process. Finch, having just suggested the travesty of a striped waistcoat with striped trousers, had gone on to surprise Edmund with a bit of genius.

"Pomegranates," Finch said.

"I'm sorry… pomegranates?"

"How do you feel about them?"

Edmund frowned at his valet, worried Finch meant to dress him in a fruit-embroidered waistcoat. "I am not overly fond of pomegranates," he said firmly.

"But neither do you find them displeasing in a bowl or floral arrangement. Would you say you are *ambivalent* toward pomegranates?"

"I suppose…"

"Your emotions prevent you from achieving an accurate reading of the light," Finch said, and Edmund's frown grew. He hadn't realized any but those closest to him were aware of his affliction. He opened his mouth on a denial, but then Finch added, "Think of pomegranates to clear your thoughts."

Despite the absurdity of it, Edmund had done as Finch suggested. He'd thought of pomegranates, and the exposures had come out right, finally. Since then, Edmund had listened more closely to Finch's opinion regarding his scientific endeavors. And to his surprise, he'd learned his valet had a better-than-average grasp of chemical processes and light refraction, though he was astoundingly blind when it came to gentlemen's fashion.

The train slowed as it neared their destination, and Edmund nudged aside the window curtains to better see their surroundings. A mosaic of sharp hills and verdant valleys spread before them. Grazing sheep dotted the meadows, and the whole was laced with drystone walls marking the lines of patchwork fields. With its rough granite edges, this landscape was markedly different from the softer, rolling chalk hills in Kent.

Steam hissed in a white cloud as the train pulled into Birthwaite. A line of small shops and establishments edged the street near the station. Many of them appeared newish, commerce's answer to the area's growing popularity as a holiday destination.

It was clear to see the appeal. The grandeur of the district's ragged fells loomed in the background, and farther east, the hazy blue silhouette of the Pennines made a majestic backdrop, their peaks shrouded in mist and casting shadows that would lengthen when the sun passed its zenith. The grand scale and stark magnificence of the tableau sent fresh optimism surging through Edmund.

Here, he would have a bit of space and subject matter with which to continue his experiments. But more importantly, this was where he would find his bride. He would see to it that his family's legacy continued.

CHAPTER SIX

—From the private journal of Miss Amelia Thorne

AMELIA LEFT HER cousin with Sir Frederick and his bevy of seamstresses and crossed the cobbled street to the Laurel Leaf Emporium. A tiny brass bell chimed as she entered, and the day's warmth yielded to the cool shadows of the shop. Her breath came easily for the first time that day, and she wondered that no one had thought to bottle the glorious fragrance that greeted her. Surely, the scent of bookshop must be as rich as the most decadent perfume.

Mr. Tidwell's head popped up from where he tended a ledger at the counter. A large, broad nose and tufts of grey hair sprouting from behind each ear gave him the look of the koala she'd read about in one of the Zoological Society's publications. The shop's proprietor was a short man, but he must have stood atop a box behind his counter as he loomed a full head above her.

Eyeing Amelia over the metal rims of his spectacles, he said, "Miss Thorne." That was all— *Miss Thorne.* All of his antipathy toward her was efficiently bundled into those two words and the tightness with which he said them.

"Mr. Tidwell." Amelia dipped her head in what was meant to be a regal nod of patience and grace but was, in all actuality, more of a twitch.

"What do you require?"

"A book, Mr. Tidwell. I would like to browse what you have on offer. But first, I should like to consult Mr. Johnson's dictionary." Belatedly, she added, "If I may."

"And will you be purchasing Mr. Johnson's dictionary, Miss Thorne?"

"I have already purchased it, and from this very shop," she reminded him.

"Then you've no need to peruse my copy, have you?"

"Mr. Tidwell," she said with forced patience, "you may rest easy as I do plan to make a purchase today. But first, there is a word I must confirm if I might consult your dictionary."

"This is an establishment of serious commerce, Miss Thorne. It is not a book museum meant only to satisfy your curious starts and whims."

Indeed, it was not. But a book *museum*… Heavens, what a lovely notion. She waited, foot tapping beneath her skirts.

Mr. Tidwell closed his eyes for a long moment, the low light catching on the lenses of his spectacles. He appeared to be weighing his irritation with her against the prospect of a sale. Her coin finally won, and he dismissed her with a curt nod. Aside from the scratch of his pen on his ledger, the shop was quiet, and Amelia turned her full attention to the stacks.

Row upon row of neatly lined books stretched ahead, and Amelia traced a finger along the dark leather spines as she walked. Mr. Tidwell's disapproval was a palpable weight between her shoulders, and she shrugged it off.

She passed the travel guides at the front to find Mr. Johnson's dictionary at the back. She opened it slowly and without intent, allowing the fates to choose her page. And the fates chose well as the book fell open to the Ps. Ps were a sheer delight. She perused the page with… palpable passion, pausing to ponder the precise pronunciations and profound poetry printed therein.

Smiling and rather pleased with her alliterative effort, she then addressed her mission, turning the pages gently backward until she found… *Insipidity*. And *insipidness*. Both forms of the word were valid. And wasn't that just the best thing about the English language? There were so many ways to say what needed saying.

A shrill whistle heralded an arrival at the nearby train station. Through the Emporium's front window, a cloud of steam and smoke accompanied the locomotive, and Mr. Tidwell's walls shook as the train rumbled to a stop. More tourists, she thought. Since new routes had been added to Birthwaite, the flow of travelers from Lancaster and London and other towns had been steady.

"Have you found a book to purchase yet?" Mr. Tidwell asked, and she jumped to find him at her elbow, peering up at her through his spectacles.

"I was just about to begin my exploration," she said as she set Mr. Johnson's dictionary aside. She moved toward one of the few shelves Mr. Tidwell had allocated to poetry.

"This is not a gallery, Miss Thorne, for *exploring*."

"Here, Mr. Tidwell." She pulled a volume from the shelf at random and thrust it toward him. By some stroke of glorious, heavenly providence, it was Mr. Wordsworth's *Prelude*. Amelia stilled, concealing her glee lest Mr. Tidwell deny her out of spite. Pulse racing, she managed a tone of annoyed disinterest. "You may hold this for me at the counter if it pleases your cold, merchant's heart. Now go and let me see what else you have on offer."

He took the book with a pinched expression and left her in peace. She worked her way through the shelves, marking the time by Mr. Tidwell's return. Every few minutes, he reappeared at her elbow to urge her along, and every few minutes she thrust another book at him. She'd acquired a tidy stack by the time the bell above the door chimed.

Had Octavia finished with Mr. Frederick so soon? Blast! She hadn't even begun to peruse the novels. She leaned to one side and peered through an opening between two shelves, but it wasn't Octavia who'd entered. Relieved, she watched as a tall gentleman approached Tidwell's desk. He wore a fine tailored coat and a sharp hat—a London buck by the look of him—and her nose wrinkled in reflex. He removed the hat to reveal dark hair, neatly trimmed and creased from his headband.

"Good afternoon, sir," Mr. Tidwell said with annoying pleasantness. "How can I be of assistance?"

Amelia suppressed a snort at the shopkeeper's toadying. She started to return to the stacks when the gentleman's reply stopped her. His voice was low and smooth, like warm, velvety chocolate, but it wasn't the quality of it that gave her pause. It was the words themselves.

"I'll be passing the next fortnight at Summerfield Cottage. I wondered if you might recommend a guidebook for the area."

Summerfield. Amelia peered more closely, wondering which of her aunt's guests she was watching. Octavia had once described Pearson and Hargreave to her as fair-haired gentlemen, so he couldn't be one of them. She'd met Mr. Temple during her season in London, but with the gentleman's back to her, she couldn't be sure if it was him.

He obliged her by turning then, angling toward her more fully as Mr. Tidwell motioned to the guidebooks. He was not Mr. Temple, so he must be the late addition, the taxidermist. Mr. Corbyn.

He was rather handsome with a firm jaw and straight nose beneath a pair of spectacles. A small cleft marked his chin. His frame was lean but not overly so, with shoulders that didn't seem padded. He wore his side whiskers well-trimmed, and he was otherwise clean shaven, without the distraction of a caterpillar above his lip that so many men sported these days. Octavia would find no hardship in charming him.

The man glanced over his shoulder then, narrowing his gaze on the stacks that separated them, and Amelia ducked behind her shelf. Her heart thumped a rapid pace.

She wasn't concerned with her aunt's demands that Amelia remain out of sight of her guests—surely, such a restriction couldn't extend to Birthwaite—but how embarrassing to be caught staring in such a fashion, like a silly schoolgirl. She was a mature female for heaven's sake.

She waited, willing her breath to slow and her heart to ease its fluttering while the gentleman completed his transaction. As he prepared to leave, he paused to make one more inquiry of Mr. Tidwell. "I don't suppose you've a copy of Mr. Wordsworth's *Prelude*, have you?"

Amelia's brows dipped in surprise.

"Why, yes," Mr. Tidwell replied. "You're in luck as I've only one copy left."

Amelia's brows reversed course at this betrayal. Such duplicity. Such perfidy! It was too much. "Mr. Tidwell!" she said as she lurched out from behind the shelves. "You can't mean to sell *my* copy of Mr. Wordsworth's opus."

Mr. Tidwell pulled himself up taller on his box as she advanced on his counter. "Miss Thorne," he said repressively. "As you've not purchased this item, it is not yours."

"But I gave it to you to hold."

"To *hold*, Miss Thorne. You said nothing about buying it."

"It was implied," Amelia said through her teeth.

The gentleman at her side cleared his throat, and Amelia swung her gaze to him. She was struck by the viridian hue of his eyes behind his spectacles—they were a rich blue-green which she'd not fully appreciated from her place behind the shelves. She swallowed and collected her wits.

"My apologies," he said in his velvety voice. "I did not realize the book was already spoken for. Please, you must have it."

Amelia opened her mouth, unprepared for capitulation. Then she realized how she must appear to him, irritable and strident. A touch mad perhaps. She gave him a gracious nod. "Thank you, sir."

Mr. Tidwell harrumphed. As Amelia reached into her reticule for payment—she would secure her purchase before Mr. Tidwell found further opportunity to thwart her—the gentleman placed a coin on the counter. "For the lady's book," he said.

"Oh, but you mustn't," Amelia protested.

The gentleman replaced his hat and smiled, and Amelia's breath caught at the sight. "For your trouble," he said with a nod before turning and striding for the door with his own purchase. He left, the bell above the door chiming, and it was a long moment before Amelia remembered to close her mouth.

She returned her gaze to Mr. Tidwell, the sneaky little rat. She would have to rethink her custom at the Laurel Leaf Emporium. Then she considered the lovely pile of books at his side, the ones she'd amassed over the last hour, and decided now was not the time for rash decisions about where to bestow her patronage. She pulled the Wordsworth toward her protectively. "Please wrap my remaining books and tally my balance," she said with more graciousness than she felt. "I find I am finished with my shopping."

There. She would not buy another book today. Let him see how he liked that. With a pinched expression, Mr. Tidwell picked up his pencil and began adding her bill.

Amelia sidled closer to the window and spied the gentleman with the heart-stopping smile across the street. He approached a servant standing near a pair of carriages and a massive hound of some sort. The dog nosed the gentleman's hand before all three—man, servant and dog—entered one of the carriages.

As Amelia watched, the dog's head appeared in the window. The animal sat regally, as high-and-lofty as a lord departing the theater. The carriage began moving, and the second vehicle followed. Amelia held her snort of amusement. Trust a London gentleman to require two carriages—two!—for a country house party. But then she considered the Wordsworth clutched in her hands, and she couldn't hold her smile.

CHAPTER SEVEN

EDMUND STROKED BLUE'S head as she settled on the carriage seat beside him. Finch inquired if he'd found a satisfactory guidebook, and Edmund responded vaguely, still distracted by the female he'd encountered in the bookshop.

He'd felt her eyes on him long before he'd seen her. And then, when the proprietor had offered to sell his only copy of *The Prelude*, she'd flown at them from behind the stacks. To be fair, she'd been justified in her pique. That Tidwell would sell a book she'd clearly set aside for her own purchase was, well, ungentlemanly.

Edmund had done the only proper thing in offering the volume to her, and she'd seemed grateful for the overture, if a little surprised.

He'd been struck by a vague sense of familiarity, as if he'd encountered her somewhere before, though he couldn't think where he might have done so. She was of average height, with regular features and honey-blond locks beneath the shallow brim of her bonnet. But she'd been dressed simply—not so simply as a maid, but a governess perhaps—and it was clear they didn't share the same circles.

The encounter might have been little more than a humorous anecdote if he'd not been rendered speechless by the lady's eyes. They were nicely set in a heart-shaped face, wide and outlined with thick brown lashes. Green but translucent, like a bit of broken glass held up to the sun. In the brief moment while he'd stood before her, they'd caught the light to shift from the bright hue of early spring leaves to the richest, deepest emerald stone, and he'd been transfixed.

Blue nudged his hand as the carriage trundled on. Edmund pulled his attention from the bookshop lady and put it to the scenery beyond the windows. The road wound through marbled, towering fells, and soon he caught an occasional tantalizing glimpse of Windermere's mirrored surface.

Finally, the lake burst into full view in its valley, spotted with pretty islands and skirted by wooded shores. In the distance, pale blue mountains lifted their heads in sleepy interest.

The carriage turned, and the lake shimmered on their right until they reached a long gravel drive. Summerfield Cottage sat an agreeable distance from the road, with sheep-dotted hills and neatly-planted fields stretching behind it. As the carriage drew up to the entrance, Edmund and Finch took in the property.

"It's hardly Redstone Hall," Finch said.

"You are a snob," Edmund retorted. Though not nearly so grand as his grandfather's seat in Kent, what Summerfield Cottage lacked in space it made up for in charm.

Thick ropes of ivy and roses clung affectionately to creamy stone walls, the flowers' petals beginning to age with the passing of the season. A slate roof topped a wide portico with tall oak doors, and near-by were gardens with more roses and thick hedgerows. Beyond, the waters of Windermere glimmered and lapped the shore, mirroring the lowering sun and completing the picture of idle, and idyllic, leisure.

If the hunting lodge he'd been assigned was half as alluring as the main cottage, he'd pass a very pleasant few weeks indeed. Then he recalled his purpose and sobered. He'd come to find a bride, not to enjoy a holiday.

Edmund descended the carriage steps and was met by Lady Worth herself. A manservant in a low knit cap stood at her back, along with a darkly-dressed lady he took to be the housekeeper.

"Mr. Corbyn," Lady Worth said. "It's a pleasure to make your acquaintance once again. We're so pleased to have you join our little gathering. I regret that my daughter Octavia is not available to greet you. She's gone for a fitting with our dressmaker—young ladies must be prepared to look their best, you know—but she'll return shortly. You will enjoy furthering your acquaintance with her, I'm certain."

"I look forward to it, my lady."

"I do hope you won't find the Vicarage too much of an inconvenience. It's close enough to the main house for comfort, but you shall have your privacy there." Lady Worth indicated the housekeeper and added, "Mrs. Kessler has assigned one of the maids to see to anything you require during your stay."

"It sounds charming," Edmund said. "And rest assured, my man and I can manage without putting your staff to any trouble. As I indicated in my reply to your invitation, I hope to use some of my time here to further my experiments." And, lest his hostess think him a poor guest, he added hastily, "When I'm not otherwise engaged, of course, with the activities you've planned."

"You're a photographer, yes! What an exciting

hobby for a gentleman to have," Lady Worth said, and Edmund's jaw tightened at the word *hobby*. He didn't correct her, though, as the distinction between hobbyist and scientist was lost on most. "Perhaps," she continued, "we can prevail upon you to capture some images of our little party. We've a full fortnight ahead of us, Mr. Corbyn. I do hope you're up to the challenge."

"As do I."

"Now, take some time to settle in. William will show you the way and then you must join us for supper. The other guests will have arrived by then, and we'll gather in the drawing room at seven sharp." She didn't wait for a response but turned to summon the man in the cap. "William, please show Mr. Corbyn to the Vicarage."

Edmund wondered if the lovely Miss Worth was as garrulous as her mother. He knew a moment of uncertainty before he reminded himself it didn't matter if she talked his ear off like a magpie. He would keep an open mind. A talkative manner was no reason to mark a lady from his list of prospective brides. But what if he found he had *nothing* in common with any of the ladies present? It did not signify. He would find common ground. He must.

He left Finch to oversee the unloading of the carriages while he and Blue accompanied William down a narrow winding path. The Vicarage, as it turned out, was just as charming as Summerfield Cottage. Situated closer to the water, it was built of the same pale stone as the main residence. He spied a small outbuilding—an old gardener's shed, William explained. Edmund glanced inside to find cobwebs and piles of old, unused implements. With a few adjustments, it might serve as a darkroom.

Edmund entered the lodge to find a small parlor with overstuffed chairs, a breakfast room overlooking the lake and a charming library complete with floor-to-ceiling shelves and a comfortable-looking chaise. A broad window seat caught the afternoon sun, and a low fire already burned in the grate.

He found the bedchamber, a cozy room in shades of blue with more expansive views of the sun-dappled lake and the fells beyond. There was an adjoining bathing room, and he was surprised to find both hot and cold taps. As he unpacked his shaving things, he allowed his natural optimism to crowd out his reservations. It brightened the room, and he wondered how he could possibly fail in his mission in such charming surroundings.

———

AMELIA SAT NEXT to Jane on Sir Frederick's gold velvet couch and waited for Octavia to finish her errand. After sliding countless glances toward them that caused Amelia's eyes to narrow with suspicion, Octavia finally deemed her business concluded.

Sir Frederick sent one of his boys to secure a carriage then began arranging Octavia's purchases for loading. There were large, silk-covered boxes for skirts and bodices, and round hat boxes and smaller packages for gloves and shawls and hair ornaments. And Sir Frederick's finely embroidered *F* topped each one to signify Octavia's excellent taste in fashion.

"You'll send the rest to Summerfield directly?" Octavia asked Sir Frederick as she adjusted her gloves.

"As soon as they're ready, Miss Worth."

The rest? Amelia, on seeing the volume of her cousin's purchases, had two thoughts. Firstly, that they might be obliged to hire a second carriage to manage them all, which would require rethinking her earlier judgment of Mr. Corbyn. Secondly, and more concerning, was whether Amelia would have any fortune left once Uncle George was finished managing it for her.

But Octavia seemed pleased with the day's effort. Octavia, who'd stood staunchly by Amelia over the last years, despite the whispers and glances and outright accusations from "polite" society. Amelia would not begrudge her cousin a few gowns and ribbons.

Octavia tucked an arm through Amelia's, and they left Sir Frederick's shop. With a glance toward Amelia's books, she said, "Judging by your fat parcel there, you've had a successful day of it."

Amelia rolled her eyes at her cousin's willful disregard of the obvious. "If I was successful, then what were you?"

"Triumphant," Octavia declared as they entered the carriage. "Oh, chin up, cousin. I've not put the merest dent into that fortune of yours. In fact, Sir Frederick and I have come to an arrangement of sorts that will benefit the both of us."

Octavia was arranging her skirts on the carriage seat, so she didn't see the narrowing of Amelia's eyes. "Us? This arrangement of yours doesn't involve me wearing a crinoline, does it?"

Octavia snorted delicately. "As if I could wield such power. No, I've merely suggested to Sir Frederick that I might have occasion to wear one of his newest creations to Lady Staveley's ball. He's been trying to secure her custom for ages, and I know she'll be positively green with envy when she sees how well the fabric drapes."

"And what have you garnered in exchange for this service?"

"Why, the gown, of course. And Sir Frederick has added an extra pair of gloves and a few other trifles to my order, at no charge to your account. So you see, Cousin, it really does benefit us both."

Amelia folded her hands over her books. "And when your mother learns you've entered into a *business* arrangement with Sir Frederick?"

"Isn't life but one large business arrangement?" she said philosophically. "Besides, there's no reason Mama need ever know of it."

"And to think, *I'm* the scandal of the family," Amelia muttered.

"The trick with scandals is not to get caught. Now, tell me of your visit to the Emporium. Was Mr. Tidwell as detestable as ever?"

"Even more so, if you can imagine." Amelia ran a finger over the embossed title in her lap, satisfied to know she'd prevailed in the end, with Mr. Corbyn's assistance. "I did encounter one of your mother's guests, though."

Octavia's brow arched. *Go on*, it said.

"It was Mr. Corbyn, although we weren't properly introduced."

Octavia's nose wrinkled. "And is he odorous and gone to fat as I suspect? Or old and balding, perhaps?"

"No," Amelia said slowly. "I believe you'll find him pleasing enough."

"Oh? Is he handsome then?"

"Some would say so."

"Would *you* say so?"

"I—yes, he is handsome. And mannerly."

"Mannerly, is it?"

"That is, he seemed so with Tidwell, and you know how difficult *that* can be." Though she and Octavia shared most things, Amelia was reluctant to disclose the full extent of her interaction with the gentleman. She clasped it to her firmly as she did her new Wordsworth, though she was at a loss to explain her reticence.

"Well," Octavia said, "I'm certain he must still have an unholy interest in... what was it? Taxidermy?"

"To be sure," Amelia agreed, smiling.

They reached Summerfield well in time for Octavia to dress for supper. As a pair of servants paid the carriage driver and began unloading her cousin's parcels, Amelia collected her books and climbed the stairs toward her room.

The corridors were quiet, but soon her aunt's guests would emerge from their chambers to gather in the drawing room. She imagined their gay laughter and droll comments as they shared tales of the last ball they'd attended or the latest scandal to grace the news sheets.

Amelia had no desire to see any of them, just as her aunt had no desire for her to be seen. On that, they were in accord.

She entered her bedchamber to an eager welcome from Lord Byron. As she removed her half boots, she wondered what Octavia would make of Mr. Corbyn, and he of her. Then, splashing water onto her face from the basin, she dismissed her musings. It was no concern of hers what her cousin thought of the gentleman.

She would take a tray in her room, and then, while her aunt's guests were occupied in the dining room, she'd escape to the Vicarage for an evening with Wordsworth.

CHAPTER EIGHT

The elements are in place;
I await the reaction to commence.
—From the scientific journals of Mr. Edmund Corbyn

EDMUND MADE A diligent effort to enjoy himself at Lady Worth's supper, though he wondered how Finch and Blue were getting on. As he'd been preparing to return to Summerfield Cottage, they'd decamped for a tavern in nearby Bowness. Even now, he imagined Finch must be enjoying a thick slab of roast beef and a tankard of ale while Edmund sipped at his consommé.

Lady Worth's party made fourteen in all, with their host and hostess seated at opposite ends of a finely-set, linen-draped table. Sir George Worth was a gruff but genial sort of gentleman and seemed content to follow his wife's lead in all things. Their daughter, Miss Octavia Worth, was seated next to Edmund. She was tall and poised, her speech more carefully dispensed than her mother's, and Edmund was relieved to think he could be charmed by her.

The Lawsons were a short, round couple of middle years, accompanied by their daughter and the lady's niece, Miss Betsy Gifford. Both young ladies were soft-spoken, and Miss Lawson was given to casting soft eyes toward her mother before replying to any question put before her.

Lady Foxgate and her daughter, Miss Rebecca Newton, were mirror images of one another, with the addition of twenty years beginning to silver the mother's hair. Both were petite with smooth skin and full lips, and Miss Newton's thick-lashed eyes put him in mind, briefly, of the governess he'd encountered in Birthwaite. The comparison ended there, however, as Miss Newton wore an elaborate necklace with diamond drops on it and matching earbobs.

Of the gentlemen, Edmund found amiable conversation with Lord Hargreave and Mr. Pearson. Temple, of course, was already known to him. He was pleasant enough, but he'd always been a bit mad for sport, and any sport would do. Rowing, cricket, boxing, hunting. Tonight, he'd already regaled the table with at least three tales of his successes on the field, and all that before the soup bowls were cleared. Temple's family had recently fallen on unfortunate circumstances, or so Edmund had heard. There'd been mention of piles of debt owing to some poorly conceived stable renovations, so he assumed at least one of the young ladies must come with a substantial dowry. Miss Newton, perhaps, who wore diamonds to a country supper.

Over the roasted fowl, Lady Worth offered the company an accounting of the activities to be enjoyed over the next weeks. And they were many, to hear the lady's exhaustive recitation. From musical evenings to cards, from picnics to charades to—and Edmund suppressed a grimace at this—a scavenger hunt, their hostess had left no amusement from her list. There was to be rowing and lawn bowling, shooting for the gentlemen and painting and archery for the ladies.

But despite all of this, it seemed few of Lady Worth's activities would take place before the noon hour, so Edmund was relieved to know he would have his mornings to himself. He'd always enjoyed exploring the early light with his camera.

When discussion of his hostess's planned entertainments concluded, Edmund turned to the lady at his side. "Tell me, Miss Worth, how did the Vicarage come by its name? Have I displaced a clergyman by chance?"

She laughed and lowered her voice to say, "My mother wouldn't have hesitated at such measures if her party demanded it, but no, Mr. Corbyn. You may ease your conscience.

"The Vicarage was christened by my uncle, Captain Alexander Thorne. He was my mother's brother and Summerfield's previous owner until his death a few years ago. The story has it that Captain Thorne was in the habit of escaping his obligations to join his friends for reading and cards in the lodge's library. I believe it began as something of a jest, to tell his wife he was off to the vicarage, for what wife would deny her husband such an outing?"

"She must have been an affable lady if he was able to jest about it."

"By all accounts, my aunt Aileen was an understanding sort, but only, I think, because she was so much in love with her husband."

Lady Worth heard this tale with a tight expression which her daughter ignored. "Soon," Miss Worth continued, "Captain Thorne's friends began telling their wives that they, too, were off to the vicarage, and the name has remained ever since."

"It's a charming story. I thank you for sharing it, and I'm relieved to know a man of the cloth hasn't been evicted for my convenience."

Lady Worth's expression eased as the conversation turned to other topics, and Edmund was left to assume she had little liking for Captain Thorne's wife.

Miss Worth smiled and leaned toward him as a servant brought round a platter of roasted vegetables. "Now, Mr. Corbyn, you must tell us what hobbies interest you. Are you a sportsman like Mr. Temple?"

Edmund wiped his mouth with a linen napkin. "Certainly, I enjoy riding and the hunt, and I look forward to the activities your mother has planned for us."

"Oh, I think you will enjoy them as long as the weather holds. There's nothing worse than Windermere when the mists roll in—it does such horrible things to one's hair. Do you dabble in any unusual hobbies? Taxidermy, perhaps?"

Her mouth formed a small smile, as if she were privy to a joke that Edmund had not heard. His brow dipped in confusion, but he replied easily. "I'm afraid I haven't spent any time studying the discipline, Miss Worth, but I do have a keen interest in scientific matters. My primary focus of late has been in the field of photography. As I told your mother, I've brought my equipment with me and hope to continue some of my experiments while I'm here."

Miss Worth's smile broadened, and her enthusiasm seemed genuine. "Photography! How diverting! Lord Hargreave, did you hear that?" she said to the lord at her other side. "Mr. Corbyn is a photographer. Perhaps we might beg him to take our portraits."

Edmund cleared his throat, uncertain how to extricate himself from such an endeavor. While he *could* do portraits, people were not his preferred subjects. They were, invariably, disappointed when the camera returned to them an image of themselves as they were, rather than as they imagined themselves to be. His hesitation was only reinforced by Mrs. Lawson's next words.

"We had our portraits done last year in a studio on Oxford Street," she said. "My expectations were higher than our photographer's talents, I'm afraid, but perhaps Mr. Corbyn can manage to capture our Letty's elegance with his camera."

"I can certainly try," Edmund said noncommittally, "but I'm afraid some ladies' charm simply defies the lens."

Miss Lawson's head bent demurely as her mother agreed. "Yes, Mr. Corbyn, I'm certain you must be right."

"Tomorrow afternoon, then," Miss Worth said with a pleased smile. "Mama's planned an archery competition, but surely there's time for portraits before we gather on the lawn. I should think the drawing room will make a suitable studio. Do you agree, Mr. Corbyn?"

All eyes were upon him, and he gave the party a short, reluctant nod. "Of course."

Conversation turned to other topics then as the meal continued. When the dessert course—a delicious trifle—was removed, Lady Worth drew everyone's attention. "Tonight, we have a special treat," she said. "Miss Newton has graciously offered to entertain us on the pianoforte."

"I look forward to hearing you play," Temple said. "Do you know any of Herr Chopin's works?"

Miss Newton gave him a nod that set her diamonds to sparkling beneath the chandelier. She indicated that she did and would be honored to play some of his compositions for their party. Temple offered to turn the pages for her.

"Do you play, Miss Worth?" Edmund asked.

She smiled ruefully. With a flutter of her slender fingers, she said, "My mother chooses to believe I'm accomplished on the pianoforte, but I'm all thumbs, I'm afraid. My cousin Amelia, though, is exceptionally talented. She plays the pianoforte splendidly, but her true gift becomes apparent when she takes up her violin."

"Oh? Does your cousin also reside in the area?"

A spark lit Miss Worth's eye. He might have thought it mischievous if his question hadn't been so ordinary. "She does. In fact, I believe you've already—" Whatever she'd been about to say was cut short as Lady Worth called for the ladies to go through to the drawing room. Edmund stood with the other gentlemen as the ladies rose.

———

EARLIER, AMELIA COLLECTED the necessities for an evening's respite—Lord Byron (the dog, not the poet, alas), her journal, her violin and her new Wordsworth—and went quietly down the back stairs, past her cousin's rooms, past the floor with the guest chambers. Lord Byron's nails clicked on the planks ahead of her, and she followed the servants' corridor that ran behind the music room. As they neared the dining room, the indistinct sounds of laughter and conversation grew.

Ahead of her in the hall, one of the maids went in carrying a large tray laden with bowls of trifle. She left the door ajar, and as Amelia went past, she slowed and peered in. Colorful silks and dark suits filled the room. There was just enough of a gap to see the far end of the dining table. She was unsurprised to find her cousin holding court with Lord Hargreave on one side and Mr. Corbyn on the other. Both men appeared pleased with the seating arrangement.

Lord Byron turned to give her an annoyed *Hur-*

ry! bark from the top of the kitchen stairs. Mr. Corbyn's head came up at the sound, and Amelia hastily scuttled past the opening.

"Hush!" she whispered to Lord Byron. She wasn't overly concerned with upsetting her aunt with her presence, but she'd no wish to be caught lurking in the shadows like some tragic character in a gothic novel.

They left through the kitchen, and a low moon lit the path to the Vicarage. Amelia used her key to let herself in the side door. Lord Byron ran ahead to his favorite spot in the library, and Amelia's breathing instantly felt lighter at the sight of the comfortable chaise before the hearth.

She knelt and rekindled the fire, surprised to see the embers still burned from when she'd been there that morning. The maids had clearly been in as the decanters on the sideboard were filled, and she poured herself a glass of sherry.

Her slippers came off as the logs popped in the grate. Then, curling her stockinged feet beneath her on the chaise, she wrapped a soft wool blanket about her shoulders and lifted *The Prelude*. She ran a slow hand over the embossed cover, feeling the edges of the letters beneath her fingertips. Lord Byron was snoring softly when she opened the volume to the delicious creak of the leather spine.

CHAPTER NINE

*I remain mindful of the
unpredictable nature of some forces.*
—From the scientific journals of Mr. Edmund Corbyn

MISS NEWTON DID indeed play the piano-forte very prettily (though her modesty over the fact rang a little false), and Miss Octavia Worth continued to be an engaging conversationalist. But Edmund grew restless as ideas for a new chemical mixture hammered at his thoughts. When the midnight hour approached and the gathering began to make noises of retiring, he was the first to take his leave of their hostess.

A full moon had turned Windermere's smooth waters into a ribbon of silver mercury, and he found the path to the Vicarage easily. The lodge's entry was dark. No lanterns had been lit, so he assumed

Finch and Blue had yet to return from their outing to Bowness.

He let himself in, surprised at the pleasant warmth that greeted him. He'd left the fire to die during supper, but a maid must have tended it, despite his assurances to Lady Worth's housekeeper that he and Finch could do for themselves.

The flickering glow came from the library, so he moved in that direction, loosening his cravat and shrugging off his coat along the way. A sideboard stood opposite the hearth, and he'd already found it well stocked. He crossed the thick carpet and poured himself a brandy. As he set the decanter back in its stand, a faint growl sounded behind him. His hand stilled as his pulse jumped.

The sound was low and throaty, but not so low as Blue's deep-chested growl. Edmund turned slowly, surprised to find the small dark eyes of a terrier watching him from beneath a scrappy white brow. Little teeth gleamed in the firelight. Though fierce in spirit, the thing appeared more nuisance than threat, and Edmund's heart resumed its normal pace. Lifting his brandy, he saluted the animal and said, "Aren't you a formidable beast?"

When there was no reply, Edmund took a step toward the dog, intent on removing it. How the animal had found its way inside the Vicarage was a mystery, but Edmund had no wish to have his sleep disturbed if the thing decided to go for his throat. The dog growled again as he drew near and Edmund stopped. That was when movement from the chaise caught his attention.

He turned, surprised to see a bundle of wool shifting about in the shadows. Edmund set his glass on the desk with a thump, and the wool jerked at the sound.

A heart-shaped face appeared from the depths of the cloth, haloed by a pale cloud of rumpled hair. The woman spied him, standing there with his mouth agape like a simpleton, and her feminine gasp broke the silence of the library.

She jerked to standing, stumbling once as she tried to untangle herself from the twisted blanket. Then, glancing about, she seized an ink jar from the table beside her. Pulling her arm back, she prepared to launch it at his head.

"Ho!" he said, holding up both hands before she spattered them both.

She hesitated then lowered her hand a fraction. "I've an excellent aim," she said in warning.

"I don't doubt it," he replied gently, in a tone he might use with an injured animal.

Sleep faded from her thick-lashed eyes and she blinked away her confusion. He relaxed when she replaced the ink on the table. "Why are you here?" she asked, her voice carrying a tinge of accusation.

She was accusing *him*? He peered more closely and recognized her then as the governess from Birthwaite. Again, something about her seemed familiar, but fiend take him if he knew what it was.

He took in the scene more fully—from the near-empty glass of sherry on the tea table to the woman's stockinged feet beneath the edge of her blanket. A worn violin case leaned against the edge of the table, and a book peeked out from under the chaise, a pink ribbon marking her place.

"I might ask the same," he said slowly. "Do you make a habit of trespassing the homes of others?"

"Trespassing!" She straightened and pulled the blanket about her more securely. The terrier took up a position before his mistress and bared his teeth once more.

"Enough," Edmund said to the dog. The woman frowned at his presumption, but to his surprise, the terrier quieted and sat abruptly at her feet. An uncomfortable possibility occurred to him, and he asked, "Have you nowhere else to go?" He'd not turn the woman out if she were in need, but where could he take her at this time of night?

"I *live* here," she bit out.

His head jerked back. "Here? At the Vicarage?" Fiend take it, matters were worse than he'd thought if she'd taken up residence.

"At Summerfield," she explained. "Clearly, my

aunt has run short of guest rooms if she's installed you here."

"Your aunt? Lady Worth is your relation?"

"Yes, though I assure you, she'll deny the connection."

Edmund wasn't certain if he should believe her, or if this were merely a ploy to escape his charge of trespass. He could hardly disturb his hostess at this hour to confirm the fact, but then he recalled something Miss Octavia Worth had said at supper. Something about a cousin… and a violin.

"You're Miss Worth's cousin," he said inanely. Of course, if she was niece to Lady Worth, then it stood to reason she was a cousin to Miss Worth.

The lady bent to retrieve her shoes from where they'd slid beneath the chaise. Her voice was muffled as she stretched for her slipper. "I am."

"May I have your name?"

She straightened. "I am Miss Amelia Thorne."

Amelia Thorne… The name tickled his memory until it came to him. A scandal, some years before. There'd been talk of a duel, though they'd long since fallen out of fashion, and an elopement. The broadsheets had described a venomous temptress, and the *ton* had taken to calling her the Poisoned Thorne. Now he knew why she seemed familiar to him. He'd seen her at various society events before her scandal, but they'd never been introduced.

"You're the—" He stopped himself before he could say the words aloud. "That is, it's a pleasure to make your acquaintance." He gave her a short bow and his own name, though he felt a bit ridiculous given the circumstances of their meeting.

She cast him a look through her thick lashes, and the impropriety of their situation struck him. It was well after midnight, and the two of them were alone in his lodgings, her rumpled from sleep and him without his coat. If anyone were to learn of their encounter, he'd not have to worry about finding a bride any longer. He'd be honor-bound to make an offer, but he didn't think the Poisoned Thorne was what Queen Victoria had in mind for the future Countess of Ashford. He swallowed as the full import of his predicament settled on his thoughts.

"You should go," he said, wincing at his impoliteness. "I don't mean to be impolite, but it's not seemly, the two of us here alone."

"You're an astute one, aren't you?"

She'd found both of her slippers, and she sat on the chaise to slide them onto her pale, silk-clad feet. As she bent in the firelight, her cheeks pink from the heat of the flame, hair coming loose from its pins to tumble about her shoulders, he was struck by the sensual intimacy of the image. He cleared his throat as she stood. Before he could bundle her out the door, though, sounds came through from the entry.

Finch and Blue had returned.

"Who else is here?" Miss Thorne whispered. The moment of intimacy was gone, her wide eyes giving her the look of a startled deer. She smoothed a hand over her hair in a feeble attempt to right the chaos there.

"My valet, Finch." Edmund's voice was tight. While he trusted Finch to be discreet, Edmund had no wish to explain the evening's tableau any more than necessary. Nor, it seemed, did Miss Thorne. She moved away from the glow of the fire and into the shadows, as if that were enough to hide her presence. In truth, the shadows only made the scene seem more illicit.

Edmund strode toward the library's open doorway and met Finch there. His valet opened his mouth on a greeting then, spying Miss Thorne over Edmund's shoulder, he promptly closed it again. With naught but a shallow nod of his head, he continued on toward his room.

Blue showed no such discretion. She entered the library, pausing to sniff the terrier who'd trotted across the room to greet her, then swung her nose toward Miss Thorne who still stood in the shadows. The lady's eyes widened as the massive beast approached her.

"Blue is harmless," Edmund assured her.

Miss Thorne cast him a look of open skepticism

before tentatively offering a hand for Blue to scent. The wolfhound's head reached Miss Thorne's waist. As Blue inspected their visitor, the lady peered more closely at her in turn. "She's one blue eye," Miss Thorne said with some surprise.

"Since birth."

"Heteroglaucos," Miss Thorne murmured.

"I beg your pardon?"

"Heteroglaucos. It's a term Aristotle used to describe the condition. From the Greek, *hetero* or different and *glaukos*, which, as best as I can tell, refers to grey or silver hues. Although, perhaps that's not the best descriptor for your dog, as she's one blue eye and one dark."

"Heterochromia," he suggested.

"Heterochromia. Different colors. I like it." Miss Thorne gave a slow smile of pleasure at the word, and Edmund's breath caught before he recalled that she was supposed to be leaving.

"Yes, well."

She jumped as if she'd been released from a spell. "Lord Byron," she said, calling to her dog.

Edmund choked on a laugh at the ridiculous name. It was far too self-important for such a scrap of a thing. Miss Thorne collected her violin case, then she and *Lord Byron* strode from the room. They made their way easily in the shadows to the front of the Vicarage. Edmund knew a moment of indecision as the pair stepped out into the night. It would be gentlemanly to escort her up the path to Summerfield, but before he could offer to do so, she stopped and turned.

"My apologies," she said, "for the intrusion."

"And you have mine, for surprising you in such a fashion."

"We are agreed then? No one need know of our encounter?"

"We are agreed."

And with that, she was gone. It was only later that night, as Edmund sat before the dying fire listening to Blue's snores, that he noticed Miss Thorne had left her book. He retrieved it from where it had slid under the chaise and the pages fell open. It wasn't *The Prelude*, as he'd expected, but a handwritten diary of some sort. He closed the volume swiftly before he could breach the lady's privacy, but not before he recognized the script that had decorated Lady Worth's invitation. A smile tipped his lips. Somehow, Miss Thorne's indulgent loops and exuberant flourishes seemed to fit the lady.

———

AMELIA SETTLED LORD Byron in his little bed then she climbed between her sheets. Morpheus didn't come, however, and she lay awake for long hours.

It wasn't the gemstone quality of Mr. Corbyn's eyes that kept her from her sleep, or the image of him with his coat off and cravat hanging carelessly. (Although, *that* sight was enough to earn a few moments' contemplation.)

Nor was it the rich, velvety tenor of his voice, although it had sent a ripple through her belly when he'd surprised her with the gift of "heterochromia."

She didn't even think overlong about the fact that he knew who she was. She was almost certain he'd nearly called her by that detestable name. The Poisoned Thorne.

She punched her pillow and turned again. No, the fact that kept her tossing until dawn was simple: in the confusion of their encounter, in the flustering aftermath of seeing him in his shirtsleeves, she'd gone and left her journal behind.

CHAPTER TEN

*Why do one's peculiarities reveal themselves
at the most inopportune times? But then, is there
ever a fitting occasion for such a disclosure?*
—From the private journal of Miss Amelia Thorne

DESPITE HER RESTLESS night, Amelia woke early, her eyes scratchy from lack of sleep. With a sigh, she realized it was too early to call at the Vicarage for her journal, so she decided to find a quick breakfast in the kitchen then pass the morning walking the fells with Lord Byron. By the time she returned, Mr. Corbyn should be up and properly dressed, unless he was the sort of gentleman who preferred to waste the best part of the day lounging about in a banyan.

She washed and donned a simple dark brown skirt and jacket and her sturdiest walking boots then roused Lord Byron, whose slumber had not been disturbed in the least by the previous evening's events.

Taking the servants' corridor once again, she crept past the public rooms, though she doubted any of her aunt's guests would be about at this hour. And yet, as she peered through the dining room's narrow doorway, she was surprised to see the object of her most recent thoughts.

Mr. Corbyn was alone at the sideboard, tall and properly dressed, with not a banyan in sight. She watched him for a long moment in the narrow opening, admiring the line of his jaw and the width of his shoulders, all of which were rather nice. He showed no signs that *he'd* passed a sleepless night, but then he wouldn't. It wasn't his journal which had been left behind.

She chewed her lip and considered how best to broach the matter of retrieving her belongings when she was meant to remain out of sight of her aunt's guests. But certainly, these were extenuating circumstances—this was her *journal*. She drew a breath and gave the bottom of her jacket a decisive tug.

Before she could announce herself, though, Lord Byron gave an aggravated bark at the top of the kitchen stairs. Amelia shushed him and ducked swiftly out of the dining room doorway, but not before Mr. Corbyn's head came up.

Had he seen her? Would he think she'd been spying? Well, she had been spying, but that was beside the point. Oh, why had she ducked into the shadows like a guilty person? And now, too much time had passed to announce herself with any dignity.

She closed her eyes and held her breath, but her silent prayers went unanswered. After a long, measured beat, heavy footsteps crossed the dining room. She remained where she stood, just out of sight on the other side of the wall. Perhaps, if he couldn't see anyone in the immediate opening, he would carry on with his breakfast without investigating the shadows.

But then Lord Byron, that bold corsair, traitor of all traitors, squeezed through the opening to trot into the dining room bold as you please. Amelia looked up to find Mr. Corbyn's gaze on her. A smile curved his lips as he studied her pressed against the wall.

"Miss Thorne," he said as if the situation weren't at all unusual. But then, once he'd found a female sleeping in his library, perhaps a woman lurking behind the dining room wall wasn't so extraordinary.

"Mr. Corbyn." She meant her tone to be one of Cool Nonchalance, but she feared the effort was lost to the hitch in her voice.

"Are you… hiding?"

"Of course not," she said briskly as she stepped away from the wall.

The smile returned to his lips, and she forced herself to ignore the way it lit his blue-green eyes. "Well then, would you like to join me for breakfast?" At her hesitation, he added, "The footman has gone to fetch coffee, but he should return soon. We won't be alone."

Her eyes narrowed with surprise. He had a concern for her reputation? Then common sense reasserted itself, and she realized his concern was more likely for his own. But Aunt Mary and the other guests wouldn't be down for some time yet, and she *did* wish to retrieve her journal.

"Very well," she conceded, "but I can't stay long."

He pushed the door open further to admit her, holding it as she went through. Her woolen skirts brushed his trousers, and there was no way she could miss the scent of his shaving soap as she passed. It was soft and spicy, like cloves and warm citrus. She'd savored a full breath of it before she knew what she was doing.

She rounded the end of the table and frowned at Lord Byron, who curled innocently on the hearth. Lord Byron, who'd been so impatient for her in the corridor but was now content to idle away his morning hours in Polite Company.

She took the chair across from Mr. Corbyn's. He sat and replaced his napkin on his lap. Amelia did the same as the footman returned with the coffee. It had been years since she'd shared a meal with anyone other than her family, and she was uncertain what to do with her hands. She was about to ask about her journal when he spoke.

"Shall I fix you a plate?" he asked with a glance toward the sideboard, and she realized *that* was what she should have been doing. Heavens, where had her wits gone? It wasn't as if she'd never taken breakfast before. She removed the napkin from her lap and rose, and Mr. Corbyn stood. She waved him back to his seat.

"I was merely considering what I wish to have this morning," she explained as she strode to the sideboard. Belatedly, she checked her long steps and slowed to a more refined walk.

"It's a weighty consideration," he agreed, although she detected the hint of a smile in his voice.

"The weightiest."

She eyed the spread of fruits, eggs, fish, ham and fried bacon, not to mention the toast, rolls, and tea cakes. It was more than the kitchen usually sent up, and leagues more than what she was accustomed to having on a tray in her room—an overly full stomach made for an uncomfortable walk, after all. Finally making her selection, she resumed her seat with a bit of poached pear and a triangle of toast.

Mr. Corbyn eyed her spartan plate before returning his attention to his own, which contained, by the looks of it, two of everything. "I don't enjoy walking the fells on a full stomach," she said, though why she felt the need to explain herself was beyond her. He was merely one of her aunt's guests, soon to be gone and forgotten.

"Do you walk often?"

"Every day, if the weather is clement."

"Excellent," he said and her brows lifted. "I imagine you must know the best prospects then."

"There are no unattractive views of Windermere, if that is what you mean."

"I imagine not, to the casual visitor, but I'm looking for strong lines and good light."

"Are you a painter?" The notion was more disappointing than it ought to have been. Windermere saw countless London gentlemen who fancied themselves artists. Painters and composers and—heaven help them—*poets* who meant to capture the sweeping grandeur of the area. Few could aspire to Mr. Wordsworth's talent, though many thought they might. She frowned to think Mr. Corbyn was just another in a long line of hackneyed imitators.

He shook his head. "No, my current interests lie in the field of photography," he said.

A photographer. Well. That was… unexpected. She'd never met a photographer before. She lowered her fork to say, "Do you mean a portraitist? Have you a studio in London then?"

He frowned and cleared his throat, and she had the impression she'd insulted him. "I've done portraits, of course—no photographer with a family can avoid them—but my work is more academic than commercial."

Ah, she *had* insulted him then. She pressed her lips against a smile. "What, precisely, does an *academic* photographer study?"

"The properties of light and how it reveals the colors of the spectrum. Photo-reactive emulsions. Exposure techniques and improved lenses. That sort of thing." As he spoke, his hands moved and his voice rose and fell in an easy cadence that betrayed his enthusiasm.

Emulsion, she thought as her lips silently wrapped the word. It had such an interesting sound to it. *Emulsion.* She picked a corner off her toast and said, in the manner of a normal person, "How does one learn about such things? Did you attend university?"

"I did, although much of my early education came from my father and grandfather. They're both astronomers with a tremendous amount of scientific knowledge between the pair of them."

Amelia smiled wistfully, recalling a time when she'd had her own, tremendously knowledgeable father with whom she might consult on literature and poetry. Philosophy and history. Captain Alexander Thorne, with his eye-crinkling humor and larger-than-life stories from his years at sea, had had a rare talent for making the dullest of topics entertaining. If only she hadn't disappointed him so with her scandal.

She nibbled a bite of pear and saw that Mr. Corbyn had made impressive inroads through his own full plate. She returned them to his question. "And you're seeking a prospect for your photography with—how did you say it—strong lines and good light?"

"Yes, I'm experimenting with a new technique, one I hope will someday be capable of capturing color."

"A *color* photograph?" she said with no little surprise. He smiled and her breath caught, much as it had during their first meeting in the Laurel Leaf Emporium. She averted her gaze so she could consider his words further. "The sky, the lake, the trees... all in color," she mused slowly.

"Precisely. My guidebook recommends several walks. I thought to try my luck at Brant Fell today for some images of the peaks across the water. "

She shook her head. "Not unless you mean to

wait until after luncheon. The morning mists will be too thick to capture anything with your camera. If you don't have time to ferry across to the Lanca-shire side, you should try the Biskey Howe route. It passes below Dragon's Breath Crag, where you'll have views of the lake's islands and the fells in the distance."

"Dragon's Breath Crag… I don't think I've come across it in my reading."

Amelia hesitated. She'd spoken without thinking when she used her father's pet name for the stone outcropping. Its proper name was Lamb's Head, but her father had always claimed the jagged and jutting rock formation looked more like the angry breath of a dragon, especially when the setting sun caught its edges.

Clearing her throat, Amelia said, "You won't find Dragon's Breath Crag in your book. The entrance to the path is hard to pick up, but you can catch it just beyond the Vicarage."

"And it can be traveled in a morning's time? I'm to return for portrait sittings after luncheon."

"You *are* a portraitist then."

"I am not a portraitist," he replied somewhat repressively as he speared a bite of sausage. "It's merely a diversion for your aunt's party."

Amelia's nose wrinkled at this reminder of her aunt's guests before she smoothed her features into a more pleasant expression. "Well, then, as to the duration, the western branch of the route can take the better part of a day to traverse. The eastern side is a much shorter path, though. It can be accomplished in two hours' time, *if* you've a sturdy constitution."

Mr. Corbyn did seem a sturdy and capable sort with his firm shoulders and lean form. But he was a tourist, for all intents, and her tone carried a bit of a point to it. It might have been her imagination, but she thought he sat a little straighter in his chair at the sound of it.

"There is nothing wrong with my constitution," he assured her. And then, "My valet and I mean to set out after breaking our fast. I would be grateful if you could provide directions."

She chewed the last of her toast, considering. "No, but I can show you where to find the path, in exchange for the return of my book. I left it at the Vicarage." Her heart thumped at this reminder of their encounter the previous night, and she forced herself to hold his gaze.

A slow beat passed before he laughed. "You drive a bargain, Miss Thorne, but I'll take it." And then, reaching into his coat, he withdrew her slim leather journal. "I brought it with me on the chance I might encounter you this morning."

Amelia gasped and reached for her book. "You

might have started with this."

She folded her fingers around the smooth leather, brushing his hand in the process. The contact was startling—there was warmth and energy in his touch—and she barely avoided jerking her hand away as he released the book. The leather, she noticed, was warm where it had been tucked inside his coat.

"Did you read it?" she asked.

"Of course not." His affront seemed genuine, and she knew a moment's remorse for her hasty tongue.

Noises sounded in the main hall beyond the dining room. The other guests would begin arriving soon. She clasped her journal to her and prepared to go. Then, recalling her bargain with Mr. Corbyn, she said, "Meet me behind the Vicarage in twenty minutes."

If her words, which sounded suspiciously like an assignation, caused a blush to rise on her throat, he gave no indication that he noticed.

"Twenty minutes," he agreed.

CHAPTER ELEVEN

*Oft before the hour of school
I travelled round our little lake, five miles
Of pleasant wandering.*
—William Wordsworth, *The Prelude*

EDMUND WATCHED MISS Thorne leave the dining room by way of the narrow servants' entrance, her journal clutched to her breast. A mixture of curiosity and intrigue filled him.

She wasn't... odd, so much as unique, and he found himself intensely curious about this lurking female who'd set London tongues wagging years before. There'd even been cartoons of the Poisoned Thorne in the news sheets, but the lady he'd encountered hardly seemed the sort to inspire such lurid accounts. She wasn't a conventional miss, it was true, but neither did she seem scandalous, their late-night encounter notwithstanding.

But for a society whose memory was as short as it was malleable, the tales about her had enjoyed an unusually long life. It seemed there were new stories to titillate the *ton* every so often, or perhaps merely old stories dressed in new clothes. But Windermere was far from London. Surely, the local society must be more forgiving, and he found himself wondering why she didn't join her aunt's party. Why she felt the need to skulk about in corridors.

As Temple and Pearson entered the dining room, he realized he must hurry if he were to meet with Miss Thorne at their appointed time. He left the gentlemen to fill their plates and returned to the Vicarage for Blue and Finch.

Finch's thoughts on learning Miss Thorne was to show them the way were plain in his tight expression. It was clear to see he disapproved of Edmund's association with the lady from the night before, though he uttered not a word of reproof.

Edmund ignored his valet's censure, and they entered the small gardener's outbuilding where Edmund's equipment had been stored. Edmund pulled his watch from his pocket. It had been a gift from his father, who recognized a scientist's need for precision, and there was a small seconds watch in the center. Edmund waited until the second hand moved toward the top before he said, "Ready?"

"Ready," Finch confirmed, and even Blue stood at attention.

"Begin."

Together they set to packing his leather carrying cases with the plates and other equipment they would require for photographing in the field. They would carry the better part of it themselves, but some months ago, Edmund had designed a small pack for Blue that allowed her to tote some of the less sensitive supplies, leaving Edmund or Finch to carry the more delicate instruments and glass plates. He and Finch worked in tandem, each focused on their assigned tasks. When all was finished, Edmund consulted his watch again.

"Five minutes, thirteen seconds," he said with a grin.

"Our best yet," Finch replied.

Indeed, there was time to spare before they were to meet Miss Thorne, but as they rounded the Vicarage, he was surprised to find her waiting for them, her little dog sitting at her feet. She carried another book—her new Wordsworth by the look of it—and she was dressed in a thick wool cloak and sturdy walking boots.

"My apologies for keeping you waiting," Edmund said.

She frowned as they stopped before her. "What is that?" she asked, motioning to their leather cases.

"Photographic supplies."

Her frown deepened as she eyed them. "You'll want to have a care for your footing. The path can be steep and uneven in places, and the stones will be slick from the mist."

To Edmund, who'd traipsed the North Downs of Kent for as many years as he could walk, and often with more equipment than they carried today, this was an unnecessary warning. "I'm certain we'll manage."

Miss Thorne gave an elegant shrug of indifference. "They're your bones."

Edmund felt they'd been measured and assessed by her knowing gaze and had come up short. The notion made him all the more determined to prove he was up to the challenge of her hills.

———

THEY WERE NOT up to the challenge of Miss Thorne's hills. Or rather, Finch was not.

They'd climbed to a high outcrop where they unpacked Edmund's camera and tripod mounting stand. The tableau spread before them was ripe with lush greens and rich blues and the first tints of autumn. It had been perfectly framed by a clear sky above and the sharp fells on either side. A broad expanse of misty meadow lay below them and the shimmering lake beyond that, freckled with an archipelago of small islands.

Miss Thorne had not been mistaken in her recommendation.

But as Edmund timed the exposure, his valet misstepped and tumbled to land in a heap at the bottom of a spiky patch of hawthorn. Fortunately, Finch had removed the leather cases from his shoulder, else they'd have heard the expensive sound of shattering photography plates along with his valet's distressed shout as he went top over tail.

Now, Edmund supported Finch's limping form with one shoulder while balancing both his own and Finch's cases on the other. Blue trotted along beside them with her own cargo as they followed the trail back to where they'd started.

"Fiend take it, Finch," Edmund muttered. "What have you been eating?"

Never had a man's name been less appropriate to his appearance. In Edmund's experience, valets were slight bird-like men with narrow shoulders, but for some reason, he'd managed to find the only valet in all of England with the frame of a medieval Norseman.

His valet must have weighed more than Edmund's own respectable thirteen stone, and Edmund felt every pound as he navigated them along the tricky terrain.

"Apologies, my lord," Finch said through gritted teeth. Sweat pearled on his waxen brow, and Edmund paused so they might both find their breath. They'd long since missed luncheon and Lady Worth's portrait sittings, but he thought—hoped—another half hour would see them back at the Vicarage where he could send for the doctor.

He didn't like the look of Finch's foot. Some twenty minutes back, he'd insisted on removing his valet's boot, and he was glad for it. Finch had paled at every bump and jerk of the leather, but now the foot was quite swollen in its woolen stocking, and Edmund didn't think he'd have gotten the boot off had he listened to Finch's protests much longer.

"Are you certain you have the case with the new lens?" Finch asked him now.

"I have it."

"And the tripod?"

"Don't worry over it," Edmund said. In truth, he'd forgotten the stand in his haste to return them to the Vicarage. But Finch would only worry over the thing if he knew they'd left it behind, or worse, he'd insist they return for it.

"Did you at least finish the exposure?"

"The exposure is fine," Edmund said, though he was certain it must be overdone. He'd be fortunate if there was anything at all on the plate once he found time to develop it.

"I hold the Thorne female responsible," Finch grumbled.

"I don't think she's the one who misstepped to land in a pile of hawthorn."

"I wouldn't be surprised if she sent us on this path just to achieve this very outcome."

"To what aim, Finch?"

"You know who she is, don't you?"

Edmund shifted. A knot was forming in his shoulder beneath Finch's considerable weight. "I'm aware," he said, "though I wonder how you're acquainted with the lady."

"Everyone's heard of the Poisoned Thorne. I recognized her likeness from the cartoons. Mark me, she'll be angling to be your countess soon enough."

Edmund barked a laugh. He couldn't help it. Miss Thorne as a countess was as incongruous a notion as Finch as gentleman's valet. As if Her Majesty would ever approve such a match.

If the scandal of the Poisoned Thorne weren't enough to render the lady ineligible, her parentage sealed it. Once Edmund recalled Miss Thorne's identity, and with Miss Worth's tale of Captain Thorne fresh in his mind, the particulars of her family had come back to him. Her father had been a sea merchant, albeit a wealthy one, and her mother an Irish seamstress—and a Catholic to boot. Miss Thorne might rise above these marks to make an

acceptable match with a pleasant gentleman someday, but she'd never be accepted as countess to an
English peer.

"I don't think you've anything to worry about
there," Edmund said. "You need only concern yourself with that foot."

"I'll be right as rain come morning," Finch assured him. "You'll not be without a valet, or a photography assistant, for longer than that."

"I can dress myself," Edmund said. It wasn't as if
Finch was much help in that regard anyway, but he
was invaluable as an assistant. Edmund checked his
sigh to think his time at Windermere might not be as
fruitful as he'd hoped.

A bride, he reminded himself. He was here to
find a bride, not to pursue his experiments.

———

LATER THAT AFTERNOON, Amelia returned from her
own walk and hung her mist-sodden cloak to dry in
the kitchen. Lord Byron tap-tapped across the slate
tiles to the stairs and she followed. With the Vicarage unavailable to her, she was intent on reaching
her room and curling up in the window seat with
Wordsworth.

She traveled the servants' corridor past the dining room and the music room. As she neared the

drawing room, Octavia stepped through the door and into her path. "There you are, Cousin," she said and Amelia stopped. "My, but you're a sight for bored eyes."

"You've grown bored?" Amelia asked with a smile. "But it's only the second day of your mother's party."

"The gentlemen are pleasant enough, but I'm afraid the ladies have little imagination." Octavia gave a little sigh of resignation before adding, "And Mama is determined we're to play charades next."

"Oh? Are the portraits already finished—" Amelia stopped, but she was too late for Octavia's astute ears.

Her cousin's brow lifted in wry amusement. "How did you know about the portraits? Have you been listening at doors?" she asked.

Amelia frowned and Octavia tapped her chin, considering. "Or perhaps… Yes, you've been conversing with our resident portraitist, I think. It's there in the color on your cheeks. But to answer your question, no. Your Mr. Corbyn hasn't joined us yet, and Mama is quite put out with him. Lady Staveley has never had a portraitist attend her house parties, you know, and it was to be quite the coup. Mama might have stormed the Vicarage for him if I hadn't persuaded her of the impropriety of such a course. What would our guests think, if their hostess were to drag one of them about by the ears?"

Amelia tucked a smile at the image of Mr. Corbyn being handled in such a fashion by Aunt Mary, who was a full head shorter than the man. But then her cousin's words settled uncomfortably. "He hasn't come to do the portraits?"

Octavia shook her head, and Amelia chewed her lip. Mr. Corbyn had been very clear that he must return in time for luncheon, and the path she'd set them on would easily have allowed for a short walk. But the ground was uneven and slick from the mist, as she'd warned them, and he and his valet had been toting about a ridiculous number of cases. She forced the concern from her brow as Octavia returned to the matter of charades.

"Go change and join us," Octavia said. "You've always enjoyed charades, and you're so much more clever at them than I."

Amelia scoffed at that tarradiddle, for no one was better at dramatics than Octavia. She shook her head, and Octavia's answering frown was immediate.

"What excuse could you possibly have? You need only appear as if you meant to join us all along. Mama won't gainsay you in front of the guests."

"There's something else I must attend to," Amelia said as she turned to retrace her steps. What her cousin failed to understand time and again was that

Amelia had no interest in rejoining Society. But now there was also the matter of Mr. Corbyn's absence. She couldn't deny she was a trifle concerned.

"What could be more important than charades?" Octavia said to her back.

Amelia ignored her and collected her damp cloak from its peg in the kitchen. She strode swiftly to the Vicarage, hesitating only briefly before rapping on the door. When there was no answer, she collected William, the coachman. He knew the fells better than anyone. If Mr. Corbyn had strayed from the path, William would know the surest way to find them.

"Whar d'ye think they started, lassie?"

"I showed them the Biskey Howe path. They picked it up behind the Vicarage, and I gave them directions to Lamb's Head."

"Aye, even carryin' gear as ye said they were, they should hae come back an hour or mair since."

Amelia gave him a tight nod and eyed the sky. It was clear for now, but storms could blow up quickly to descend upon the lake. Perhaps she ought to have been more forceful in her warning to them. Tourists were forever becoming injured on the paths as they underestimated the steepness or overestimated their own agility. Yes, she most definitely should have issued a stronger warning. The sooner they located Mr. Corbyn's party, the better.

Of course, it was possible he'd simply been captivated by the view and had decided to forgo the portrait sittings in favor of something more transcendent. Amelia knew what she would have chosen were the choice hers to make.

She and William rounded the first curve in the path with determined steps. They hadn't gone more than a hundred yards along the graveled trail when the missing trio appeared around a bend ahead. The giant wolfhound led the way, but not far behind, Mr. Corbyn carried all of their equipment on one side as he supported his valet's weight on the other.

William hurried forward to assist them, and Amelia's eyes widened at the sight of Finch's swollen, wool-clad foot. The valet gave her a dark scowl as if she'd been personally responsible for his injury. She returned his frown with one of her own, though with less force than she might have done.

"I'll send for the doctor," she said as the gentlemen passed her.

CHAPTER TWELVE

D R. PEMBROKE'S KNEES creaked as he rose from the chaise where Finch had been placed in the library. "Broken," he said, and Amelia's stomach sank to hear the diagnosis. "Thankfully," Pembroke continued, "the skin is intact. I'll apply a splint, but you'll need to stay off that foot."

Finch shifted, wincing as he pulled himself higher on the low-backed seat. "For how long?"

"You don't wish to sustain permanent damage. I'd say a few weeks at best. A month or more at worst."

"A month!" Finch's glance shifted to Mr. Corbyn, and Amelia could read the concern on his face. He probably worried for his position—an immobile valet wasn't much of a valet, after all, and a London gentleman wasn't likely to dress himself.

Mr. Corbyn's expression was inscrutable. Her ire rose in tandem with her guilt as she wondered if he'd turn the man out. Finch wouldn't find work in his current condition. Why, he probably had a family to support. An ailing aunt or a lonely mother at the very least. To turn him out now would be unconscionable.

Mr. Corbyn frowned at his valet, and Amelia's sense of injustice was fueled on Finch's behalf. "Mr. Corbyn," she began stoutly, just as he spoke to Finch.

"You must do as Pembroke advises," he said in his low voice, and Amelia's ire eased just a bit.

"But there's work to be done," Finch protested. And then, curiously, he cast a glance toward Amelia and muttered what sounded like, "Perils to defend against."

Mr. Corbyn frowned at his employee. "And there will still be *work* to do when you're recovered."

Amelia looked at Mr. Corbyn more closely to gauge his sincerity. He rubbed a hand along the back of his neck, his blue-green eyes angled in concern beneath the dark slash of his brows. He appeared earnest.

Finch opened his mouth to say more, and Mr. Corbyn's gaze turned to one of exasperation. "I've already told you, Finch, I have things well in hand," he assured his valet, which earned him a tight-lipped silence.

As Dr. Pembroke applied a salve to Finch's hawthorn scratches, Amelia leaned toward Mr. Corbyn. "I think," she whispered, "your valet would prefer to know his services are not so easily dismissed."

Amelia waited while he considered her words. In her experience, London gentlemen were not inclined to heed a lady's advice, no matter how sincerely it was given. So, it was something of a surprise when he gave her a short nod of acknowledgement and turned back to his valet.

"Finch," he said evenly, "there's no need for concern. While I can select my own waistcoats—temporarily, of course—I will feel your absence behind the camera keenly. But it's a sacrifice we both must make if you're to return to full health. I can't have my assistant hobbled."

Finch frowned a moment at this speech, causing Dr. Pembroke to pause in his ministrations. But then the valet's face relaxed. "Very well, my lord."

Amelia's brows shot up at the valet's address. She'd been calling the man *Mister* Corbyn. Had she gotten it wrong? But no, Aunt Mary also referred to him as such, and when he'd introduced himself to her the night before, he'd given his name simply as Edmund Corbyn.

She considered him as he strode to the leather bags and cases he'd left at the library's entrance. He lifted a pair of them and exited the room, the wolfhound following at his heels. Amelia hesitated, at a loss for what more she could do to aid the gentlemen but drawn by that fiendish companion of hers, curiosity.

When man and dog crossed the lawn to the gardener's outbuilding, she bent to retrieve the remaining bags. They were heavier than she expected, and she lurched beneath their weight.

"Careful!" Finch called from the chaise. He started to rise to assist her, but Dr. Pembroke pressed him back down with a firm hand.

Amelia moved with deliberate steps to follow Mr. Corbyn. Blue greeted her with a sniff when she opened the door to the low stone shed. Mr. Corbyn's back was to her as he unpacked his cases, but at her entrance he turned. Seeing the burden balanced on her shoulders, he hurried to relieve her. She wasn't certain if he was being gentlemanly or if he simply had a concern for the state of his equipment. Their hands brushed when he took the cases from her, and the same energy she'd felt at breakfast zipped along her arm.

"Thank you," she said as she rubbed at her

sleeve.

He gingerly set the cases on a worktable, and Amelia turned her gaze with some surprise to the orderly state of the room. What had once been haphazard storage at best, and poorly managed chaos at worst, was now a tidy photographer's closet. The cobwebs had been cleared and old gardening implements neatly organized along one wall to make room for Mr. Corbyn's equipment. And there was quite a bit of it. Trays and tanks and bottles. Stands made of brass and wood and more cases like the ones she'd carried. It was little wonder the man required two carriages.

Mr. Corbyn gave her a rueful glance. "It's a lot, I know."

"You'll certainly be hard pressed to make a swift escape, if one is ever warranted."

He stared at her for a beat as if uncertain, and then he laughed. The sound was warm and she felt the echo of it in her belly. "Is that a concern for you, Miss Thorne? The ease of a swift escape?"

"It's merely a practical observation."

"Well, I dare say you're right. I'll not be fleeing to the Continent with any haste if I mean to take my equipment with me."

Unable to deny her curiosity any longer, she asked, "Why does your valet call you 'my lord?'"

He turned his attention to a tall stack of wooden

boxes and aligned the edges. "It's merely a jest," he replied, "and a poor one at that. Finch's humor leaves much to be desired."

Amelia frowned, thinking it an odd sort of jest, but she was relieved, nonetheless. Befriending a London gentleman was bad enough, but a London lord? Then she nearly laughed aloud at the path her thoughts had taken. *Befriending*, as if they might become bosom bows. They were merely sharing conversation.

Then, to his surprise as much as her own, she blurted, "I'll bring a pair of crutches for your valet."

"I beg your pardon?"

She cleared her throat. "There are some crutches in the attic at Summerfield. I'll bring them to aid in Mr. Finch's recovery."

He smiled. "While I thank you for the sentiment, we don't wish to impose on your aunt and uncle's hospitality. If you or Lady Worth could recommend a suitable shop—"

"It's *my* hospitality," Amelia said and immediately cursed her tongue for its waywardness. But at his confused silence, she felt compelled to explain. "The Vicarage, Summerfield—and the crutches—they belong to me."

"I see," he said, though it was clear he did not. "And your aunt and uncle...?"

"My uncle has been tasked with the management

of my property until my next birthday."

"Well, in that case, I accept your generosity on behalf of my valet. We would be grateful for the loan of your crutches."

She gave him a brisk nod and turned to go, but he spoke again.

"Miss Thorne, I apologize for my presumption, but may I ask another question?"

Her lips twitched. "Presumptuous questions are the best sort, Mr. Corbyn, followed closely by impertinent ones."

He smiled and pushed his spectacles up with one finger, and she was reminded how close the gardener's shed was. What was she thinking, to flirt with the man? Had she not learned anything five years before?

"If Summerfield belongs to you, then why do you not join your aunt's party?"

The question was unexpected. Did he really not know her history? Was it possible he was unacquainted with the tale of the Poisoned Thorne?

But no, everyone had heard the stories. Many had trimmed them with their own embellishments. And for those who had forgotten, the papers revived them every year or so. Even Mr. Tidwell at the Laurel Leaf Emporium had once commented on the drawings he'd seen in *Punch*.

No, Mr. Corbyn simply hadn't made the connection yet between the siren known throughout the *ton* as the Poisoned Thorne and the sensibly attired Miss Amelia Thorne.

She hesitated, the truth a bitter pill on the end of her tongue. Finally, she said simply, "I have little use for large gatherings." Before he could follow that with another query, she turned his question around. Casting her eye toward his stacks of photography supplies, she asked, "Why, Mr. Corbyn, have you come to Summerfield? It's clear you've other interests. I can't imagine a fortnight of cards and scavenger hunts is to your liking."

He nodded, and she was surprised by how easily he admitted it. She thought he might dissemble or offer a polite denial at the very least, but he merely said, "It's true. I'd rather be pursuing my experiments, but I find myself in need of a wife."

The air in the shed stilled as she took this in. It shouldn't have come as a surprise. Matrimony was one of the primary aims of house parties, after all, and her aunt's house party in particular. But the stark admission unsettled her, as did the way in which he'd said it. He *needed* a wife. He hadn't said he *desired* a wife, nor that the time had come for him to take a wife. He *needed* a wife.

Was he a fortune hunter, then? She resisted the urge to groan aloud at how easily she'd told him Summerfield belonged to her. Was it any wonder her father had given her fortune into her uncle's keeping?

"Well, then," she said tightly, "you'd best join the others, as you'll not find a wife standing about in here."

CHAPTER THIRTEEN

*Beware the unforeseen variable, which can threaten
any sound experiment's intended course.*
—From the scientific journals of Mr. Edmund Corbyn

A FROWN PULLED Edmund's brows together as he watched Miss Thorne depart. He thought they'd got on rather well, but then she'd neatly set him in his place with her parting words. But one thing was certain: when he asked why she didn't join her aunt's party, she'd delivered him a bit of flim-flammery. As a man with three sisters, he knew fluff and nonsense when he heard it, and Miss Thorne had given the truth a cautious berth.

She claimed a dislike of large gatherings, but he'd sensed a bit of longing in her. Not for her aunt's party, *per se*, but for a bit of amusement. Interaction with other people, perhaps. She wasn't meant to lurk about in corridors. He'd felt her loneliness, and the weight of it had muted the already low light in the gardener's outbuilding. But whether it was her scandal that kept her from others or something else, he couldn't say.

He returned to the Vicarage to find Pembroke had departed. He checked his watch and sighed. There was no time to retrieve his mounting stand from the path where Finch had fallen. He'd already missed his hostess's luncheon, and he feared missing tea might be an unforgivable slight.

He'd brought an additional stand with him, of course, but the one he'd left on the path was crafted of ash with brass stretchers, so it was both firm and lightweight. It worked far better on uneven terrain than any of his other tripods. He resigned himself to putting its retrieval off until the following day—and hoped it would still be where he'd left it.

After confirming that Finch didn't require anything, he changed his clothes and set out for Summerfield. He was the first to arrive in the drawing room, so he occupied himself with studying the painting above the mantel. It was of a ship, *The Aileen*. He thought it must have been Captain Thorne's, named for his understanding Irish wife. As he examined the painting's wide brushstrokes, the low murmur of voices came to him from the other side of the wall. Two women, if he weren't mistaken, and at least one of them was displeased. Her words were clipped and harsh while her companion's manner was hushed and placating.

Edmund wasn't in the habit of listening at doors, or walls, as it were. He was about to move to the other side of the room, but then he heard the unmistakable phrase, "Poisoned Thorne," and he did the unthinkable. He moved closer to the wall.

"You wrote me that she would not be here," the displeased woman said shortly, "and yet, I spied her not ten minutes past in this very hall." That voice belonged to Lady Foxgate.

"I said she would not be joining our party, and you may rest assured that she will not." And that, Edmund realized, was Lady Worth.

"You're splitting hairs, Mary. I cannot take a risk with my Rebecca's reputation. Why, what would people say to know she's spent so much time in proximity to such a female?"

More words were exchanged, but they were too low and indistinct to make out. Edmund moved away from the wall before he could be caught eavesdropping and shortly, the brisk sound of footsteps signaled an end to the ladies' conversation.

He had just taken up a position near the window when his hostess glided in. Lady Worth gave him a smile he recognized as false, even without the knowledge of her encounter with Lady Foxgate.

"Mr. Corbyn," she said evenly. "Ah, and here come Misters Temple and Pearson."

"Lady Worth," Edmund said.

"We will make a smaller group for tea," she said with a practiced sigh. "Lord and Lady Foxgate have been called away unexpectedly, and I'm afraid they must depart directly with Miss Newton."

Temple and Pearson made the expected sounds of disappointment, and Edmund's own brow dipped at the news that Lady Foxgate would leave the house party altogether before suffering a fortnight *in proximity* to Miss Thorne. The small-mindedness of it set his teeth on edge, though it did shed some light on Miss Thorne's reluctance to join her aunt's activities.

Lady Worth then waxed effusive over Finch's injury. Miss Thorne, it seemed, had already apprised her of it. "Of course, you must not hesitate to ask for anything you require as your man recovers."

Edmund thanked the lady for her hospitality, but the words felt a bit wooden now that he knew it wasn't her hospitality to offer. "You have my apologies for missing luncheon," he told his hostess. "I hope the other guests weren't too disappointed at not having their portraits made."

"We are all just that relieved to know you're safe," she said, though he detected a hint of irritation about her eyes. "But perhaps you might try again tomorrow."

Edmund, who knew a direct order when he heard one, nodded. "Of course."

——

AFTER HER ENCOUNTER with Mr. Corbyn in the gardener's shed, Amelia went walking again. The mirror-smooth lake with its purple-mountain backdrop had a way of soothing her when she was feeling out of sorts, and there was no denying that Mr. Corbyn had a talent for putting her in such a state. Her usual disposition was an easy one, without an excess of upset or discomfiture, but it seemed a mere glance from the gentleman was enough to throw her off her balance.

She regretted her hasty assumption about his intentions at Windermere. Belatedly, she recalled her aunt's words about his income—six thousand a year if Aunt Mary's intelligence was reliable. A man with such prospects would not be hunting a fortune, and he certainly hadn't deserved her harsh words.

So, when she came across a finely made tripod atop a rocky outcropping near Dragon's Breath Crag, she didn't hesitate. After a brief examination to see how the thing worked, she folded the legs and toted it back down.

She left the stand in the Vicarage's sheltered portico—a peace offering of sorts—and returned to her room at Summerfield. There she found Lord Byron curled on his little bed and a pile of unexpected boxes at the foot of her own bed. Covered in pale peach silk and with an elaborate *F* embroidered atop each one, they looked suspiciously like the sort of boxes Octavia had brought home from Sir Frederick's shop.

She opened the first one and frowned to find a skirt of the softest blue wool. It was the precise color of Windermere's glassy waters on a summer's day. Another box revealed a skirt and matching bodice in spring green and another, a walking set in a cheerful pale coral.

The last box was larger than the others, and her breath tightened in her chest as she carefully lifted the lid. Inside, nestled on a bed of fine tissue wrapping and secured with satin ribbons, lay a taffeta silk confection in aged gold. She lifted it and the fabric slipped over her hands, cool to the touch. It was soft and luxurious with a subtle sheen to it. A full evening dress, as if she meant to attend a ball.

She was waiting in Octavia's window seat by the time her cousin returned to dress for supper.

"I take it Sir Frederick's boxes have arrived," Octavia said after a cursory glance at Amelia's face.

Amelia cast her Wordsworth aside and swung her stockinged feet to the floor. "What are you doing,

Octavia? You know I've no intention of joining your mother's party, much less attending Lady Staveley's ball. You're only wasting money— my money—on unnecessary purchases."

"Oh, pish. These are my gift to you. Remember the arrangement I made with Sir Frederick?"

"You said gloves! He provided you with an extra pair of *gloves*."

Octavia waved a dismissive hand, which only sent Amelia's irritation higher. "And a few more items besides," her cousin said. "Sir Frederick found himself burdened with a canceled order and was only too happy to make other arrangements for it. And it certainly can't hurt for you to have some new things in case the occasion calls for something a bit less… drab."

"You have overstepped," Amelia said tightly.

Octavia eyed her for a long moment. "Amelia. I'll say this because no one else will, but don't you think it's time to end this self-imposed penance? No one will judge you harshly for wearing nice things."

Amelia snorted in denial. "Just because you and Sir Frederick have conspired against me doesn't mean I have to wear them."

"Oh, now you're just being childish," Octavia said airily. A lift of her brow said, *Go on, stamp your foot. You know you wish to.*

Amelia ignored the fact that her cousin was right. She pinched her lips together and spun on her heel, but she—heroically—did not stamp her foot. As she left, her cousin called after her.

"Just try the gold silk, Amelia. If you still don't approve, we'll donate the whole lot to the parish home."

And Amelia, not one to let others have the final word, said, "I've a mind to donate the whole lot *now*, and yours as well."

So much for her easy disposition.

———

WITH DETERMINATION, EDMUND renewed his bride-hunting efforts at supper, where he was seated next to Miss Letty Lawson. He tried—he really did—to engage the young lady in conversation. He asked after her family and her home, her acquaintances in London and her favorite pastimes. But with each attempt, she glanced first to her mother then to her hands before responding in whispered tones. He was forced to lean closer just to hear her soft replies, and his neck had grown stiff from the endeavor.

It required some effort to maintain his smile as he imagined Miss Lawson as his bride, still consulting her mother years from now on which meal to serve their guests and what names to give their children.

When his hostess declared they were to have an evening of cards, it was a relief to find himself paired with Miss Octavia Worth. That lady was immeasurably more confident than Miss Lawson. He found her to be an astute whist player and an easy conversationalist, with not a single glance cast toward her mother for the duration.

They played at a table with Temple and Miss Gifford, and Edmund found flirting with Miss Worth to be an easy matter—much easier than the simplest of conversations with Miss Lawson. She carried a charming conceit about her, but he sensed there was more to the lady than she would have any of them believe.

Edmund wondered if Octavia Worth might be the bride for him. She certainly had an elegant, assured bearing about her. One might even go so far to say she was countess-like. Could his admiration grow to something more?

"How does your valet go on?" Miss Worth asked as Temple dealt the next hand.

"The physician says the foot will heal, but Finch is distressed over his enforced inactivity."

"How did you find yourselves so far from the Vicarage?" Miss Gifford asked. "I dare say I can't tell one walking path from another and should find myself hopelessly lost were I to venture out on my own."

"Yes," Miss Worth said, putting her chin in her hand and eyeing Edmund across the table. "You said you'd taken the path to Dragon's Breath Crag. How ever did you find it?"

She was a crafty one. He was certain, or very nearly so, that she knew precisely how he'd learned of the path. But given Lady Foxgate's poor reaction on learning of Miss Thorne's presence, he'd no wish to be the one to reveal it to the rest of the party. Miss Thorne deserved better.

He laid down the king of hearts and said casually, "I encountered a local resident on my arrival in Birthwaite who was kind enough to point me in the right direction."

"Ah," Miss Worth said knowingly. "No one knows the paths as well as our local resident."

Edmund didn't miss her use of the singular *resident*. She laid down her matching queen and the trick went to Edmund. He frowned, certain Miss Worth still held several lower cards. Why the lady would sacrifice her queen when he'd already played high made no sense, but then he was beginning to suspect Miss Worth enjoyed her own game.

"Ho, Miss Worth," Temple said with a frown for her discarded queen of hearts. "That was a bold move."

"Did you expect any less?"

"Boldness? No, but if I didn't know better, I'd say you weren't attending the game. Or... perhaps you're casting your heart about for some fortunate gentleman to pick up." Temple gave her a flirtatious smirk which Miss Worth ignored.

"Ah, but you do know better," she said.

Edmund laughed. "Perhaps Miss Worth is simply of the noble belief that a queen and king should never be parted."

The lady gave a delicate snort as she played another card. "You are a romantic, Mr. Corbyn. I suspected as much."

Her assessment caught Edmund by surprise. He tucked his chin as he inspected his remaining cards. "I would not have described myself as such, but I sense your disapproval."

"Oh, I'm all in favor of romance, when it's inflicted on others. But I'm of a much more practical mind myself."

"Throwing your queen hardly seems a practical move."

"You're mistaken, Mr. Corbyn. I threw my queen to knock Mr. Temple off his game. It seems to have worked, too, as you'll notice we've taken the last three tricks. I aim to win, you see."

Edmund laughed. The lady was right, and Temple sat straighter at her words, his eyes narrowing on his pretty adversary. "That's rather Machiavellian of you," he grumbled as Miss Gifford tittered behind her hand.

Miss Worth merely smiled and returned them all to the topic of Windermere's paths. "What did you think of our pretty lake, Mr. Corbyn? Before your valet's tumble, that is?"

"The view was sublime," he said. "The landscape here is unlike anything I'm used to." Then he wondered if he could persuade her to walk with him sometime. Surely, like her cousin, she must be familiar with some of the lesser-known paths, and it might be a pleasant way to further their acquaintance. "Do you enjoy walking the fells, Miss Worth?"

Her mouth curved before she said, without apology, "I do not. I've no wish to turn an ankle or suffer the mist in my hair. These loops do not curl themselves, you know."

All right. No walking then.

"And yet, you seem rather knowledgeable about Windermere's… secrets."

She gave him a knowing glance, and he regretted the words as soon as they left his mouth. It had been a careless thing to say for someone reluctant to betray Miss Thorne's presence. He waited to see if she would take the opening he'd given her.

She did not, saying only, "Secrets, Mr. Corbyn? I assure you, we're not so gothic as that."

"Gothic? Oh, I do love a good novel," Miss Gifford interjected.

Edmund sat back. As the conversation turned and play continued, he felt oddly relieved for Miss Gifford's interruption. Then it occurred to him that although he'd been flirting with Miss Worth, beneath it all he'd been *thinking* of Miss Thorne. Some might even argue that he'd been flirting with Miss Worth *about* Miss Thorne. His bride-hunting technique required some polish, it would seem.

———

IT WAS NEARING midnight by the time Edmund left his hostess to return to the Vicarage. A full moon cast its silvery glow on the lake's smooth waters, and leaves rustled in the ancient beech wood that bordered Summerfield. The breeze that rolled off the lake was cool, and he dug his hands in his pockets as he navigated the lantern-lit path.

He'd left a lamp burning at the Vicarage, and as he neared the lodge's ivy-draped stone portico, he slowed his steps. There, propped before the heavy oak doors, was his camera stand.

Finch had certainly been in no condition to retrieve it, but he wondered if his valet had sent one of Lady Worth's servants up the path. The coachman, perhaps. But no. Somehow, he knew this was the work of Miss Thorne. Despite her curt words to him at their last encounter, it seemed the lady wasn't as prickly as she appeared.

Retrieving the stand, he let himself in. He loosened his collar as he entered the library, and Blue lifted her head from where she'd been dozing before the fire. She received his ear-scratch sleepily before dropping her head back onto the rug. Edmund fought his own yawn, but then he thought of his camera and the image he'd been trying to capture before Finch's tumble.

The plate had certainly been overexposed while he assisted Finch from the hawthorn. There'd not been time to develop it before supper, and though he doubted his camera had caught anything worthwhile, the plates took too long to prepare not to see each one through to the end.

He left Blue snoring and made his way to the gardener's outbuilding. It wasn't an ideal darkroom. There was no lock to prevent someone from inadvertently ruining his developing images, for one thing, and he preferred a warmer space to speed the reaction of his chemicals. But the thick stone walls kept out the worst of the lake's damp and chill and, more importantly, its seams were tight enough to prevent any outside light from seeping in.

He lit a single oil lamp and turned the wick low before draping a red cloth over it. The lamp cast its familiar dim glow as he donned gloves and a leather apron then set about preparing an acid solution in a shallow porcelain dish. With a precision born of practice, he added several grains of silver nitrate then carefully retrieved the glass plate from the back of his camera. He used tongs to gently slide the plate into the dish then left it to its solution.

While the image developed, he cleared a space at the end of the worktable and prepared another tray, this time with a solution that would fix the developed image onto the plate. After an adequate amount of time had passed, he checked the glass, lifting the plate gently to see what, if anything, his camera had managed to capture.

His photographer's eye was accustomed to viewing negative images on his plates, where light was dark and dark was light, and he frowned to see it was just as he suspected. The once-promising Windermere landscape was emerging as little more than an indistinct haze. The colors, were he to attempt to render them onto paper, would be naught but muddied shades of grey.

He sighed, but just as his disappointment was urging him to seek his bed, a subtle shape began to emerge from the misty chaos on the plate. He peered more closely as the figure of a woman materialized. Hazy and ephemeral, she took the form of a ghostly shadow, and the pale mist wrapped her like a flowing cloak sewn from light.

It was a hauntingly beautiful image. Stark and eerie but soft at the same time. Evocative. He wasn't one for spiritualism or fanciful musings, but even he had to admit to the chill that climbed his spine. Somehow, chance had conspired to turn a photographic mishap into an intriguing composition. He waited as the image continued to develop until, alongside the woman, emerged the figure of a small dog. A smile tipped the corner of his mouth as he recognized Lord Byron, which meant the dreamlike woman could only be Miss Thorne.

Miss Thorne, who seemed to be everywhere and nowhere at once.

CHAPTER FOURTEEN

Unlike books, cloth does not stimulate the mind. Truly.
—From the private journal of Miss Amelia Thorne

THE NEXT DAY, Edmund dutifully presented himself for the morning's portrait sittings. Lady Worth wished to have them completed in time for the guests to enjoy an afternoon of lawn bowling, so he'd set up his camera directly after breakfast. Now, Miss Worth gazed at him serenely from her pose on the drawing room settee while her mother watched from across the room. Miss Worth was to be the morning's final sitting, and she'd donned a finely trimmed ensemble for the occasion.

Edmund had found Summerfield's drawing room surprisingly well-suited for portraits. With tall ceilings and pale walls, the light moved easily around the room. A low fire burned in the grate, and he'd asked that the curtains be drawn to filter the light coming through the windows. The effect was a room as properly balanced as any portraitist's studio.

"I wonder, Mr. Corbyn," Miss Worth said, "should I stand before the fire instead? Would it not add a nice element to the picture?"

"I'm afraid not, Miss Worth. While it would make a pretty scene for us today, such a bright light will overpower a photograph. It will leave you cast in shadows."

Her lips curved in amusement. "We can't have that, now, can we?"

"Indeed not," he replied with his own smile.

Just as Edmund was framing her in his lens, Miss Worth leaned forward with sudden inspiration. "Mama," she said. "We must send for Amelia. She shouldn't miss the opportunity to have her portrait made as well." Miss Worth angled her head back toward Edmund. With an explanation he suspected was for her mother's benefit, she added, "Amelia is my cousin, sir. You've no objection to one more portrait, do you?"

Edmund returned her gaze with an even one of his own. "Of course not, if you're certain your cousin wishes it."

She hesitated for the merest second. In truth, Edmund didn't know what her cousin wished, much less what game Miss Worth played. But beyond the lady's cryptic conversation from the evening before, this was the only time any of the Worth family had acknowledged Miss Thorne's presence, and that must count for something.

Lady Worth drew up, her lips pinched. Her jaw was rigid as she said, "I am certain Amelia does not want to be disturbed."

"But Mama, surely, she will wish to have her portrait made. I'll just send Jane to fetch her." Miss Worth rose from the settee to pull the rope before her mother could offer further objection.

Lady Worth, who'd had nothing but praise and accolades for her daughter's virtues since Edmund's arrival, now appeared decidedly put out with her. Irritation was not an attractive addition to her features, and Edmund suppressed a frown on thinking she might one day be his mother-in-law. Miss Worth's attractive qualities dimmed a little, and he reminded himself that Kent and Redstone Hall were a fair distance from Windermere.

Miss Worth spoke in low tones to the maid who answered her summons, then she settled herself back onto the settee. Silk rustled and shimmered as she arranged her full skirts about her. Edmund would never understand the current fashion for ladies to don an excessive number of petticoats, though he couldn't argue the effect on Miss Worth's appearance was a pleasing one.

"Shall we proceed?" he asked. The solution on his plate wouldn't bear much more delay.

Miss Worth beamed at him. "Of course. Please continue, Mr. Corbyn."

——

AMELIA GAZED AT the silk-covered boxes stacked in a shadowy corner of her bedchamber. She'd not donated them to the parish home as she'd threatened, but neither had she permitted Jane to empty them into her wardrobe.

But now, the boxes beckoned like the last sweet on an empty tea tray. With reluctant steps, Amelia approached them. Arms crossed, she stood and frowned at the offending pile. *Self-imposed penance,* indeed.

And then, because it couldn't be helped, she traced the swooping line of Sir Frederick's embroidered initial before tipping the lid back on the blue wool. *It's only a skirt,* she told herself. Nothing but thread and buttons and yards of dyed wool. It would probably require *three* petticoats to support the heavy weight of it. Four, possibly. Society was nothing if not predictable in its love of excess.

Ten minutes later, Amelia stood before her mirror, surprised to discover that two petticoats were all that were required. She smoothed a palm over the bottom of the skirt's matching bodice. It was finely fitted while the skirt's folds draped her form with an elegance and grace she'd forgotten.

Perhaps she might keep a few of the items. It had been years since she'd seen herself so attired, and before she could stop the thought from forming, she wondered what Mr. Corbyn would make of it all.

———

AS SOON AS the exposure finished on Miss Worth's portrait, the lady stood and shook out her skirts. "I'll be interested to see what your camera has made of me," she said.

Edmund smiled. Before he could offer a flattering response—for surely, one was expected— the sound of tiny nails tapping the wood floor reached them and Miss Thorne appeared with Lord Byron.

"What's wrong?" she asked her cousin breathlessly, one hand pressed to her heart. She was dressed today in soft blue. It was a more fashionable ensemble than any he'd seen her in so far, and it set off her fair hair and creamy skin to perfection. A dainty scowl pulled at her features when she spied

Edmund with his camera and Lady Worth near the fireplace.

"Jane said you required my assistance straight away," she said. "I believe she used the phrase 'mortal peril.'"

Miss Worth gave a low trill of laughter. "Oh, Jane—she does have a penchant for the dramatic," she said, which only caused her cousin's scowl to deepen. "I only sent her to fetch you so you might have your portrait made. And I see you're wearing one of Sir Frederick's new ensembles, so it's fortuitous, really. You can hardly miss such an opportunity. Here, have my place on the settee. May I introduce Mr. Edmund Corbyn, our visiting portraitist?"

The introductions were prettily done, but Edmund didn't think Miss Worth's innocent expression fooled anyone.

Miss Thorne looked first to Edmund and then to her aunt, who'd remained silent during this exchange. Although Lady Worth gave no verbal hint of her displeasure, it was clear enough to read on her face. Irritation filled Edmund for the disapproving manner in which the woman treated her niece. He thought of his own family, and he couldn't imagine what act he might commit to warrant a similar disdain.

Edmund stepped forward. "Miss Thorne, I've

still another plate with me. It will only take a few moments to prepare if you would like to have your portrait made."

"Yes, Amelia," Miss Worth said as she pulled her cousin toward the settee. "Even if you've no desire for it, I should like to have your portrait for the mantel." She directed a pointed tone toward her mother as she added, "We would all like it, wouldn't we, Mama?"

Trapped, Lady Worth could only agree with her daughter, which she did with a single, tight nod of her head. "Of course. If it's not too much of an inconvenience for Mr. Corbyn, that is."

"It's no trouble at all, my lady."

By the time Edmund finished preparing the additional plate, several of the guests had wandered back into the drawing room. Miss Worth was playing hostess, making sure all the proper introductions were performed, while her cousin stood stiffly in her pretty blue skirts. Her discomfort was matched only by Lady Worth's pinched expression, and he wasn't certain who was the more miserable of the two of them. He imagined Miss Worth might receive a dressing down or two for her role in the day's events, but that lady seemed blissfully unaware or uncaring of her fate.

The guests' reactions to making Miss Thorne's acquaintance were mixed. The gentlemen, as one might expect, were curiously polite about the new female in their midst, but Mrs. Lawson examined Miss Thorne with suspicious eyes. She kept herself firmly positioned between the newcomer and her own daughter, like a knight shielding a princess from unpleasantness.

Edmund invited Miss Thorne to take her place on the settee. She looked at him as if he were the tooth drawer. "I will endeavor to make it a painless experience," he whispered.

Her eyes widened at his teasing and her lips quirked up on one side. "I'm afraid you're a bit too late for that," she murmured, but she sat on the striped cushion, nonetheless.

"Think of Wordsworth," he said, pleased to see how the simple words eased some of the stiffness from her shoulders. "Ah, and here's Lord Byron to keep you company."

The little dog hopped onto the settee and settled himself on Miss Thorne's lap.

Edmund moved back to his camera and adjusted the lens. "Do you join us for today's entertainment?" he asked conversationally.

"Am I not the entertainment?"

Temple chuckled from where he stood near the fireplace and Edmund smiled. "I believe your aunt has planned an afternoon of lawn bowling," he said.

"Your appearance is timely, Miss Thorne," Temple said. "You can make up our numbers since Miss Newton has decamped with Lord and Lady Fox-gate."

"Oh, but I expect it will rain," Mrs. Lawson was quick to say as she tucked her daughter more firmly behind her, and Edmund's irritation with the lady grew.

Miss Thorne lifted her chin the merest fraction and gave Temple a stiff nod. "Thank you for the suggestion, Mr. Temple, but I'm afraid I have a prior commitment."

Edmund admired her grace under the older woman's obvious discourtesy. "Do join us," he urged, "if the weather favors us and if your plans should change." Then he lowered his voice and added for her ears alone, "I imagine you must have a fine aim."

The smile she gave him, though it was faint, caused warmth to flood his stomach. "It is rather admirable," she said. The light in the room shifted and brightened, and Edmund moved away from her to regain his composure.

He made one final adjustment to his camera, pivoted the shutter plate and took Miss Thorne's portrait. She remained motionless, one hand holding Lord Byron in place until Edmund released them with a nod. "Well done, Miss Thorne."

She stood hastily and Lord Byron leaped to the

floor. By the time Edmund had gathered his equipment back into his case, Miss Thorne was gone. And, true to Mrs. Lawson's prediction, the sky had begun to darken.

CHAPTER FIFTEEN

I was taught to feel, perhaps too much,
The self-sufficing power of Solitude.
—William Wordsworth, *The Prelude*

AMELIA KNEW SHE'D been tempting fate to leave Summerfield in haste and without her hat, but she'd needed to escape her aunt's guests. To breathe freely without the scrutiny of others constricting her lungs.

But Mrs. Kessler had been complaining about her knees when Amelia left the warm kitchen. The housekeeper's knees always ached just before the lakes delivered one of their soaking rains. And now, true to Mrs. Kessler's knees and Mrs. Lawson's prediction, the sky had darkened and purple clouds billowed and shifted over the fells.

Amelia was still a mile from Summerfield, and

the grey shadow of rain already veiled the south-western peaks. She always enjoyed the rain when it came, but Lord Byron was not overly fond of baths. And rain meant mud—lots of it.

"Hurry," she urged. And Lord Byron, who'd been pausing to scent every bit of scrub along the path, finally sensed her urgency and picked up his pace.

Half a mile later, the first raindrop landed to slide down her cheek in a cold trickle. Another followed and then another, until the sky unlocked a torrent. Thunder rumbled and she was laughing by the time the Vicarage came into view, Summerfield looming behind it beneath a curtain of rain. Then a jagged arc of lightning flashed over the lake, chased by an echo of thunder that shook the ground.

She glanced toward the Vicarage's small gardener's shed. Mr. Corbyn, she imagined, would still be with her aunt's guests. She hesitated as the rain continued to fall, but when another jagged bolt lit the sky, she called to Lord Byron. Veering off the path to Summerfield, she raced for the Vicarage's shed. They'd wait out the storm there before returning to the warmth of Summerfield's kitchen.

She turned the knob and pushed on the door, relieved when it opened easily. She stumbled inside on a gust of wind and rain, urging Lord Byron inside before the storm could follow them.

———

THUNDER ECHOED AND rolled outside the gardener's shed, and Edmund frowned to know Mrs. Lawson had been right about the weather turning. Not that he attributed any powers of prediction to the lady — he was certain she'd only foretold rain on account of Temple's invitation to Miss Thorne. But the rain had come, nonetheless, and put an end to any plans for lawn bowling.

Now, Edmund had nearly finished developing the day's portraits and transferring the images onto paper. He had only the final plate to complete — the one of Miss Thorne. He wondered if her drawing room portrait would prove as captivating as his overexposed image of her.

As soon as the thought occurred, he knew it for the nonsense that it was. The imagery captured that day near Dragon's Breath Crag was nothing more than a trick of the light — a disaster by photography standards. A fellow photographer would merely click his tongue and lament Edmund's poor luck at ruining the plate. He was at a loss to explain why he didn't just toss it into the rubbish bin.

He used the tongs to lift a corner of today's glass

plate and inspected the emerging image in the dim light. It needed another forty seconds. Forty-five at most.

Just then, the door to his makeshift darkroom shuddered open to admit a slashing burst of rain and wind. He fell over the developing dish to block the light, but it was no use. The image was ruined. He blew a lock of hair from his forehead and looked up to find Miss Thorne silhouetted in the doorway.

He stared. He couldn't help it. Her blue skirts were drenched, soaking the stone floor of the gardener's shed. Her hair was limp and dripping, but still she managed to look like… Joan of Arc. Bold and vibrant and determined, her soul larger than her physical body could hold. It was just as well his portrait of her was ruined, as a drawing room pose would never have done her spirit justice. He shook his head at the fanciful thought and straightened.

Her eyes widened when they found his. "My apologies," she said, taking in his solutions and the cloth-draped lamp behind him. "It appears I've trespassed again."

"Miss Thorne, you seem to have a special talent for it."

Her lips quirked at that, and he thought she might smile. He was disappointed when she conquered the urge. The wind and rain continued outside and she pressed the door closed, though she didn't move away from it. Lord Byron shook vigorously, sending water and mud to spatter the slate floor.

Miss Thorne furrowed her brow at the line of porcelain dishes he'd spread atop the worktable. At the completed photographs he'd hung to dry behind him. "What are you doing?"

"I am—I was, rather—developing the portraits from this afternoon."

She pushed away from the door and approached the worktable. "Why do you have a cloth over the lamp?"

"To create red light," he said. At her frown of confusion, he clarified. "The solutions are less sensitive to red light than to other colors. Back in London, I have a lamp with a red chimney, but a cloth suffices in a pinch. It allows me to work without exposing the plates to wavelengths that affect the developing images."

"Oh...," she breathed, realizing the significance of what he'd said. "And I ruined your images when I opened the door."

"No. That is, only the last one—yours."

She straightened. "Well, that's all right then. I've no need for a portrait."

"It is not all right," he said, removing his gloves. Her green eyes were wide and fringed with thick, rain-soaked lashes, and he nearly drowned in them.

Swallowing, he added, "I would say you, Miss Thorne, owe me another portrait, in fact."

What was he doing? His words, his manner, had all the feel of a flirtation. And Miss Thorne was not the sort of lady with whom he ought to be flirting. She was certainly not the sort of bride Queen Victoria and her advisers would approve.

"I *owe* you a portrait? No," she said, laughing. "I do not."

He ought to have been relieved that she was releasing him from his idiocy. And yet, he dipped the tongs into the dish and angled the ruined plate toward her. "Do you see? It's ruined. My very reputation as a photographer hangs in the balance. Yes, the way I see it, you owe me a portrait."

Her eyes narrowed at this speech, and he noticed anew her limp, honeyed curls and damp skirts. Rain trailed from her hair down her cheek, down the smooth, pale column of her neck, to soak the wool of her bodice. He pulled his gaze up and offered his handkerchief. She blinked slowly, as if the simple courtesy were unexpected. Had she always been so wary, he wondered, or was this hesitancy the result of her scandal?

She reminded him of a wild kitten he'd once tried to tempt with a dish of milk. Miss Thorne, though, was a notch above feral as she took the linen from him and dried the rain from her cheeks and neck. He recalled his earlier impression of her as Joan of Arc before she realized she wasn't alone. *That* seemed a more fitting analogy than a wild feline.

"Will you show me how it works?" she asked with another glance toward his dishes.

"You wish to know about photography?"

She nodded, and it was his turn to be surprised. Most people, on learning of his experiments, wished to know how soon he could take their portrait or what was best to dress their children in for *their* portraits. He generally tempered his enthusiasm, at least in company, because most people, he'd found, didn't care about the science of photography itself. But Miss Thorne seemed genuinely… interested.

He couldn't help noticing, though, how her gaze went to the closed door when thunder rumbled overhead once more. Her thoughts were as transparent as one of his clean glass plates. She wondered at the propriety of them being alone together. But she couldn't return to the storm blowing outside with its wind and lightning. He could go, he supposed. The distance to the Vicarage's kitchen door was nothing to the path she must travel to Summerfield.

Yes, he ought to go.

He opened his mouth to say as much, but instead, he lifted one of his finished glass plates. "I begin by coating the glass with a light-sensitive solution...."

———

MR. CORBYN PUSHED his spectacles up with one finger in what Amelia now recognized was habit for him. He probably wasn't even aware he did it, but the gesture gave him the look of a scholar. It was very appealing.

She listened as he explained the rather cumbersome process of photography. She'd never had much interest in the subjects of natural philosophy—preferring words and music to spectrums and chemistry—but he made the concepts interesting. He was a natural teacher, patient with her questions and clear in his explanations without being overly pedantic.

There was something unique about him that she couldn't name, something that encouraged conversation. And it had been a long while since she'd enjoyed that with anyone other than her cousin or the servants at Summerfield.

"It's remarkable," he said with feeling, "that we can arrest a single fragment of our time on this earthly realm—a cloud, a face, a flower—with the sheer power of light. And advancements are being made all the time. We'll soon capture the hue of a lady's eye or the joyful colors of a child's toy…"

"You speak of light and color as if they're living things," Amelia said. "As if they've the ability to… shape our emotions."

His jaw ticked for a moment before he replied. "For some, perhaps they do. For me, it's not so much a shaping as a… reflection."

She tilted her head to give him a considering look.

He hesitated as if weighing a decision. Finally, he said, "You'll think me touched, perhaps, but I… see… my emotions."

Amelia tucked her chin, intrigued by his words. "You *see* them. I'm afraid I don't understand."

He ran a hand through his hair, disordering it slightly. "Whatever I'm feeling appears to me in varying degrees of light and color. Boredom, for example, casts a dim, grey light on my surroundings, whereas happiness and joy make everything seem brighter, more vibrant. My mother suffers a similar affliction, and my research and correspondence suggest we're not the only ones. The composer Franz Liszt is another, though his experiences vary from mine."

"How so?"

"As I understand it, he *hears* colors. He's been known to direct his orchestra to play 'a little bluer, if you please' or 'not so rose,' when the music, to his ear, should really be more of a deep violet."

Amelia couldn't hide her frown as she took a long moment to consider this. His explanation did sound a trifle unbalanced but at the same time, rather lovely. "You see in... poetry," she whispered. He began to shake his head and she rushed on. "A poem that describes the world in shades of grey and shadows takes on a melancholic tenor. But works that evoke the joys of nature and pure love—they've a sound to them that's vivid and radiant. It's rather marvelous, I should think, to see the world in such a unique way."

He appeared skeptical. "It's rather inconvenient," he countered, "for a photographer, at any rate. I'm constantly required to adjust my exposures to account for any shift in sentiment."

"It's why you study light and color," she said in sudden realization. "To understand yourself better."

"Do you know, I've never considered it that way. My father—"

"The astronomer."

"Yes. He's of a scientific mind, but my mother is a painter who sees things like I do. I've always thought my interest in photography was merely my two halves coming together, but perhaps there's something to what you say."

His voice was rich, his wonder tangible, and Amelia became aware of the close intimacy that had formed about them in the gardener's shed. He'd removed the red cloth from his lamp, but the light was turned low. It cast long shadows on the walls and made Mr. Corbyn, who was already a tall man, seem even larger in the low-ceilinged room. His shirt sleeves had been pushed up to reveal strong forearms. Amelia hadn't realized how near they stood to one another, but now, the small space was overly warm. She took a tiny step backward.

"What"—she stopped and licked her lips—"what are you seeing now?"

He smiled as he studied her, and she held her breath. It was irresponsible, really, the way he wielded his smile without a care for where it landed. "I do not see grey," he said softly.

Amelia swallowed. His words weren't flirtatious. They were simply earnest, and she felt them in the deepest part of her. She turned away and inspected his array of tools, from tongs to trays to low porcelain dishes. On one corner sat a small crate into which he'd organized his finished glass plates. But poking out from behind them was a thick piece of paper. A finished photograph, by the look of it.

Eager for a distraction and curious to see the results of his work, Amelia tugged and it came free. It was a portrait of a family. She studied it, counting at least four generations, seated and standing in various positions in what appeared to be a very fine and expansive drawing room. The eldest, an esteemed gentleman in a wheeled chair, sat in the center next to an elegant older lady.

Everyone faced the camera, and their ease with the world and with one another was clear in their postures and an unnamable quality that had been captured in their eyes. Contentment, perhaps. Love, even, if such a thing could be captured with Mr. Corbyn's light. She thought, perhaps, it could.

"My family," he said, leaning over her shoulder. "My mother and father are there," he added, pointing, "and my sisters—Aster, Helen and Eloise. Their husbands and children. And there, in the center, my grandmother and my grandfather, Edmund St. James." There was a quality to his voice that made it clear his family was an affectionate one. She wasn't surprised. She didn't know him well, but she couldn't envision him arising from anything less than a warm and loving home.

"You were named for your grandfather?"

"I was."

"You're not in the photograph," she said.

He smiled. "A photographer's lament, always to see, never to be seen."

He took the photograph from her to inspect a tiny imperfection only he could see in the background. As he peered at it, he explained the solution he'd used that day and the exposure time that had been required to balance the tricky light in his grandmother's drawing room. When he looked up and caught Amelia watching him, his lips tilted sheepishly to one side.

"My sisters tell me that when it comes to photography, I have a tendency to go on—in their words—past the point of normalcy. Given my passion for the discipline and my odd perceptions, you must think me a bit mad."

She couldn't help her small smile. "'No great mind has ever existed without a touch of madness,'" she murmured.

"Is that more of your Wordsworth?"

"I do have wider interests," she said with a frown. "It's Aristotle. Never say your studies neglected the classics."

"I wasn't the most attentive student, I'm afraid. At least, not when the subject was anything other than maths or natural philosophy." He set the photograph aside then added, "I met him once, you know."

"Aristotle?" she said on a surprised laugh.

He pressed his lips in annoyed amusement before he said, "Mr. Wordsworth."

Amelia straightened, all laughter escaping her. "You met him? When?" More than once, Amelia had gazed across the smooth waters of the lake toward Grasmere, trying to imagine what verses the day's tranquil scene might have inspired in the poet's thoughts. Mr. Wordsworth had always been a bit elusive, and his social circles had not intersected with those of her parents. Clearly, Mr. Corbyn moved in exalted company.

"It was naught but a brief encounter some years ago. I chanced to meet our poet laureate during one of my mother's exhibitions at the Royal Academy."

"What was he like?" Amelia's chest was tight as she awaited his response.

Mr. Corbyn set the photograph aside and rubbed a hand along the firm line of his jaw as he considered the question. "I recall that his countenance carried a bit of weight to it—the burden of a contemplative mind, I suppose. And his conversation leaned toward the poetic, as one might expect. I confess, I didn't make much of the encounter at the time, but there seemed a certain authenticity about the man, an earnestness in his expression, which couldn't be denied."

Amelia released a slow sigh of regret that she'd never had such an opportunity. Then she recalled Mr. Corbyn's interest in Wordsworth at the Laurel Leaf Emporium. "I've nearly finished my first reading of *The Prelude*," she said slowly. "If you've still an interest in it, I… I could lend it to you."

"Your *first* reading, Miss Thorne? Will it require more than one?"

She huffed a laugh at his joke—it couldn't be helped—but then she realized he wasn't jesting. Recalling his earlier words, she returned them to him without contrition. "When it comes to poetry, Mr. Corbyn, I've been told I have a tendency to go on past the point of normalcy. So yes, it will require more than one reading."

He laughed. "Well said, Miss Thorne. And thank you. I promise to have a care for your book. I've a clear recollection of how much it means to you."

His eyes—that unique not-quite-blue, not-quite-green shade—flashed behind his spectacles. His teasing reminder of their first encounter when she'd nearly launched herself at him from behind Mr. Tidwell's stacks brought a flood of warmth to her cheeks. He gave her a smile that was at once genuine and conspiratorial, and it came to her then—the quality that made him seem different.

Mr. Corbyn didn't treat her like an outcast, an entity to be avoided at all costs. There was no judgment in his gaze or his words. Unlike Mrs. Lawson, who had bodily shielded her daughter from Amelia's presence in Summerfield's drawing room. Or Lady Foxgate, who'd been so small minded she'd taken her daughter and gone. (Octavia had shared *that* tale with a good measure of loyal affront on Amelia's behalf.)

It seemed that Amelia would never overcome

one single, silly, wretched mistake, which made Mr. Corbyn's kindnesses all the more remarkable.

He turned to replace the tongs in a case behind him. Amelia took the opportunity to study him, tracing the strong line of his profile with her gaze and noting the deftness with which he handled his photography implements. His shoulders seemed broader in the close confines of the outbuilding, and she wondered what activity gave him such strength. Boxing, perhaps? Or did toting his camera about have such a sculpting effect?

When she'd encountered him at the Vicarage that first night, she'd been nearly certain he knew who she was. But now, she wondered if she'd been mistaken. Given his easy manner with her, he must be unaware of the scandal surrounding her. His attitude would certainly change once he knew she was the female all of London called the Poisoned Thorne.

The rain continued outside, a steady *rat-tat-tat* on the roof of the gardener's shed, but the thunder had stopped. She should go. Her damp skirts and petticoats and the high collar of her bodice were beginning to itch. She drew a breath and prepared to leave but found herself reluctant to do so until her curiosity was sated.

"Do you know who I am?" she asked.

CHAPTER SIXTEEN

The elements are volatile. Proceed with caution.
—From the scientific journals of Mr. Edmund Corbyn

EDMUND STILLED AT Miss Thorne's question. Though it was simple enough on the surface, he suspected what she really wanted to know was whether he knew of her scandal. He was uncertain how to respond.

Should he laugh and make light of the question? *Why, you're Lady Worth's niece, of course.*

Or perhaps he should play the gentleman and claim ignorance. *Miss Thorne, I'm afraid I don't take your meaning.* No lady wished to be reminded of past unpleasantness.

He looked up from where he'd been ordering his instruments to find her watching him. She'd been doing so for the duration of their conversation—stealing glances at his profile when she thought he wasn't looking. Her furtive interest had sent warmth spiraling through his stomach, but now, she held her green gaze steady on his. Despite the confession he'd given her about his unusual affliction, or perhaps because of it, they'd found an accord. He was loath to end it with polite evasion or false ignorance.

"I do," he said.

Her lips parted slightly at his admission. Then, with what looked like a spark of challenge in her eye, she clarified, "You know I'm the one they call the Poisoned Thorne?"

He winced inwardly to hear her put it so plainly, but he nodded. "It's an unfortunate name and undeserved, I'd wager."

"Do you think so? Did you not see the sketches in *Punch*? You must not have, or you wouldn't make such a claim. Many have said they painted a rather clear picture of my character."

"I require more to assess the nature of another person than a few poorly done cartoons."

"You, sir, seem to be in the minority."

A lengthy silence passed between them. He wondered if there were some polite, acceptable way to put an end to the discussion. It wasn't proper to discuss a lady's past so openly, even with the lady herself, and he didn't wish to cause her any discomfort. But nothing he'd seen in Miss Thorne thus far aligned with the venomous temptress the satirists had made her out to be. From their first encounter, she'd seemed nothing more than what she appeared—a slightly lonely, rather unique, wholly intelligent female with a delightfully off-center sense of humor. And, heaven help him, he was curious to know more.

"The news sheets are notoriously unconcerned with accuracy," he said. "They claimed you inter-vened in a duel, but I suspect there must have been more to it. I would like to hear the story of what truly happened, if you would care to tell it."

She hesitated before giving him an elegant lift of one shoulder. "I intervened in a duel."

——

MR. CORBYN'S CONFIDENCES had emboldened Ame-lia. It was the only explanation for why she shared the entire story of The Great Disgrace with him. And he, gentleman that he was, listened politely for the duration.

She explained how her father, despite his unend-ing love for her late mother, wished for more for his only child. He'd sent her to the best schools and clothed her in the best silks. And when it came time for her come-out, he'd taken her to London.

She wished to please him, so she danced and smiled, made calls and drove out with eligible gentlemen. And she thrilled to the excitement of the glittering balls with their nose-tingling champagne and elegant men in their dark suits. That her father had made a fine fortune at sea—and that Amelia was his only child and heir—certainly wasn't lost on anyone, though they were quick to whisper that her mother had been naught but an Irish seamstress.

Amelia enjoyed dances that season with a number of fine London gentlemen, but one in particular, Lord Snowdon, had been charmingly persistent in his pursuit of the unknown miss from Westmoreland. She also made the acquaintance of another gentleman that season, Mr. Palmer. Though Mr. Palmer had little fortune or family to recommend him, he'd recently had occasion to visit Windermere, and they'd fallen into an effortless acquaintance over their shared love of the Lake District.

But then, one evening as they lined up for a *contredanse*, Amelia had pressed Mr. Palmer on his quiet mood. The figure of the dance took them apart, but when they came together again—and under much gentle prodding—he shared the surprising news that her name had been placed in the betting book at White's.

She laughed. "The betting book? You must be mistaken."

"I saw it myself, in the middle of the page just below a wager on the weather for Lady Vincent's masquerade."

"But whatever for?"

"Snowdon claims you're to elope with him," Mr. Palmer whispered. "He says it will be 'a done thing' by the end of the week."

"Ha!" she said a little too loudly. "Please, Mr. Palmer, record a bet for me in this book, if you will. Put fifty pounds on me *not* eloping, with Lord Snowdon or anyone else."

His step faltered and she realized with a wince that others were attending their conversation. She lowered her voice to say, "I'm afraid Lord Snowdon has misunderstood me. He made a joke about eloping and I—I thought we were merely teasing one another."

The dance ended and Mr. Palmer led her back toward the chaperone her father had hired. Before they reached Mrs. Brownlee's hearing, he said, "It wasn't idle flirting, not to hear the way Snowdon tells it. But worry not. I will see to it."

"Of course, you will not, Mr. Palmer. I must speak with Lord Snowdon myself. I will explain that it was only a harmless bit of flirtation."

"I should not wish to see you upset by all of this,"

he said. "Please, disregard my heedless words." They'd reached the rim of the chalked floor, and he left her with Mrs. Brownlee. Amelia sat, and the colors of the ladies' full gowns swirled like a drunken kaleidoscope before her.

The set soon ended and her next partner appeared. Lord Snowdon. She allowed him to lead her out.

When she broached the matter of the wager, he didn't deny it. Instead, he was aghast to know she'd ever learned of it, and he and Mr. Palmer exchanged words the following day. Amelia wasn't certain how matters escalated so quickly, but before nightfall, the gentlemen had named their seconds. They meant to fight a duel. Over her! It was the most ridiculous thing, and so she told them.

"Snowdon can't be permitted such liberties with a lady's reputation," Mr. Palmer told her grimly.

"But a reputation is not so important as a life. Either one of you could be injured, or worse."

"And it would be an honorable death."

She'd scoffed at such nonsense and left Mr. Palmer in an irritated huff. In hindsight, she should have told her father what had transpired, but she had only herself to blame for the predicament she'd gotten herself into. Her father had always praised her sound mind, but she'd let the season go to her head. If she'd not flirted with Lord Snowdon, he'd never have placed his wager in the first place. And her father, who had weightier matters to sort with his vast shipping enterprise, didn't need the added distraction of his daughter's folly.

When dawn arrived on the heath above London, so had she, riding up boldly on her father's mare. Mr. Palmer and Lord Snowdon argued her presence, united in their shared affront that a lady should interfere with a matter of honor.

She'd stupidly stood her ground between them as they took their paces, but before either of the men could fire, the authorities arrived, whistles blowing, and called for them all to "Stand down!"

Punch and the *Times* had been the first to print their cartoons, but others soon followed. *The Manchester Guardian. The Illustrated London News. The Morning Chronicle.* All the caricatures depicted Amelia as a bold and unapologetic temptress who'd dared to stand, quite literally, in the path of gentlemanly honor.

The drawings of her—with eyes flashing and hair flowing from beneath her hat—resembled a mythical goddess. Medea, perhaps, with her poisons, or Circe with her enchantments. The first caption in *Punch* read, *A Poisoned Thorne,* and the papers described her, rather unfairly, as "a rattle and a flirt." Some blamed her actions on the lack of a "softer influence" to guide her while others claimed with derision that an Irish seamstress for a mother wouldn't have made any difference. And her father, seeing no way to salvage the season, had ordered their trunks packed without delay.

Lord Snowdon, with the influence and resources of his family name, escaped with little more than a stern warning from the magistrate. But Mr. Palmer, who had no fortune or illustrious family to appeal on his behalf, had been forced to flee to the Continent to avoid Newgate. And all because she dared to interfere in a duel. Or rather, because she'd flirted with Snowdon in the first place.

"So, you see," she finished, palms up, "the Poisoned Thorne name is well earned."

He frowned. "I hardly think your actions warrant such a punishment. Was there nothing your father could have done to smooth things over?"

Amelia's lips twisted. "I doubt there was anything anyone could have done. The story had a pulse of its own, and no amount of explanation, no defense, would have helped. And my father... though people admitted him into their homes because of his fortune, their favor was fair-weathered. He was naught but a ship's captain to them—a merchant."

Amelia realized she'd been clenching her fists, and she forced them to relax. She could still hear the whispers from behind gloved hands and feel the heat of judging eyes on her back. The speed with which she'd fallen had been dizzying.

"At any rate," she finished, "my father returned to sea a week later. His ship later foundered and was lost off the coast of Cathay. If not for my scandal..." She stopped, unable to say the words aloud, though they played often in her mind. *If not for my scandal, he would have remained in London.*

Mr. Corbyn was silent for a moment, and she welcomed the chance to regain her composure.

"What of your aunt and uncle?" he said. "Certainly, Sir George and Lady Worth must have connections—"

"My aunt does all she can to distance herself from the matter, though I can't fault her for it. Octavia will never make a match if my scandal taints her, too. It wasn't until my father's ship was lost—and the full extent of his fortune became known—that my aunt found a sense of familial duty, though it pains her."

He frowned and she felt compelled to explain.

"My uncle's title is an impoverished one. My aunt married to please her family, but my father married to please his heart. My aunt has her title, but not the means to circulate in Society. And my father, though he married an Irish seamstress, went on to make his fortune. My aunt has never quite forgiven him for it."

Mr. Corbyn's jaw tightened, and she knew a

moment's remorse for unburdening herself to him. Then he said, staunchly, "You are well quit of Snowdon. A true gentleman never would have placed a lady's name in the book at his club, and Palmer only made matters worse. One of them should have done the honorable thing and made you an offer."

"Pish. Why compound the disaster even further with an ill-advised marriage?"

"You're not… angry, then?"

"With the gentlemen?" She'd always wondered if things would have been easier for her if Snowdon had suffered just a bit, or if she'd had the opportunity to confront him, but none of that would have changed matters. A confrontation, had the papers learned of it, would only have made things worse. "There were plenty of mistakes made all around," she said, "so no, I'm not angry with them." There was an edge to her tone which she'd not been able to soften, and he heard it.

"But you are angry," he said. "At the news sheets? No one can fault you if you hold them in contempt."

Amelia sighed. "I am angry," she said slowly, "at a society that values individual misfortune for the collective amusement of its members. At the sort of world that would harshly judge a person sooner than forgive her mistakes."

He remained silent as rain continued to drum the roof. Then, in his low, velvety voice, he said, "I think it showed a bit of courage, to ride between two duelists as you did."

She snorted softly and glanced away. "And perhaps an uncommon lack of sense."

"That too," he agreed.

She cast a glance at him from the corner of her eye, wondering what he must be thinking. What he must *truly* be thinking, that was, for certainly he couldn't believe that nonsense about courage. He was merely being polite.

Would he, she wondered, whisper about her to her aunt's guests or laugh if one of them dared to resurrect the old scandal? She pressed her lips, sharply irritated that, despite everything, she still cared about the opinion of others. And perhaps more distressing was the knowledge that she cared about the opinion of *this man* in particular.

She turned to go but as she did, she knocked a cloth from the worktable. She bent to retrieve it and he did as well, their heads bumping in the small space. He chuckled as they stood, holding his head with one hand and the cloth with the other. Their fingers tangled and she released her grip on the linen. When she looked up, it was to find him dangerously close, his eyes intent on her. The space was warmer, as if his gaze had electrified the air. The tiny dimple in his chin was close enough that she could touch it if she wished… She did not wish. Absolutely not. She'd come to escape the storm, but it seemed one was brewing now inside her makeshift sanctuary. One of them should leave, and yet, she made no move to step away.

It was Mr. Corbyn who acted first. He lifted a hand toward her temple as if he might touch her before lowering it slowly to his side. He straightened and took a step back, his face assembling into lines of polite apology as he cleared his throat. "The rain continues. I will leave you and Lord Byron to the shelter of the shed." He collected his hat and ducked beneath a low beam, intent on the door.

"I—" she began, stopping him, but her voice was hoarse. Licking lips that had gone dry, she finished, "I'll go. There's no need for the both of us to become soaked." He looked as if he might argue for the sake of chivalry, if not good sense, so she added a bit untruthfully, "My aunt is expecting me."

After a moment, he nodded. She collected Lord Byron and turned for the door.

"Miss Thorne."

She paused, glancing back at him over her shoulder.

"Do not forget that you owe me a portrait." He smiled, his eyes finding hers in the dim light, and she could do nothing but smile in return.

CHAPTER SEVENTEEN

TWO DAYS LATER, Amelia was unable to avoid her aunt's picnic outing to St. Mary Holme, to both her and Aunt Mary's dismay. But Octavia's account laid it out thusly: Mr. Temple inquired at breakfast if Miss Thorne would join them. Aunt Mary demurred with some vague nonsense, but Mr. Temple politely insisted that the younger set wouldn't be complete without Miss Thorne, especially as Lady Foxgate had taken her daughter off. When Lord Hargreave, who outranked them all, agreed, Aunt Mary's defeat had been complete.

"I have Mr. Temple to thank for this?" Amelia asked her cousin.

"Yes. He seems rather taken with you. I think he

must be in need of a fortune," Octavia said as Jane pinned her hair.

Amelia might have taken offense at her cousin's comment, but it was only a testament to Octavia's innate practicality rather than an opinion on Amelia's attractive qualities.

"I think you must be right." Amelia looked up from her book and checked the clock on Octavia's mantel. "Are you nearly finished?" she asked. "The guests will be ready to depart soon." Though she had no eagerness to join her aunt's party, she also had no wish to arrive late and draw everyone's attention.

"It won't hurt for the gentlemen to wait a bit." Then Octavia eyed her critically in the mirror. Amelia, who had already donned a dark brown walking dress for her morning walk, hadn't seen the need to change just so she could walk about the ruins on St. Mary Holme. Octavia's gaze turned speculative as she asked, "Which bonnet will you wear?"

"My straw poke, I imagine."

Predictably, Octavia shook her head, her unpinned curls bouncing about her shoulders. "I've the perfect capote," she said. "It's trimmed with a ribbon of brown velvet and will complement your dress perfectly."

Amelia cast a dubious glance toward her simple wool skirts, but a small bit of vanity had her agreeing to Octavia's offer. "If it's not too excessive," she said.

Octavia's brow lifted in mild surprise at her easy capitulation, and Amelia returned her attention to *The Prelude* before her cousin could comment. She was only at the tenth book, and there were fourteen in all. If she meant to lend the volume to Mr. Corbyn *and* ensure he could return it before he left, she must remain diligent.

Thoughts of the gentleman caused her to lose her place on the page, and she frowned. She still wasn't certain why she'd told him all she had about her scandal, but whenever she thought of their time together in the gardener's outbuilding, her cheeks grew uncomfortably warm.

"What do you think of Mr. Corbyn?" Octavia said, and Amelia sucked in a breath for her cousin's prescience.

A glance at the mirror over Octavia's shoulder indicated that, yes, there was a bit of betraying color in her cheeks. She willed it away, unsuccessfully, and said, "What do you mean?"

"What do you think of him? You met him in Birthwaite and again when he took your portrait. Do you still find him handsome?" As she spoke, Octavia rubbed a bit of color onto her lips. This time, she didn't wipe it away.

"I—yes, of course. Anyone can see he's rather

handsome."

"He doesn't wear a mustache like Mr. Temple and Lord Hargreave."

"A point to his favor," Amelia conceded.

"I've found him to be kind."

"He seems amiable."

"He's grandson to an earl, so you would think he would be more top-lofty. I wonder what his family is like."

He has sisters, Amelia thought. *Three of them and nieces and nephews. A scientist father and a mother who's an artist. Grandparents. He loves them very much. It's in his voice when he speaks of them.*

"I wouldn't know," she said.

Octavia's brow rose in silent question. *Wouldn't you?* When Amelia kept her silence, Octavia shrugged. "It's a shame he's not in line for the earldom, though. A title would make him all the more attractive. Irresistible, I should think."

"I disagree," Amelia said before she could stop herself. "I think a simple 'mister' suits him much better than a burdensome title."

"Only you would think a title is burdensome," Octavia said. "But I dare say his lack of one certainly makes him more attainable. If one wishes to attain him, that is."

"Really, Octavia. You make him sound like a prize at the fair."

"What use is the game if there's no prize to be won?"

In a corner of her mind, Amelia wondered what her cousin *truly* thought of Mr. Corbyn. Surely, she must see him as more than a prize to be won. She wouldn't ask, though. Only to herself would she admit the danger in that. For if she asked, and if she learned Octavia was enamored of Mr. Corbyn, then Amelia wouldn't be able to entertain thoughts of him any longer.

Amelia swung her legs down from the window seat. "We should join the others. Your mother won't wish to keep her guests waiting."

She collected her shawl and her Wordsworth with a frown. Her cousin's words had struck a nerve. Like the wrong meter in an otherwise perfect verse, or a discordant note pulled across a fine violin, she felt them in the pit of her stomach. But for one brief moment, she wondered what it would be like to "attain" Mr. Corbyn for herself.

———

EDMUND DEBATED WHETHER he should attempt to take his equipment on Lady Worth's picnic outing. Without Finch to help carry the cases, it was rather too much to pack and tote about, especially as they'd be traveling the lake by rowboat. And he could hardly continue his bride search from behind a camera. With a last, lingering glance toward the gardener's outbuilding, he left his cases behind and strode along the path to Summerfield.

He arrived in the drawing room to find several guests discussing the carriage arrangements. Lady Worth had hired several coaches to convey their party to the ferry landing at Bowness. From there, they would row across to St. Mary Holme, where they would enjoy a picnic luncheon and the chapel ruins that gave the small island its name.

Mrs. Lawson was angling for the last two seats in Pearson's coach for herself and her daughter. Miss Lawson's head was down as her mother made obvious overtures toward the gentleman on her behalf. Edmund felt sorry for her, but relieved that he would not be required to spend time in her mother's company. The woman's poor opinion of Amelia had lodged beneath his skin like a splinter.

The rest of the guests soon appeared, although Miss Worth was not yet down. That lady, he'd noticed, followed her own tune. Her calm demeanor must surely be a mark in her favor, but as the clock ticked off the minutes, Edmund couldn't help wishing she were a little more considerate of the other guests.

"I say," Temple said to the group, "Miss Thorne can ride in my carriage if she needs a place."

"Miss Thorne means to join us?" Edmund asked.

Temple nodded. "I reminded our hostess that Lord and Lady Foxgate's defection has left us with a shortage of ladies. We're fortunate to have Miss Thorne to round out our party."

The thin line of Mrs. Lawson's upper lip indicated her disagreement with this sentiment, and Edmund wondered at Temple's new interest in Summerfield's elusive resident.

"Here they are," Pearson declared.

Edmund looked up to see Miss Worth making her entrance. She wore a fetching cornflower-blue walking dress beneath a manteau in a darker shade. It was trimmed with velvet ribbons that matched her bonnet. Pearson bowed over her hand as the other gentlemen lined up to greet her, but it was Amelia, coming quietly behind her cousin, who captured Edmund's eye.

She wore brown. Though she probably thought it made her appear a wren to Miss Worth's bright kingfisher, the hue suited her. The simple dress was a deep, rich shade, and her honeyed hair was pulled smoothly back beneath a bonnet trimmed with velvet ribbon. It was a more elegant confection than he'd seen on her before, but tastefully so.

She smoothed her gloves along her arms as she eyed the assembled party with a stoic expression, and he thought again of their time in the rainstorm in the gardener's shed. Of her trusting confidence and her interest in his photography. Of how close they'd stood to one another and how much he'd wanted to kiss her. He forced the thought aside.

When her eyes reached him, her features relaxed enough to form a tiny smile. Temple moved to greet her with a bow, blocking Edmund's line of sight. But when Miss Worth claimed Temple's attention some moments later, Edmund stepped forward.

"Miss Thorne, I'm pleased to see the lure of your aunt's party has managed to separate you from Mr. Wordsworth."

Her mouth twisted with a secret humor that only he could see. "Never underestimate a lady's reticule, sir." She lifted the accessory, which appeared to have a bit of book-shaped heft to it, and he smiled.

There was no time for more than that. The guests readied themselves to go, and Temple announced again that Amelia and Miss Worth must ride with him.

"And Mr. Corbyn," Miss Worth said. "We've room for one more. You must join our carriage."

"Thank you," Edmund said. "I would be delighted."

Temple cast a speculative look at Miss Worth, and then at Edmund, before the group began a slow migration toward the doors. As the ladies passed through, Temple slowed. "Corbyn," he said.

Edmund turned an inquiring gaze on the man.

"Is it fair to assume you've taken an interest in Miss Worth?" Temple asked as he adjusted his cuff.

Surprised by the question, Edmund could only say noncommittally, "She is a charming lady."

"Charming and poor as a church mouse, according to my solicitor," Temple agreed with a regretful sigh. "It's a pity we can't all marry where we wish, but it relieves me to know you don't require a rich wife. Leaves the field open for the rest of us."

The words were said without malice or rancor, but Edmund's jaw tightened. Ashford had certainly been thorough in his campaign to make Edmund's financial prospects known. Temple's comment, though, confirmed the rumors Edmund had heard in London. Temple must have been disappointed when Miss Newton and her diamonds left the party.

"What, precisely, are you saying?" Edmund asked.

"I'm merely confirming we don't compete for the same end."

Edmund quirked a disbelieving brow at Temple, who enjoyed nothing more than the heat of competition. "I've no wish to do battle for a lady's affections," he said, "if that's what you mean."

"We are agreed then," Temple finished with a friendly clap to Edmund's shoulder.

He followed the others to the carriages, leaving

Edmund to wonder just what it was they were agreed upon.

———

AMELIA SETTLED NEXT to Octavia for the short ride to the ferry landing below Bowness. The gentlemen—Mr. Corbyn and Mr. Temple—were both long-limbed, and there was a bit of shuffling required to accommodate their persons as well as the ladies' full skirts. When everyone was arranged, Mr. Corbyn rapped on the roof to signal the coachman and they were off.

"Miss Thorne," Mr. Temple said as the passing trees drew patterns on the carriage walls. "You look particularly fetching today. What color do you call your gown?"

"I call it brown, Mr. Temple." Amelia avoided her cousin's gaze, certain Octavia's brow must be angled in mocking humor at the gentleman's feeble attempt.

"Ah, but it's not just any shade of brown, is it? It has a charm of its own, and I dare say the hue sets off your eyes to perfection."

"Thank you," Amelia said, unable to fashion a more elegant reply.

They soon passed Bowness with its school and villas, and the ancient parish church lifted up its square tower in the distance. Mr. Temple continued, undeterred by Amelia's lackluster response. "It has the softness of a sparrow's feather and the... er, grace of her wing."

"Soft *and* graceful, Mr. Temple?" Octavia put in. "My, Amelia, who knew the humble sparrow could inspire such admiration?"

Amelia shifted on the seat and took a moment to mourn her younger self, who would have been entertained by such obvious and ineffectual flattery as that which Mr. Temple offered. The girl who'd danced and flirted in London would have lapped up his attempts with good humor and returned them measure for measure. She'd not been easily gulled, but she'd certainly been up for the game of courtship, for all the good it had done her.

Now, though, Mr. Temple's attentions only saddened her, for it was clear he'd determined to overlook her scandal in favor of her fortune. His situation must be dire, indeed, and she frowned to think her cousin had been right.

Her gaze passed over Mr. Corbyn, and there was the merest tightness about his mouth before he said, "Miss Thorne, I'm certain there's not an inch of the lake you haven't explored. What can we expect to see today?"

Amelia inhaled, relaxing against the back of the upholstered seat. The sun was out, and a breeze hummed through the open carriage window to cool the air. Sycamore groves went past, and beyond, the sky was a vibrant blue. She hoped Mr. Corbyn saw it in a similar light for surely, the day held promise despite Mr. Temple's attempts at flattery.

With a smile, she replied, "I believe you'll enjoy the day's outing, Mr. Corbyn. Mr. Wordsworth always held that Windermere ought to be seen from its surface as well as its shores. The lake is so transparent that even at ten fathoms, you can make out the distinct colors of its pebbly bottom...."

She went on to describe the islands they would encounter—first Belle Isle, the largest of the lake's islands with its round house positioned like a cherry on the top. They'd find their destination, St. Mary Holme, just beyond it while two Lily of the Valley Holmes lay near the opposite shore.

"The Lilies are an unparalleled sight in the spring, with the white heads of their flowers bobbing and bowing to the breeze. I've always wondered what it must be like to visit the island at night and see them silvered by the moon."

"Miss Thorne," Mr. Temple said, "you make the lilies sound enticing indeed."

They neared the ferry landing where a line of passengers had formed at the small pier to await the next crossing to the Lancashire side or to Ambleside at the lake's head or Newby Bridge at the foot. On the opposite shore, at impressively wide intervals and tucked neatly among the trees, lay several manor homes. Octavia pointed out Stonecroft just beyond the ferry house.

"I understand we're all invited to attend Lady Staveley's ball at week's end," Mr. Temple said.

Octavia nodded, her enthusiasm for the event clear. "We'll take the carriage road round the lake to Stonecroft. All the families of any distinction will be there, and a number of visitors, I expect, who will come up from London especially for it. Lady Staveley's balls are always the most delightful crush. I dare say, we might even convince Amelia to attend this year."

Amelia stifled a sigh for her cousin's persistence.

"You do not usually attend, Miss Thorne?" Mr. Temple asked.

"No, Mr. Temple. I do not."

A small frown pinched his brows as if he were just now realizing the full extent of her exile from Society. He looked as if he might try to persuade her, but Mr. Corbyn spoke first. "If you decide to make an exception this time, I would be honored if you would save a dance for me."

Warmth flowed through her for his kindness, and she nodded her agreement.

Octavia sat back on the seat, looking all too pleased with herself as the carriage slowed. They came to a stop near a line of rowboats that had been pulled onto the pebbled beach. The water, rippled by a slow breeze, lapped against their bows, and the calls of the boatmen as they negotiated the boats' hire carried on the air.

Their driver lowered the steps and Mr. Temple went first. He handed down Octavia, who led him away with an exclamation over the landing's lively bustle. Mr. Corbyn left the carriage next before offering his hand to Amelia.

As she stepped down, he leaned close and murmured, "A peaceful wood at dawn." At her inquiring look, he added, "That's how I would have described the color of your dress."

A smile twitched at the corner of his mouth, and Amelia was powerless to stop her lips from curving in reply. "How so, Mr. Corbyn?"

"There's something… lyrical about the dawn's light. It's soft and tranquil. Hopeful, even." His hand felt warm, despite the leather of his gloves and the thin cotton of hers. He held her gaze as he added, "The air is cool and still, but there's an expectant vibrancy to it, as if the wood awaits the sun with a lover's eagerness."

Amelia caught her breath, her eyes widening at his description. The moment stretched between them until, finally, she murmured, "Heavens, that's a lot to say of a… a dress."

He straightened, a fleeting emotion clouding his features. It was almost as if he'd forgotten they were speaking of cloth. "I'm a student of color and light, Miss Thorne." He pressed her hand briefly before releasing it, and it was only then that she realized he'd held it overlong.

——

LADY WORTH HAD sent her man ahead to negotiate the boats, and several were secured for their use. It had been decided that the elder Worths and Lawsons would carry the picnic supplies in theirs, with a man to row them, while the other gentlemen were determined to ferry the young ladies.

"We must make it a race," Miss Worth declared.

Miss Gifford clapped her hands together once in anticipation. "Of course!"

"An excellent notion," Temple said. It had been some years since Edmund and Temple had competed on the water, and Temple's grin suggested he looked forward to it.

"Wait—where are we rowing to?" Pearson asked. He shaded his eyes as he gazed up the lake where several small islands dotted the water.

"St. Mary Holme is just there," Amelia said, pointing toward a moderately sized clump of trees and rock beyond the much larger Belle Isle.

By Edmund's estimation, it was no more than a mile and a half distant. He and his university mates had rowed greater distances at Cambridge against their archrivals from Oxford, and many of those races had been on the Thames with the incoming tide. But the lake was smooth as glass. It would be an easy matter to row the distance. Edmund turned his gaze toward Temple, who lifted a brow in silent challenge.

"What say you, gentlemen?" Lord Hargreave asked. "Are we up to the task?"

"That must be nearly two miles away," Pearson said. "The prize must be worth the effort."

A gleam lit Miss Worth's eye. "The prize," she declared, "will be a favor from the gentleman's lady passenger—"

"Within the bounds of propriety," her mother interjected from some feet away.

"Of course, Mama. Within the bounds," Miss Worth said with a nod for her parent. "Certainly, gentlemen, that must be sufficient motivation."

And so, it was decided: they would row to the southernmost point of St. Mary Holme, and the winning gentleman would have a favor from his passenger, within the bounds of propriety.

Edmund selected his boat from the line awaiting them at the shore. It was a smart craft with tight seams and a red hull. As he checked it over, he considered which lady he should invite to join him.

Miss Worth was the clear and obvious choice. Of all the ladies, she seemed the most likely candidate for the future countess of Ashford, and she didn't seem opposed to his suit. He knew he should ask her to ride in his boat, but a contrary urge had him wishing for more time in Amelia's company. But of course, that wouldn't do, given his purpose at Summerfield. While he debated with himself, Temple claimed the adjacent craft and settled the matter for him.

"Miss Thorne," he said, "will you do me the honor of allowing me to row you ashore?"

Edmund stilled, bent low over the bow of his boat, and watched from the corner of his eye. There was a long pause as Amelia considered Temple's invitation. He thought she might refuse—part of him hoped she would even though *he* could not ask her. Given Temple's current lack of funds, the reason for his excessive attentions was clear, but Amelia deserved better than a suitor interested only in her fortune.

To his disappointment, though, she gave Temple a short nod of acceptance. "Of course. Thank you, Mr. Temple."

"Mr. Corbyn." Startled from his eavesdropping, Edmund stood abruptly as Miss Worth approached him. "Mr. Temple tells me the pair of you used to row at university, and I think you are my best hope of winning."

"And here I thought the competition—and the prize—were meant for the gentlemen."

She patted him on the forearm and gave him a flirtatious smile as she stepped lightly over the edge of his boat. "You've much to learn, Mr. Corbyn. Much to learn."

CHAPTER EIGHTEEN

EDMUND REMOVED HIS coat and folded it, rel-
ishing the sun's warmth on his shoulders.
Windermere stretched before them, mirror-
smooth and reflecting the clear blue sky. Amelia
had been correct, and he could easily see the pebbled bed of the lake several feet from the shore.

He watched as Temple assisted her into the
stern of his boat then spent some moments stretching his arms. With a confident smirk, the other man
turned to Edmund. "Ready to suffer the anguish of
defeat once again, Cambridge?"

"Your memory fails you, Temple. Cambridge

took the trophy my final year as stroke."

Temple chuckled. "That may be, but perhaps you've grown soft behind your camera."

"If I have, then you've grown soft between the ears," Edmund added with what was, admittedly, a touch of juvenile glee.

As he bent to retrieve the oars from the bottom of his boat, Amelia looked over and met his gaze. Her lower lip was caught between her teeth and laughter lit her eyes. Edmund winked—he couldn't help it—and her smile unfolded.

He climbed into his boat and positioned himself in the bow. The craft bobbed on the low surface of the water, and he used the blades of his oars to hold it steady. Hargreave and Pearson readied themselves as well, then Miss Worth gave the signal for them to start.

Edmund pushed off from the shallows. Soon, his oars slipped easily through the water, propelling them toward St. Mary Holme. Temple had been fortunate—or unfortunate, depending on one's perspective—to snag a boat painted in Oxford Blue. He kept a constant pace next to Edmund's red craft.

Miss Worth leaned forward, her encouragement clear as she held the strings of her bonnet against the breeze. "Go, Mr. Corbyn! You can out-row him!"

Shouts also rose from Miss Lawson and Miss Gifford as they urged their gentlemen on, but Amelia's voice was curiously absent from the clamor. It occurred to Edmund then that if Temple won, Amelia would be obliged to provide a favor. A favor "within the bounds of propriety," of course, but a favor, nonetheless. And, judging by the placid expression on Amelia's face, that was not something she anticipated with any eagerness.

The realization propelled him far more than his longstanding rivalry with Temple. Edmund's focus sharpened, and he rowed with more vigor. His red boat surged ahead, slicing the water as Miss Worth cheered him on. Edmund deepened his strokes, and his arms and shoulders began to burn with the effort. He ignored the strain, focusing only on the rhythm of his rowing.

"Left!" Miss Worth shouted from the coxswain's seat. "No, my left. Right! Right!"

Like any experienced rower, Edmund could navigate with only the feel and motion of the boat to guide him. But at Miss Worth's enthusiastic-but-inexpert direction, he glanced over his shoulder to gauge his position. The action was enough for the Oxford Blue to narrow the gap by another foot.

"They're gaining!" Miss Worth exclaimed as Temple pulled ahead of the others to glide just behind Edmund. Edmund glanced toward Amelia as their boats drew closer. Her eyes met his. They were bright with pleasure as she held fast to the sides of her seat, and he felt her silent encouragement. Edmund pulled harder.

The ladies' shouts rose above the sound of the oars to urge the gentlemen forward. The boats approached St. Mary Holme, and Edmund's heart raced in time with his rhythm. Temple, undeterred, matched his pace and soon, their boats were side by side. Edmund dug deeper, his oars cutting the water cleanly.

The boats scraped the pebbled beach of the island's shore, and it was Edmund who edged out Temple by mere inches. A cheer erupted from the ladies, and Amelia's smile seemed one of approval. It stole what was left of Edmund's breath.

He assisted Miss Worth onto the shore then secured his boat as the others did the same.

"Well rowed, Cambridge," Temple said. "Treasure the feeling while it lasts." He extended his hand and Edmund shook it.

"My, Mr. Corbyn," Miss Worth said with a glint in her eye and becoming color on her cheeks. "Who could have known my favor would be so motivating?"

"Oh, yes!" Miss Gifford said. "What prize will you claim with your victory?"

Edmund stilled. He'd prevented Temple from winning a favor from Amelia, but in his fervor to do so, he'd forgotten his own prize. A bird soared overhead, calling to its mate in the silence. The group awaited his reply, and it was Miss Worth herself who stepped in to save him.

"Of course, you'll wish to think on it," she said. "My favors aren't given easily, you know."

He breathed more easily and dipped his head toward her. "If I may have some time to consider it—I wouldn't wish to waste such an opportunity."

——

AMELIA ACCEPTED MR. Temple's assistance from his boat and willed her heart to slow from its scared-rabbit pace to something more human. But really, she could hardly be faulted. Mr. Corbyn with a set of oars was something to behold.

The other boats soon arrived with the picnic supplies and a welcome distraction. At the ladies' direction, the gentlemen laid out folding chairs and blankets on a grassy spot overlooking the lake.

Despite Aunt Mary's shortcomings, the lady knew how to organize a picnic, and she couldn't have demanded a better day for it. The sun washed everything with the golden warmth of late summer while the day's gentle breeze carried the earthy scent of the wildflowers that grew at the edge of the island's narrow beach.

Amelia and Octavia set to work unpacking large

wicker hampers of food. There were finger sand-
wiches of thinly sliced cucumber and butter. Salads
of tomato and lobster and pear. Summerfield's
cook had sent paper-wrapped scones and a cloud-
like sponge. Pots of clotted cream and strawberry-
and-currant preserves. Miniature tarts filled with
apricot and tumblers for crisp lemonade. And
Summerfield's best china—delicate pieces acquired
in Shanghai by Amelia's father—hadn't been spared
the occasion.

Before Amelia could prepare a plate for herself,
Mr. Temple surprised her with one he'd already
filled for her. Unable to decline the offering without appearing rude, she took it.

"Thank you, sir," she said as he claimed the
place next to her. When he wasn't looking, she gave
him an assessing glance, which was rather more
than she'd done thus far. He'd removed his hat to
reveal gold hair a shade darker than her own, and
his long-limbed form was nicely made. With kind
eyes above a well-proportioned nose, he wasn't an
unattractive gentleman by any stretch, but she
thought his appearance might be improved with a
pair of spectacles.

Octavia settled herself on a nearby chair and arranged her skirts about her. Her cousin was
resplendent in Sir Frederick's blue poplin master-
piece. Aunt Mary must have been over the moon.

"Mr. Corbyn," Octavia said when he joined them, "you must try the Victoria sponge. I think you'll find it some of the best you've ever tasted."

Mr. Corbyn's smile was genuine. "I shall be sure not to miss it, as you have impeccable taste, Miss Worth."

Octavia's response to this was a giggle. A full-debutante *giggle*. Amelia's cousin was not a giggler, and Amelia narrowed her eyes.

"Miss Thorne," Mr. Temple said, drawing her thoughts. "I count myself fortunate to have secured a place at your side."

Amelia held her sigh, though it required some effort. She wished he wouldn't try quite so hard. It might make him easier to like, were his efforts more sincere. Still, it wouldn't do to set tongues wagging with her rudeness, so she strove for a polite de-meanor. "It's a lovely day for a picnic, is it not?"

"Indeed, it is. But I must admit, the beauty of this place pales in comparison to your own."

Warmth filled Amelia's cheeks and she said tightly, "You're too kind, Mr. Temple." *Really,* too *kind.*

Octavia appeared to be restraining a smile while Mr. Corbyn wore a slight frown. He appeared as uncomfortable with Mr. Temple's overdone compli-ments as Amelia felt. She couldn't escape the im-pression that Mr. Corbyn had been rowing for *her,*

Amelia, rather than Octavia, but that was absurd. Octavia had been his passenger, and it was Octavia who sat beside him now.

And none could deny they made an attractive pair. As Amelia took a sip of her lemonade, Octavia passed a plate to Mr. Corbyn. The act was simple but domestic, and it spoke of an intimacy between the two. A pairing.

Amelia stared at her own plate, procured for her by Mr. Temple, and slowly set it aside.

"Can you tell us anything of the island's history, Miss Thorne?" The question came from Mr. Corbyn, and Amelia straightened, relieved for the distraction.

"Of course. You can see it's not but a small spot of land, no more than an eighth of a mile at the longest point, but St. Mary Holme is named for the chapel that once stood on the grounds in honor of the Blessed Virgin. The structure itself has long since disappeared, but some of the foundation stones are still visible beneath the vines.

"It's said that, in centuries past, a couple of priests were installed on the island by a local lord to pray for his family. Not much more is known of the chapel's history, but it dates as far back as Edward the Third."

"Is there any wildlife about?" Mr. Temple asked. "Foxes or pheasants, perhaps?"

"A colony of cormorants have made their nests in the trees at the other end," Amelia said, "but the island's not much used for game hunting, if that's what you're asking."

Mr. Temple frowned, and it was clear the island's charm had lessened in his eyes.

Mr. Corbyn leaned back on his hands, his long legs extended before him on the blanket and his neckcloth just a trifle loose from his rowing exertions. Amelia's breath felt a little fluttery in her chest.

"Regardless of the island's vague history," he said, "or perhaps because of it, there seems an easy serenity about the place. An unexpected calm."

"You feel it too?" Amelia said with some surprise.

"Of a certainty." Mr. Corbyn's eyes caught hers and held for the briefest of moments.

"We should go exploring," Octavia said, drawing Amelia's attention. She turned to her cousin in confusion, as Octavia was not one to participate in, much less suggest, nature excursions.

"Come, Amelia." Octavia leapt up with more haste than Amelia was used to seeing in her. "You must lead the way."

"An adventure," Miss Gifford said. "That sounds perfectly splendid."

There was general agreement all around, and

Aunt Mary and Mrs. Lawson demanded assurances that the group would stay together during their exploration. Two people could easily call to one another from opposite ends of the small island, but they gave their assurances anyway then set off.

Amelia led them along vague, barely-there paths, around clusters of oaks and along the ragged shore. When they reached the island's high point where the chapel had once stood, she pointed out bits of the foundation stones, barely visible through the shadows of the foliage.

"Mr. Temple," Octavia called, "can you assist me over this fallen trunk?"

Amelia snorted. It wasn't the first such entreaty her cousin had made to Mr. Temple. For whatever reason, Octavia was determined to explore every leaf and stone on the island, and it seemed she required Mr. Temple's assistance to do so. Amelia couldn't say she was disappointed by her cousin's newfound interest in nature, though, as it relieved her of the gentleman's company.

A breeze had picked up, and she tucked an errant lock of hair back into place. Footsteps approached as she watched the smooth roll of the lake through the leaves of an oak tree. She turned.

"Mr. Corbyn, I didn't have a chance to congratulate you on your victory."

He grinned and she detected a bit of color in his

cheeks. "Temple is a formidable opponent."

"The two of you rowed at university, I take it."

He nodded. "Temple was at Oxford, so we were on opposing crews, but it was a friendly rivalry for the most part."

It occurred to her then: "Rowing… that's how you came by your shoulders." An embarrassed grin flashed across his face, and she realized she'd spoken aloud. She hastily returned her gaze to the shoreline below.

An awkward silence passed between them before he rescued her with a change of topic. "You've a commendable knowledge of the island," he said.

"St. Mary Holme was my father's favorite of all the islands. We used to come here often when I was small. Or as often as his travels allowed, rather." She smiled, remembering. "He always created stories about the fairies that lived beneath the oaks, and I hung on his every word."

"Are you certain they were stories? The island seems a bit enchanted."

"It's one of the few places that remain so," she said softly. She'd long since given up believing in fairies, but there was an unmistakable peace and contentment about the island that never failed to set her heart at ease. "St. Mary Holme was the first place I visited when I returned home after… well, after my London season."

"I'm sorry you had a difficult time of it."

She had no one to blame but herself, but that sounded a bit too self-pitying, so she held her tongue. He stood beside her, silent, hip to hip as they watched the water below shift and glide. A sailboat went past, its white canvas taut.

Mr. Corbyn worked something in his hand, and she cast another glance at him. He held a smooth stone he'd picked up from the lake's edge, and she was captured by the deft motion of his fingers as he turned it.

"It's for my nephew, John," he explained, though she'd not asked. "He collects rocks, to my sister's consternation—his pockets are always full of them—but he's a particular liking for the smooth ones."

Amelia smiled as a memory came to her. "I used to collect buttons," she said. "My father would bring me one from each of his ports of call. Ivory, silver, wood, it didn't matter. He said they were proof he thought of me on his travels."

"Did you require proof?"

"No," she said automatically. "Perhaps. Regardless, I always looked forward to his button more than any other gift. Your nephew is fortunate to have you for his uncle."

"Do you think so? I would argue that I'm the fortunate one."

Octavia's laugh came to them from a few yards

away, and they both turned toward the sound. Though Amelia had been trying not to think of it, she wondered what favor her cousin would grant Mr. Corbyn for his rowing victory. Knowing Octavia, it would be just this side of the pale. Nothing too objectionable, but whatever it was, it would be bold enough to capture the gentleman's interest.

An unexpected jealousy stabbed at her. Amelia had never felt envy toward her cousin before, and now was not the time to start. There was nothing but discontent to be gained by that course.

"Miss Thorne," Mr. Corbyn said softly, though there was an edge to his voice that drew her eyes back to him. "I'm not one to gossip, but I feel I must caution you about Mr. Temple. There's no mistaking he's a pleasant gentleman and a fair rower, but I understand he seeks an advantageous marriage. To put it bluntly, he requires a bride of means."

Amelia's chest tightened and she swallowed. With an effort, she held her gaze on his. "Thank you for the warning," she said, pleased with the steadiness of her voice.

He nodded, and a flicker of emotion crossed his face. "I thought you should know. Please accept my apology and forgive me if I've overstepped."

"There's no need for apologies or forgiveness, Mr. Corbyn. I appreciate your concern, but I'm aware of Mr. Temple's intentions."

He nodded with what seemed like a twinge of regret, and Amelia left his side to rejoin the others. She held her shoulders back, head high, though her emotions were swirling.

It was bad enough to hear the warning from Octavia, but to hear it from Mr. Corbyn, too, caused an uncomfortable lump in her throat. The consensus was clear, though: she was so far beyond respectability that only the most desperate of gentlemen would consider a match with her.

CHAPTER NINETEEN

She was a phantom of delight
When first she gleamed upon my sight.
—William Wordsworth, *Perfect Woman*

THE NEXT FEW days were a dizzying course of al fresco luncheons and parlor games. Edmund found more occasions to be in Miss Worth's company, though he'd be hard pressed to say he knew her any better. The lady was a bit of an enigma, and Edmund suspected few knew anything of her that she didn't wish known.

Meanwhile, Temple's attentions toward Amelia continued. To her credit, though, Amelia didn't seem overly interested in encouraging him, which gave Edmund more pleasure than it ought to have done.

He wondered if she'd had any local followers—

gentlemen who might not have heard of her London scandal or seen the cartoons, or who might at the very least be willing to overlook them. Perhaps she might find herself a fellow Wordsworthian, although the notion of Amelia sharing her enthusiasm with another gentleman caused an uncomfortable itch to start beneath Edmund's collar.

Late Thursday afternoon, there was a reprieve from the party as no activities were planned from tea until supper. The hour had that unique quality of in-betweenness when the sun's golden warmth still washed the landscape while the stars began peeping out from the darkening sky. Edmund left Blue to console a restless Finch while he collected his camera and plates and ascended the path behind the gardener's outbuilding.

The evening mists had already begun to form in the cooling air. They were a living white fog that rolled and wrapped the trees and the lake below. He couldn't even make out St. Mary Holme or her sister islands.

The path rose until it seemed he'd climbed above the clouds, although he couldn't have been walking more than ten minutes. Soon, he heard the faint strains of… music. A violin. The sound was unexpected in such a setting, but oddly appropriate.

He slowed, quieting his steps to better hear. The notes flowed like melted honey, and as he rounded a curve in the path, he was unsurprised to find Amelia at the source.

She stood atop a small rise, violin tucked beneath her chin. Mournful notes echoed off the fells as she played. Tendrils of her gilt-and-honey hair had escaped their pins to curl above her collar, and despite the chill in the air, her shawl lay puddled at her feet. She wore a sensible grey walking skirt, but the unremarkable hue only highlighted her bright features. They seemed lit from within, outlined against the darkening cobalt sky.

She was a study in texture and contrast, in light and shadow, and Edmund's lips twisted in rueful wonder at the poet he was becoming. It must be the Cumbrian air. It was easy to see how the lakes had moved Mr. Wordsworth to such elegant verse. He lowered his camera from his shoulder and let her music play over him.

She'd chosen a perfect composition for the setting. Haunting and evocative. Symmetrical and concise, it echoed the surrounding beauty with an arrangement of notes that was both elegant and simple. The only thing he had for comparison was a well-crafted equation, but her music was that perfect.

He stood motionless as she pulled the last plaintive notes from her bow. When she stopped, he opened his eyes to find her gaze upon him. She was the first to break the silence.

"Mr. Corbyn," she said without a bit of hesitation. This wasn't the lady who skulked about in the servants' corridor.

"You play beautifully. I've never heard anything like it."

She knelt to replace her instrument in the case at her feet. "I merely play what I feel, and I certainly can't take the credit for Herr Mendelssohn's fine composition." There was no artifice to her words, unlike Miss Newton, who'd seemed all too aware of her talents on the pianoforte despite her maidenly modesty.

Amelia clicked the latch shut on her case and stood. With a glance for the camera at his feet, she said, "What do you photograph today?"

"You," he said with inspiration, "if you'll permit me."

"Me?" She pulled her head back to give him an uncertain look. At his nod, she glanced at the landscape around them. "What... here?"

"You can't deny the setting is sublime. Not all portraits need be taken in a drawing room or studio."

"But there are far more interesting things to which you might direct your camera."

"I can't think of any."

Her eyes widened and she pulled in a breath.

He wondered if he'd been too forward, but he knew this was an opportunity he would regret missing. There was something about the light of this woman that he needed to capture. He pressed his advantage and, with a lifted brow, he added, "You do owe me a portrait, after all."

She frowned at that, but he knew he had her when the lines of her mouth eased. Glancing about the path, she said, "There's nowhere to sit."

"You can remain standing just as you are. The lighting from this angle is perfect." He bent to unpack his camera and mounting stand.

She shifted uncomfortably from one foot to the other. The subject of a standing portrait was typically a gentleman, who had a cane or a chair or a wife's shoulder on which he might rest his hand. But Edmund could see that Amelia must be wondering how to arrange herself.

"Tell me more about Wordsworth's *Prelude*," he said in an effort to distract her. "I imagine you've brought it with you?"

She snorted a disbelieving laugh, and some of the tension left her frame. "Of course, I brought it with me. You really know nothing of Wordsworth if you have to ask that."

He smiled and finished attaching the camera to its stand. "And which has been your favorite part thus far?"

"That's rather like asking which star in the heavens pleases me the most."

"Well, then… which do you think I'll enjoy if I ever have the good fortune to read it?" He bent to view her through the lens in time to catch her narrowed eyes.

"Do you mean to rush me?" she asked with a sniff. "One cannot race higgledy-piggledy through Wordsworth."

"'Higgledy-piggledy,' Miss Thorne?"

"Yes. It means pell-mell. Hurly-burly or —"

"I know what it means. It's only that, in my experience, it takes a rare talent to work 'higgledy-piggledy' into a conversation, and yet you do it with aplomb. But regardless, I would never suggest you proceed with Wordsworth in such a… raggle-taggle manner."

He wiggled his brows at her, and she eyed him for a beat as if to gauge his earnestness. He must have satisfied her assessment because she smiled and returned them to his original question.

"Very well. Since you asked, I've found *The Prelude's* sixth book to be sublime in its depiction of the Alps. Although, I would argue Mr. Wordsworth's verse evokes a stronger sense of peace and tranquility in the fourth book. Once you've read it, you'll have to tell me if you agree."

"He had a fine turn of phrase, didn't he?"

"He wielded words like a painter with a brush." She bent to retrieve the volume from the folds of her shawl. "Just listen to this," she said as she turned to a marked page. "'Magnificent the morning rose, in memorable pomp, glorious as e'er I had beheld—in front, the sea lay laughing at a distance; near, the solid mountains shone, bright as the clouds.'"

Edmund's hands stilled on the camera as she read, and he was hard pressed to say which was more entrancing—Amelia's violin playing or her reading of Wordsworth. He didn't share her fervent appreciation for words—he was much more interested in empirical facts and scientific truths—but he couldn't deny how the sound and cadence of them rolled easily from her tongue.

"'The sea lay laughing,'" she repeated. "Have you ever heard anything so perfect? Only the most joyful of hearts would phrase it thus." She closed the book and held it to her chest.

In her reading, she'd shifted a little out of his camera's frame. "Can you please step to your left?" Edmund said.

She stiffened slightly at the reminder of his camera before doing as he requested. She stepped too far, though, and now she was off center in the other direction. Edmund left his camera and reached her in three long strides. Lifting his hands toward her shoulders, he said, "May I?"

She hesitated the merest of moments before giving him a nod. He set his hands atop her shoulders and pushed gently, positioning her. He might have imagined the warmth of her beneath his hands. There were layers of fabric between them, after all, but he felt it, nonetheless. His hands lingered on the softness of the brushed wool, and she looked up at him with eyes bright behind her thick lashes. When her gaze dipped lower, toward his mouth, he was lost.

He lowered his head slowly but with intention, giving her an opportunity to shift or move or retreat. When she remained still, he touched his mouth to hers. Her lips were cool against his, but they warmed as he kissed her. He tasted the contours of her mouth, feeling the gentle bow of her top lip and the wide fullness of the bottom.

His hands moved from her shoulders down her arms and back up again. Then farther, along the smooth column of her neck to cradle her head, one thumb stroking the gentle curve of her cheek. She smelled of sunshine and soap, and he savored the taste of her as their breath mingled. Minutes passed —he didn't know how many—before he lifted his head.

Eyes closed, he leaned his forehead against hers and tried to collect his thoughts. After a long moment, he straightened and opened his mouth, uncertain what to say after such a kiss. Then a line from the volume of poetry he'd read on the train came to him and he recited it softly. "'She was a phantom of delight.'"

Amelia's lips curved with pleasure, and warmth unfurled within him. "'And yet a spirit still,'" she added with a whisper, "'and bright with something of angelic light.' Well done, Mr. Corbyn."

Edmund released her with reluctance. "Miss Thorne—"

"Mr. Corbyn," she interrupted before he could continue, which was just as well as he had no notion what he'd meant to say. "Shall we finish this portrait of yours while the sun still shines?"

Her gaze was steady on his. He pulled in a slow breath then returned to his camera to find Amelia perfectly framed in the square view. She was bright and vivid, and he forced his mind to still so he might calculate the exposure correctly. *Pomegranates,* he thought, though the trick did little to ease the rapid beating of his heart.

"Hold, please."

———

IT WAS ALL Amelia could do to hold herself still while Mr. Corbyn—Edmund—completed his portrait. With both hands gripping her Wordsworth, she managed to still their shaking, but good heavens!

His kiss was even better than she'd imagined, and she admitted the truth that she *had* imagined such an event. More than once.

She could still smell the faint, warm-spicy fragrance of his soap and feel the press of his lips against hers. They'd been gentle but sure. There'd been an unexpected energy to Edmund's kiss, but a peacefulness as well, like coming home after a long time away. Not the sort of homecoming one had after a disastrous season in London, but a return to one's self. To one's heart.

Nothing in her experience had prepared her for it. The novelists and poets offered hints and tantalizing glimpses into a realm beyond the ordinary—from Lord Byron's passionate outpourings to Mr. Keats' poignant yearning for an unchanging, eternal love, to Mrs. Browning's heartfelt sonnets. But none of their words—delightful though they were—had even approached the stark, elemental sensation of Edmund's lips on hers.

It was as if his soul had touched hers and, in that meeting, a star was lit.

There was no denying Edmund was different from all the other gentlemen of her acquaintance. To exchange a kiss as they had, with such meaning shared between them in the merest touch—surely,

he must see something more of her beyond her fortune or the lines drawn by her scandal.

———

THAT EVENING, EDMUND passed a distracted few
hours at Summerfield, with little more than thoughts
of Amelia's kiss capable of occupying his brain.

That changed, though, when he returned from
supper to find a letter for him at the Vicarage. He
recognized his sister's handwriting on the direction
and retired immediately to the library with a glass
of brandy.

Dear Edmund,

*Mama sends the enclosed letter regarding
Grandpapa's health (of which there is little
change). I don't think his condition can be
helped, though, by articles like the one I've included from the Illustrated London News. I can't
imagine how they come by their information.
Grandpapa's staff are the most loyal to be found
anywhere, so I know they can't have been the
source.*

*Needless to say, we've gone to pains to keep it all
from Ashford, but he grows suspicious about the
missing pages from his papers. What else can we*

do? Are you any closer to finding a bride? These things can't be rushed, I know—it took Andrew <u>forever</u> to come to the point—but we all worry for Grandpapa.

My children send all their love to their favorite uncle, and John has asked that I extend this request: if you find the time, can you please bring a stone from Westmoreland for his collection? I would not impose on your bride-hunting, but we've been practicing please and thank you, and he's asked very prettily. (Knowing your nature as I do, it would not surprise me to learn you've already secured an acceptable specimen in anticipation of John's delight.)

Yours fondly,
Aster

Enclosure from the *Illustrated London News*:

This author has heard whispered tidings of the Earl of Ashford's fading health amidst the stark and all too somber reality of the Heirless Noble. The eyes of the beau monde are drawn to the poignant narrative of the Ashford legacy, veiled in uncertainty, where the delicate threads of lineage seem destined to dissolve.

Alongside these whispers, an intriguing subplot unfolds with the conspicuous absence from London of the earl's grandson, the inventor Mr. E. Corbyn. Speculation sweeps through drawing rooms as all of Society puzzles over the reasons behind this retreat. Some have wondered if it signals the final refrain in this noble lineage, but this author has reason to suspect we may anticipate a Royal assist.

Edmund studied the full glass before him, noting how the cut crystal caught the light from his candle to cast prisms along the wall. He shoved the glass away, and the amber liquid sloshed onto the desk. Though he would appreciate the oblivion to be found in a bottle of fine brandy, it wouldn't solve his problem.

Problems, in the plural. There was the matter of Her Majesty's matrimonial mandate, for one, always lurking at the top of his mind. And today, he'd added his heart-stopping kiss with Amelia to the pile. Amelia. When had he begun to take such liberties in his mind, to think of her by her Christian name?

Removing his spectacles, he scrubbed his face hard with both hands. Blue, sensing his mood, rose and bumped her large head against his thigh. He stroked her ears, but even that was small comfort.

The sound of wood thumping wood preceded Finch's arrival at the library. His valet stood framed in the doorway, Amelia's wooden crutches balanced beneath his arms.

"I can't suffer any more stillness," Finch announced. "I'll be in the outbuilding if you need me."

Edmund nodded distractedly then straightened as Finch turned to go. "The outbuilding? For what purpose?"

Finch paused to look at Edmund over his shoulder. "To develop your plates from this afternoon. You went walking, did you not?"

"Leave them," Edmund said. He'd not taken any more photographs after his encounter with Amelia, and he wasn't sure he had the heart or the desire to develop her portrait at this point. In fact, it would be best if he set his photography aside altogether until he secured a bride. That was his purpose at Summerfield, after all.

Finch's brow climbed toward his hairline at Edmund's tone. "But—"

"It's late," Edmund growled. "I'll see to them myself."

Finch narrowed his eyes in a very unvaletlike way. "It's the Thorne female that's caused your poor mood, isn't it?" He shook his head with a mixture of concern and disbelief shadowing his features. "I suppose I was right, though it pains me to say it. She's vying to be your countess, isn't she?"

"She knows nothing of my situation." Edmund said, turning his sister's letter in his hand. "Now, go brush my coats or organize my neckties or something. There's nothing on the day's plates worth developing." His chest tightened as he said the words, and he couldn't hold Finch's gaze.

After a long silence, his valet finally left him, though his grumbles could be heard in the hall after he'd gone.

Edmund released a slow sigh. No matter how strong the impulse, it had been wrong to kiss Amelia. To taste her lips. To feel her soft skin beneath his fingers. To draw her breath inside himself as if he might absorb her poetry. It had been an unguarded moment, one he *should* regret, though he was finding contrition hard to come by.

But Amelia was not a willing widow or a friendly actress. A gentleman who kissed her ought to be free to court her in earnest. And the fact that he was *not* free to court her, he did regret. Very much.

He recalled his conversation with his mother in the gardens at Redstone Hall. He'd had the naïve arrogance to assure her he could manage his heart. What an ignorant fool he was, and she'd been right to be concerned.

He knew what he must do, though the thought

of it caused a tightness in his chest. He must apologize to Amelia. His actions had been thoughtless and careless, for no matter how his heart swelled at the mere sight of her, no matter how she brightened the world around him, nothing had changed. Amelia would never meet with Queen Victoria's approval, and Edmund would never forsake his family for his own happiness.

CHAPTER TWENTY

Would that a kiss could be so easily forgotten as one's hat.
—From the private journal of Miss Amelia Thorne

TWO DAYS PASSED before Edmund was able to find a quiet moment with Amelia. Temple had increased his pursuit, insisting to Lady Worth that her niece join the group's activities when Edmund suspected Amelia would rather be walking the fells with Lord Byron. So, although Edmund saw much more of her during Lady Worth's entertainments, her new suitor was always at her elbow.

Today, Temple had arranged to partner her at pall mall, determinedly ignoring the frequency with which Amelia's ball sent his own out of bounds. Edmund silently applauded her strategy as the pair fell swiftly behind the others in points, and Temple's face darkened with growing frustration.

Just now, she'd hit her ball with enough force and angle to knock Temple's far off course of the ring. It was a move that required skill and no little patience to execute. Edmund covered his smile with one hand as Temple stared at the field, dumbfounded.

Amelia's eye caught Edmund's, her humor evident as if they shared a secret jest between them. Edmund's own smile slipped, his stomach twisting at the thought of the conversation to come. But if he meant to apologize for their kiss—and he did—then he must find a moment away from the others.

Taking a page from her own book, he hit his ball wide to send hers careening into the hedgerow at her side. "Apologies," he called to the group. "I have it." As expected, Amelia strode to his side to assist in finding her missing ball.

"Miss Thorne," he murmured.

"Mr. Corbyn."

"You once told me you have an impressive aim, and now I've seen it for myself."

She fought a smile as she poked her mallet into the bottom of the thick hedge. "But I've missed the ring every time."

"Precisely."

Her smile won, appearing at once to light her

face, and he swallowed. "Thank you for the loan of *The Prelude*. Finch said you brought it round while I was out the other day."

"Never let it be said that I am a slow reader, Mr. Corbyn, though I must apologize for the scribbles in the margins. I like to mark my favorite lines, and with Wordsworth… well. That's nearly every one of them."

"Perhaps it would be easier to mark your *least* favorite lines."

She smiled. "Perhaps."

Then, because he couldn't put it off any longer, he began earnestly, "Miss Thorne, I feel I should… that is… or rather…"

She straightened. "Yes?"

"I must apologize for my actions the other day. They were inconsiderate and unthinking. Despite that, I… I hope you can forgive me."

He delivered this carefully practiced speech and waited, breath held. She tilted her head to one side and studied him. He knew a sudden wish to take his words back. To return to their easy banter and contemplate another kiss. He kept his jaw firmly locked against the impulse. Then, to his relief, her smile returned.

"Of course," she murmured. "Consider it forgotten."

Forgotten? Well, that was a bit strong.

"Ah, here it is." She bent to retrieve her ball from the middle of the hedge, holding it up for the others to see. "We found it," she called before striding back to the group.

And, if it were possible, Edmund felt even worse.

———

"LET ME SEE if I have this right," Octavia said, unscrewing the lid from a porcelain jar on her vanity. It was late. They were in Octavia's room in their braids and dressing gowns, and Amelia had just told Octavia she meant to give Mr. Temple a chance. She might as well have said she meant to flap her arms and fly round the room, for the disbelief that pulled at her cousin's features. "You *like* Mr. Temple?" Octavia said.

Amelia stretched her legs on the window seat and stroked the fur of Lord Byron's neck. "I wouldn't put it in those terms," she said, "but there's no reason not to keep an open mind, is there?"

The words made sense to her logical self, but as she spoke them, they sent a pang to squeeze her heart. She still couldn't believe she'd mistaken the growing accord between her and Edmund for something more. That she'd allowed hope to wedge its way beneath her skin while he'd been regretting their kiss.

Her cheeks burned as she recalled his apology.

Octavia dipped her fingers into the jar. "An open mind, yes, but not an empty one," she said as she smoothed white cream onto her neck. "Besides, I thought you were content to pass the remainder of your days alone, among your hills and rocks."

"I am," Amelia insisted. She was. But Octavia would marry one day—soon, if her mother's party had its desired effect—and Amelia would reach her twenty-fifth birthday. The responsibility for managing Summerfield would become hers, and her aunt and uncle would return to their home in Surrey. Solitude should have been an exciting prospect, but the notion left her feeling a bit flat. When had being alone started to sound so… lonely?

"So," Octavia pressed. "You'd leave Summerfield for Mr. Temple? You do realize he makes his home in London?"

Amelia shook her head. "It will be a condition of the marriage terms that we remain here, at least for much of the year. He'll agree if he wants my fortune badly enough."

"Ah, it's to be a contractual arrangement then. How very *haut ton* of you."

Amelia gave her cousin her best arch look. "Don't patronize, Octavia. I dare say it's no different than the sort of marriage you imagine for yourself."

"Yes, Cousin, but I'm *me* and you're, well, *you*."

"Meaning?"

"Meaning you will not be happy with such a match. Not *truly* happy. You require poetry in your life."

Amelia swallowed. Lord Byron shifted on her lap and she relaxed her hold on him. "We're putting the proverbial cart far ahead of the horse," she said. "In fact, I think you've pushed the cart clear to Ambleside while the horse still sleeps in his stall. I said only that I will *consider* Mr. Temple. He hasn't even asked for my hand."

Octavia frowned. "You're determined in this? There's no one else you would rather 'consider?'"

Amelia hesitated, but when Octavia eyed her intently in the mirror, she nodded. "I am, and there is not."

Octavia shrugged. "Then I shall see to it that you're paired with Mr. Temple for the scavenger hunt."

"Your mother won't be pleased to have me paired with anyone."

"Well, she's little enough choice in the matter with Mr. Temple's insistence on your company at every turn. She should take heart you're not setting your sights on Mr. Corbyn's flush pockets. The rest of us wouldn't stand a chance."

Amelia's cheeks heated, and she looked away. "You're ridiculous," she said.

"I won't deny it, but I must congratulate you: you've done a smashing job thwarting all of Mama's carefully laid plans. It's been the most devilish fun to watch."

"I aim to entertain."

Octavia studied herself in the mirror. "What favor do you think Mr. Corbyn will request for his rowing victory?"

Amelia blinked at the change of topic and then again at Octavia's disclosure. "He hasn't claimed his favor yet?" The question was out before she could think better of it.

"The man is nothing if not thorough in his deliberations. Perhaps I should press him during the scavenger hunt."

Amelia nodded as if this were an agreeable plan.

Octavia shifted her ministrations to her mouth and applied a softening balm with one finger. She smacked her lips together once in the mirror before adding, "I do hope it's a kiss. Mr. Corbyn strikes me as a man who knows his way around one."

Lord Byron gave an annoyed yip, and Amelia loosened the grip her fingers had on his fur. "Your mother said the favor must be within the bounds of propriety," she reminded her cousin in a voice that sounded depressingly like Aunt Mary's.

CHAPTER TWENTY-ONE

I will like Mr. Temple.
I will like Mr. Temple.
I will like Mr. Temple.
—From the private journal of Miss Amelia Thorne

THE SUN SHONE brightly on Aunt Mary's scavenger hunt as the guests assembled on the lawn in front of Summerfield. Puffy clouds dotted the late summer sky, and the verdant scents of grass and water and moss surrounded them. They'd nearly reached the end of the house party, and spirits were high. Tomorrow, the guests would travel to Lady Staveley's ball on the opposite side of the lake, and the day after that, they'd board carriages and trains to return to their homes.

True to her word, Octavia had seen to things, and Amelia found herself paired with Mr. Temple.

It was no surprise that Octavia would partner Edmund. Aunt Mary had announced that pairing with more syrup than usual, as if Edmund were visiting royalty and Octavia the choicest wine from the cellar.

In fact, Aunt Mary's manner toward Edmund had shifted in the past days, from courteous hostess to fawning acolyte. Amelia could think of only two reasons for the change in her aunt's demeanor.

One, Edmund's suit for Octavia's hand had progressed. Perhaps he'd already proposed, although she rather thought Octavia would have mentioned that bit of news.

Or two, Aunt Mary had reason to believe Edmund's six thousand was a gross understatement. Either way, poor Lord Hargreave—a titled baron to Edmund's mere mister—barely rated a consideration as Aunt Mary doled out the team assignments.

"I count myself most fortunate to have you for a partner, Miss Thorne," Mr. Temple said.

To which she replied, "Thank you, Mr. Temple." And then, because she meant to give him a little encouragement, she added, "And I am fortunate as well."

Mr. Temple's eyes widened at her concession before a smile came to his face. It appeared genuine, and Amelia reflected that there wasn't so much that was objectionable about Mr. Temple, if one ignored his tendency to over-flatter. And if one didn't count his light pockets. Or the fact that he wasn't Mr. Corb— She stopped her thoughts before they could go any farther down that path.

But perhaps, if she allowed herself to see Mr. Temple in a new light, she might find something of sincerity beneath his character, if not his pursuit. Perhaps he might be someone for whom she could come to feel an affection.

Aunt Mary clapped her hands to gain the group's attention. "Ladies and gentlemen," she began. "I'm delighted to see everyone so eagerly anticipating our little adventure. Sir George holds before you the first clues to our scavenger hunt." At her nod, Uncle George lifted a short stack of sealed cards, his manner more resigned than eager. "Each team will begin with a different clue," Aunt Mary continued, "and each clue is a riddle you must decipher in order to find the next."

Miss Gifford raised a gloved hand.

Aunt Mary frowned at the interruption. "Yes, Miss Gifford?"

"Are the rooms of Summerfield fair game?"

"No, Miss Gifford. And it goes without saying that the proprieties will be observed at all times. To that end, the clues will be found on the grounds only. None have been hidden in secluded locations or the rooms of the house, so there is no need for any… unnecessary investigations." Aunt Mary's gaze swept the participants, and Amelia wondered if Octavia still meant to press Edmund for his favor.

"Once you solve a clue," Aunt Mary continued, "be sure to leave it for the other teams to find. There will be no irregularities. Bring your completed answer sheets to Sir George, who will be our judge. The team which deciphers all ten clues first will be declared the winner. Remember, this is a test not just of speed, but of wit and perseverance! Play fair"—Amelia barely held her snort at that bit of hypocrisy—"and may the best team win." This last was said with an overlong glance in Octavia and Edmund's direction.

Mr. Temple cleared his throat. "And what is the prize for winning this test of wit?"

Before anyone could suggest another favor from the ladies, Aunt Mary said, "The prize, Mr. Temple, will be nothing less than the noble glory of victory."

"And the knowledge that we've bested Corbyn this time, eh?" Mr. Temple murmured to Amelia.

Amelia's answering smile was weak, and she tried to prop it up with a reminder of the lovely day. Low spirits were never any match for a Windermere sun.

"At the very least," she said, "we'll enjoy an afternoon spent out of doors." That it was unlikely anyone but Octavia would win, Amelia kept to herself.

Uncle George came round with the clues, and Mr. Temple took one, cracked the seal and read it aloud to Amelia. "'I am solid, yet I do not move. I am large and green, yet I can be overlooked. By the water's edge, I forever reside.'"

Really, Aunt Mary.

"It's the large moss-covered rock down by the water," Amelia said. "The one you can see from the drawing room windows."

"Shh," Mr. Temple said with some urgency as he peered over his shoulder to where Octavia and Edmund were investigating the trunk of an old oak. He turned back to Amelia and cleared the annoyance from his features. "That is... well done, Miss Thorne."

They did indeed find their next clue at the moss-covered rock, though not without a bit of subterfuge on Mr. Temple's part. He was determined that no one witness their success and steal it for themselves, so he made a great show of inspecting the grass, the surrounding trees and a large pile of leaves while sending Amelia in to retrieve their clue. "Quietly, now," he advised.

Amelia extracted the sealed paper from a gap between the mossy rock and its neighbor—quietly, of course—and returned to her partner.

Nearby, Octavia's laughter rippled, drawing

Amelia's gaze. Edmund smiled down at her cousin, and Amelia reminded herself of her new aim regarding Mr. Temple.

"We have the advantage of them now," Mr. Temple murmured as Amelia wrote in their first answer. "I dare say we have them between a *rock* and a hard place."

This shockingly poor attempt at wit, accompanied by a self-satisfied grin, startled a laugh from Amelia. *You must try harder to like him,* she told herself. "Indeed, Mr. Temple. One might even say fortune favors the *boulder.*"

——

EDMUND TURNED AT the sound of Amelia's laughter. She cast her smile up at Temple, and a growl started low in Edmund's throat. He swallowed it and returned his attention to his partner.

"'What grows when fed but dies when watered?'" Miss Worth read. Her eyes were warm with humor and he tried to share her enthusiasm for the game, but his thoughts were constantly being pulled in other directions. Or *one* other direction, rather. He studiously avoided looking at the water's edge where Amelia stood with Temple and considered Miss Worth's clue instead.

"Grows when fed and dies when watered," he

repeated. The answer was rather too obvious. "A fire," he said. "Perhaps our next clue lies behind the stones of one of the chimneys?"

"How clever you are, Mr. Corbyn," Miss Worth said, though the glint in her eye was suspicious. "Let us try the chimney on the south end first and see if you're right."

"Why do I have the feeling you know the answer already?"

"Oh, pish." Her hand rested on his sleeve as they walked to the end of the house, and he tried to imagine it there for decades to come. Then he imagined a lifetime of verbal dances like the one they engaged in now, wherein Miss Worth spoke but said nothing. She had a rare talent for it, which was why her next words caught him off his guard.

"Your attention seems elsewhere, Mr. Corbyn, and I can't help but wonder if your distraction has anything to do with a certain article in the *Illustrated London News*."

He tucked his chin on an inward wince. "You saw that?"

"Oh yes, and I have to say, my mother has been in high feather ever since."

Well. *That* explained the shift in Lady Worth's demeanor. She'd always been courteous, but in the last days, her manner toward him had become embarrassingly attentive. Just last night, Edmund had complimented her cook's syllabub, and she insisted on sending one of the kitchen maids to the Vicarage with extra servings of it in case he grew hungry in the night.

They reached the library's outer wall, and he began a search of the chimney stones, hoping Miss Worth might abandon the discussion. He was not so fortunate, though.

"I do believe I have you squarely in my debt, Mr. Corbyn."

He lifted a brow as he passed another folded clue to her. "I do not doubt it, but how so?"

"My mother was determined to show the paper to Mrs. Lawson, but I convinced her that as soon as the other ladies know the full extent of your prospects, the competition for your hand will become rather fierce. That is not to downplay your personal attributes, but it is a plain fact. A title *and* means will always trump a fine countenance. Mama sees the truth of this, so she has hidden the paper from her guests, but you will want to lock your doors, sir, lest she compromise you herself and seal your fate."

A short laugh escaped Edmund for Miss Worth's bold speech. "Your efforts on my behalf certainly have my gratitude, though you've a rather direct way of lowering a man's opinion of himself." And then, because he couldn't help the question, he said, "Did... that is... does Miss Thorne know?"

Miss Worth eyed him for a long moment. "Am I to understand from your question that you have not explained the situation to her?"

"I—no."

"Hmm. I thought perhaps that was the reason for her new interest in Mr. Temple. At any rate, my cousin avoids the Society pages whenever she can, so make of that what you will. Now, what do you think of this riddle?"

Edmund took the clue from her, but he didn't read it. Instead, he looked over Miss Worth's shoulder to where Temple stood near the hollowed-out tree of an old oak, trying to appear as if he'd not just uncovered another clue. Amelia wore a pleasant smile, though it wasn't the full one she used when she spoke of Windermere or Wordsworth. But to judge by the confident grin on Temple's face, they must be nearing the end of their clues. Either that, or he was making inroads in his pursuit of Amelia.

Edmund released his breath on a slow sigh. His apology had been poorly done. He knew that now. He'd offered regret he didn't feel for a kiss he'd never forget, but it wasn't enough to put an end to the growing connection between them. He must explain to her *why* he wasn't free to marry to suit his heart. Perhaps then they might put whatever was between them aside.

As he watched, Temple took Amelia's hand in his and pulled her toward Sir George. They passed their answer sheet to Amelia's uncle and, after a cursory review of the clues they'd uncovered, Sir George announced, "Ladies and gentlemen, it seems we have a winner." He paused, and there were disappointed groans from the others. "The clear victory goes to Mr. Temple and Miss Thorne."

"Mr. Corbyn," Miss Worth said, recalling his attention. "You surprise me with how easily you yield the game to Mr. Temple. I thought the rivalry between you more robust than that."

Edmund smiled, though it felt forced. "Some games, Miss Worth, simply aren't winnable."

"Nonsense. If you're not winning, then you must simply make your own rules."

———

AMELIA GLANCED TOWARD her cousin as Mr. Temple accepted their congratulations from the others. That they'd won was rather surprising, given it was Octavia who had all the answers. Perhaps her cousin had been too engrossed in her conversation with Edmund to give the game her full attention. Were they even now discussing Octavia's favor, perhaps? She pulled her gaze away from the pair and forced a smile for Mr. Temple.

"It was Miss Thorne's sharp wit that won the day," he was saying to Lord Hargreave. "That and a good strategy of stealth and secrecy on my part."

"Well played, Temple," Mr. Pearson said.

"Now, perhaps we might enjoy more of this fine day with a leisurely walk about the gardens," Miss Gifford added.

The others agreed, and Amelia took the opportunity to escape. She began walking toward the house, but as she neared the kitchen, footsteps sounded behind her and she turned.

"Mr. Corbyn."

"Miss Thorne." His expression was thoughtful as he stopped before her. "I see congratulations are in order for you and Mr. Temple." He must have considered how his words sounded, for he amended, "For the scavenger hunt, that is."

"Yes. I believe Mr. Temple is pleased with our performance."

He opened his mouth as if he might say more but hesitated. A frown tugged at his brows and the thumping in Amelia's heart increased its pace.

"Mr. Corbyn?"

Laughter sounded from the path behind him, and Amelia looked over his shoulder to where Octavia approached with Mr. Pearson. Edmund saw them too. Leaning toward Amelia, he whispered, "There's something I should like to explain. Will you meet me in the gardener's outbuilding in ten minutes?"

She looked at him in surprise. His expression wasn't that of a lover anticipating an illicit tryst. It was… determined, if a little sad, as he watched her, waiting.

They were to say their goodbyes then.

She'd hoped to have more time to prepare herself. After all, the guests wouldn't leave for two more days—not until after Lady Staveley's ball. But she agreed with a slow nod and then he was gone, striding down the path past her cousin and Mr. Pearson.

"Amelia," Octavia called. "Do you walk with us in the garden?"

"I—no. There's something I must attend to."

Amelia waited a respectable amount of time before turning her steps toward the Vicarage. She rounded it to the gardener's outbuilding at the back, turned the knob and entered. Her eyes took a moment to adjust to the dim light, and when they did, she saw that Edmund's photography supplies were already packed. She swallowed as he straightened from the far wall.

"You came." He walked toward her, hands in his pockets, and she nodded. "I wasn't sure if you would."

"You've packed your supplies already."

He looked at the tidy stack of cases behind him, his jaw tight. "I thought it best to give your aunt's party my full attention."

"You… you said you had something to discuss?" *Explain.* He had something to explain. What could it be? *Please don't let him apologize again.*

"Have you seen last week's issue of the *Illustrated London News*, by chance?"

The question was unexpected and she frowned in confusion. "No."

He took a folded paper from the worktable and extended it to her. Her stomach dropped. Heaven help her, had she made it into the papers again? She took the news sheet despite the dread pooling in her center and began to read.

"This is about you," she said when her lungs began working again. He nodded, and she handed the newspaper back to him. "The writer suggests an unforeseen turn in your family's history. Are you to be named your grandfather's heir?"

He swallowed, and the lantern light glinted off his spectacles as he pushed them higher. "That is my grandfather's hope."

"And yours, I imagine?"

He gave her a single, tight nod.

"It's why your valet calls you 'my lord.'"

"Despite my instruction to the contrary, Finch insists on practicing," he explained. "My grandfather is also Viscount Randolph, so his heir, if one is named, will have the courtesy title."

"And if no heir is named?"

He shrugged, though his tone carried the weight of his words. "Then the earldom will revert to the Crown. The tenants and servants will be impacted, and my family's legacy… six hundred years' worth… will end. All for want of an heir."

She knew enough of this man to know he would not allow that to happen, not if it were within his power to prevent it.

"Queen Victoria has agreed to amend the letters patent to name me as my grandfather's heir," he explained, "but only after I've made a match she deems suitable. It's why I've come to find a bride."

A suitable match. A match worthy of a queen's approval. Suddenly, all became clear to Amelia, but he continued speaking.

"Matters would be far different if it were up to me to marry where my heart—" He stopped, and Amelia held her breath. "That is, if it were up to me to choose my path."

"But it's not up to you," she said. "You're part of something much larger than yourself."

He nodded, eyes closed. He opened them again, his expression complicated as he said, "I cannot fail my family, but I… I wanted you to know."

A long silence stretched between them until, finally, she said, "I understand." And she did, on an intellectual level at least. Her heart was another matter, though, refusing to see reason though it had been laid before her in sharp-edged black and white. But there was no future for her with Edmund. She knew this. She just needed to accept it.

He lined the newspaper up with the corner of the gardener's workbench, and she wished she could even up her emotions just as easily.

"Do you go to Lady Staveley's ball?" he asked, and she frowned at the change in topic.

"I don't know," she said honestly. "I've not been out in Society for five years. I'm not certain they're ready for me." It was one thing to socialize with her aunt's guests. To play pall mall and race rowboats with them. Another altogether to present herself at a to-do like Lady Staveley's ball.

He lifted a hand as if to take hers before dropping it again. "I think you punish yourself unfairly," he said softly.

His words were eerily reminiscent of something Octavia had said, but without the sharp edges. *It's time to end this self-imposed penance.*

Was her solitude some form of self-punishment or was it a necessary retreat? If she were honest, she must admit the possibility that she'd been a bit cowardly to hide herself away at Summerfield. Perhaps, if she meant to give Mr. Temple a proper bit of encouragement, she ought to consider attending the ball.

"Regardless of what you decide," Edmund said, "know that there are people who will stand with you."

Warmth filled her for his simple acceptance, for his friendship. "Thank you." Her voice was barely audible around the lump in her throat.

He picked up something from the shadows behind him and offered it to her. Wordsworth's *Prelude*. "I've nearly finished it," he said, "but I doubt I'll find more time to read before I go."

She shook her head slowly. Her eyes burned, and she blinked. "Consider it a gift."

He lowered his hand. "I will treasure it. Thank you."

She pulled in a slow breath, savoring the soft clove-and-citrus scent of his soap in the close space. Smoothing her hands along the wool of her skirts, she prepared to go. Then, licking her lips once for courage, she said to him, "Octavia would make a fine countess, if you're determined to find one at Windermere."

He stilled for a long moment before giving her a slow nod, and she left before tears could threaten once again.

CHAPTER TWENTY-TWO

My head aches and my stomach turns, but I dare say a waltz
with Edmund will be worth the evening's trial.
—From the private journal of Miss Amelia Thorne

IT HAD BEEN years since a ball gown had given Amelia pleasure, but she had to admit Sir Frederick's creation did just that. It was perfectly fitted to her form, and the deep gold silk caught the light when she moved. She took another step before Octavia's mirror, just to see the skirts swing as Jane and Octavia looked on. Her cousin caught Amelia's eye in the glass, and the smile she wore was less sardonic than usual.

"Thank you, Octavia," Amelia said softly.

Octavia dismissed her words with an airy wave of one hand as her mother sailed in clutching her watch. "It's nearly time, Octavia," Aunt Mary began then stopped. Her lips pinched to see Amelia dressed, her hair braided and curled and threaded with tiny pearls.

"You're determined to go?" she said.

Amelia smoothed a hand along the cool silk of her bodice. Her stomach gave an uncomfortable lurch as she said, "I think I must. It's time to put the unpleasantness of the past years behind me." It was time to stop punishing herself.

"They have not forgotten," Aunt Mary said, "and your presence tonight will only revive the gossip."

That was precisely what Amelia feared, but she'd grown tired of hiding. And Sir Frederick's gown was really too magnificent to remain in its box.

And... she didn't want to miss seeing Edmund in his evening finery. She'd promised to save him a dance, after all, the day they'd rowed to St. Mary Holme.

She could no longer deny he'd touched a place deep in her heart, and not only with his kiss. Edmund was the sort of gentleman who, in the shadowy, not-quite-acknowledged part of her mind, she'd always imagined falling in love with, but with one rather glaring difference: she'd never thought to be so tragic to love a man who was forbidden to her.

If she'd fallen for Edmund after learning the full

extent of his situation, she might have blamed her feelings on contrariness. On some perverse desire to have that which was denied to her.

But, truth be told, she'd fallen a little bit in love him that very first day in Birthwaite when he'd purchased *The Prelude* for her.

She was a fool, but it couldn't be helped.

"All will be well," she assured her aunt with more certainty than she felt.

Aunt Mary gave her a look full of idioms.

As you sow, so shall you reap.

You're making a rod for your own back.

Foolish ladies who make their own beds must lie in them.

Amelia couldn't disagree.

———

FOUR COACHES HAD been secured for the journey to Lady Staveley's ball. Edmund sat across from Amelia and Miss Worth as light from the lanterns bounced over the carriage interior. Temple, seated next to him, took more than his share of the bench. The route around Windermere was a well-traveled one, and they soon passed the lake's head to come down the Lancashire side.

"Miss Thorne," Temple said, "you're in fine looks tonight. I dare say you'll outshine the other ladies." It was not Temple's first such compliment of the evening, but it seemed he'd already run through his repertoire and was determined to begin again.

"Thank you, Mr. Temple."

Miss Worth did her part to keep the atmosphere inside the carriage light with her droll commentary on the evening ahead, but Edmund was filled with what could only be called sober contemplation.

He was pleased Amelia had decided to attend. Her spirit was too bright not to be shared. He watched as her fingers plucked at the tips of her gloves, the only hint that her nerves weren't as steady as they appeared. He longed to settle a hand atop hers and offer words of comfort, but he settled for stealing glances at her profile as she watched the darkness beyond the window.

Her manner was all that was proper, without a hint of the scandal that stained her reputation. Added to that, she wore an elegant gown of dark gold silk that had him imagining her as a proper countess. And that thought, of course, prompted their last exchange to repeat itself in his mind. *Octavia would make a fine countess.*

He couldn't dispute it. Miss Worth *would* make a fine countess, if she were agreeable to the match. But time was running out, and he'd not given her a clear indication of his intentions. He would find a quiet moment tonight away from the dancing to gauge her feelings on a marriage between them. It would be best to have things settled before he returned to London.

The carriage slowed as it joined the queue outside Stonecroft's white marbled entrance. Finally, the steps were let down and Edmund extended a hand to Miss Worth. Temple did the same for Amelia, and Edmund couldn't help but notice how her breath caught as she looked up at the well-lit entrance towering before them. Uncertainty filled her, though she hid it well.

They handed off their hats and cloaks, and the chamberlain announced them. Heads lifted throughout the ballroom. On seeing the new arrivals, fans began waving and whispers rose to circulate. Amelia clasped her hands before her, and Edmund stepped closer to her side.

"Your elegant manner does you credit," he murmured for her ears alone.

"I should not have come. Do you see how they whisper?"

Edmund eyed the assembled guests dressed in their best ball finery—dark suits and colorful silks, feathered headdresses and patterned waistcoats. More than one matron caught Edmund's eye as his gaze roamed the room, and it came to him then.

"Miss Thorne," he said with a smile for those watching. "I dare say they've been reading the news sheets. They're whispering about *me*."

Her eyes widened and she examined the ball-room once again. "Oh! Do you know, I think you must be right."

"There will always be small-minded Lady Fox-gates to contend with," he said, "but I think you may be assured your own scandal has begun to fade from the collective memory." More tension left her frame, which only showed how much she'd been dreading the evening. Edmund knew an over-whelming urge to embrace her, to hold her tight in his arms as she recalled she was more than a story to be told for the amusement of others.

"Miss Thorne," Temple said. "The musicians are preparing for a new set. Will you do me the honor?"

Edmund flattered himself that she hesitated be-fore placing her gloved hand in Temple's. It was with reluctant acceptance that he watched her go.

"Well, Mr. Corbyn," Miss Worth said from his side. "Shall we show them how it's done?" He hid a smile for her forwardness. Miss Worth was no de-mure debutante, and he wondered how she'd avoided a scandal of her own. But then, she had an astute cunning about her that Amelia lacked. She would know precisely what she could say and to whom so she might skirt the edge of propriety without tipping over it. It was a compliment to Amelia that she lacked such wiliness.

Couples were taking their positions for a quadrille, and Edmund allowed Miss Worth to lead them to one corner. The music began and they moved through the steps. She was an accomplished dancer, her motions fluid. Her laughter and conversation were easy as the steps brought them back together, and when they were apart, she charmed those around her. He could easily picture her as mistress of Redstone Hall.

——

THE STEPS OF the dance brought Amelia back to Mr. Temple, but it required an effort to keep her attention on her partner. Her gaze kept straying to Lady Staveley's other guests, none of whom seemed overly interested in the scandalous woman in their midst. She'd not heard one whisper, in fact, of the Poisoned Thorne. Could Edmund have been right?

She'd been a mass of writhing nerves all evening, and her neck had grown sore from holding her head at such a confident angle. But now, for the first time, she allowed herself to relax just a tiny bit.

It had been a long time since she'd danced, and she'd forgotten how much she enjoyed the rhythm and motion of it. The gold silk of Sir Frederick's gown shimmered beneath the low gas lights of Stonecroft's ballroom. The effect, combined with the dawning realization that she wasn't the topic on everyone's lips, was a heady one.

She wasn't the only one to benefit from Sir Frederick's talent. Aunt Mary wore another of his gowns in deep burgundy—supported by no less than five petticoats, Amelia would wager—and Octavia looked especially resplendent in cream silk adorned with Honiton lace. If the admiring and envious glances being cast Octavia's way were any indication, Sir Frederick had found a profitable ally in her cousin.

The dance ended and Mr. Temple offered to lead Amelia back to her aunt. Before they'd taken more than half a dozen steps in that direction, a gentleman approached them. He was young and earnest-looking with a fine head of auburn hair. Amelia recognized him as Lady Staveley's nephew, a respectable gentleman with a respectable fortune at his disposal.

"Temple," he said with a nod.

"Daventry."

"I wonder if you might do me the honor of introducing your companion," the gentleman said with a smile for Amelia.

Mr. Temple performed the introductions with some reluctance, but before Mr. Daventry could come to the point and invite Amelia to stand up with him, Aunt Mary joined them.

"Mr. Daventry," she cooed. "And Mr. Temple. Might I beg my niece's company for a turn about the room?" Amelia checked her frown as Aunt Mary wasn't in the habit of begging for anything, and certainly not where she was concerned.

"Of course, Lady Worth," Mr. Daventry said with a gallant nod. He stepped back to permit Amelia to pass, and Aunt Mary seized her arm with a vise-like grip.

"Have a care, niece," she said when they were alone. "You wouldn't want your behavior to cause old tales to resurface." She nodded as they passed a pair of feather-adorned acquaintances.

"My behavior?" Amelia said with some surprise. "I merely shared a dance with Mr. Temple, and then he introduced me to Mr. Daventry. It was all very properly done, I assure you."

"Yes, well, memories are long and unforgiving." Aunt Mary nodded again, this time at a pair of gentlemen who watched their progress. Once they'd passed, she hissed beneath her breath, "Everyone knows Temple is pressed for funds. It's the only reason he pursues you so openly, but I'll not have you compromising Octavia's chances with Mr. Corbyn—not when she's got him so close to the mark."

Amelia swallowed. For a few brief moments, she'd allowed herself to forget about Edmund and his intentions toward her cousin. Now, though, the room felt too hot, the gas lights too bright. They'd reached a group of her aunt's friends and Amelia tugged her hand free.

"I think I will find some refreshment," she murmured. She turned away before her aunt could argue, but not before catching the pursed and wrinkled lips of her aunt's companions as they eyed her. Much of Society may have forgotten about the Poisoned Thorne, but not all, it would seem.

Amelia found the refreshments table and collected a cup of punch from a footman. Moving to an alcove off to one side, she sipped the beverage in an effort to calm her irritation. It wasn't working. She cast an annoyed glance back toward her aunt's corner, but Aunt Mary had left her friends.

Amelia noticed then the weight of several pairs of eyes, and her breath froze in her chest to realize a number of ladies and gentlemen were looking her way. She heard—imagined?—their whispers above the strains of the string quartet. She held herself straight, though her stomach tightened and her blood flowed hot beneath her skin. Edmund had been wrong, after all.

She forced a calmness to her features she was far from feeling. Searching the ballroom again, hoping to prove herself wrong, she soon found the rich burgundy of Aunt Mary's gown. Her aunt stood with her back toward Amelia as she spoke with Mr.

Temple and Mr. Daventry, the jet beads at her ears bobbing in time with her words.

Amelia watched over the rim of her cup as Mr. Daventry looked up and over Aunt Mary's shoulder. His frowning gaze found Amelia and quickly slid away, and it didn't take an enormous effort to guess at their topic of conversation.

Of all the... Amelia's cheeks lit with mortification and sudden, disbelieving anger to think that her aunt—her father's sister—would add fuel to the gossip about her.

The sweet punch soured in her stomach, and she carefully set her empty cup on a footman's passing tray. The night's surprises weren't finished, though. As she turned to leave her alcove, she came face to face with Lord Snowdon of The Great Disgrace.

The ballroom stilled, or perhaps Amelia imagined the fading of the music and the heaviness that settled on her shoulders. It was no consolation that Snowdon seemed equally surprised to meet her. He was older now, obviously, and it occurred to her that she'd thought him little more than a boy all these years.

Had her aunt known Snowdon would be in attendance tonight? Aunt Mary was a frequent caller at Stonecroft, so it was possible.

She might have given Amelia some warning, but then, to do so probably wouldn't have served her own scheme, whatever that was.

The heat of the ballroom was at Amelia's back, and it pressed heavily as she waited for Snowdon to acknowledge her. A nod or a word between them and they might convince Lady Staveley's guests that the old scandal wasn't worth recalling.

But then, Snowdon flicked a glance over her shoulder at the crowded ballroom. His gaze caught on an acquaintance, and she knew with a sinking feeling that he meant to cut her. She wasn't having it. The past years of avoiding Society, of suffering the weight of stares and whispers, and now, Snowdon's poor manners—it was all too much.

"Lord Snowdon," she said before he could move around her. "It's a pleasure to see you once again. I hope you're enjoying your visit to the Lakes." She knew it wasn't done, to speak so to a peer before he'd acknowledged her, but she didn't think he'd go so far as to ignore a direct address. She hoped not, at any rate.

Several people had developed a sudden thirst and clustered around the nearby refreshments table. Amelia held her smile in the face of their hushed scrutiny and gripped her hands to still their shaking.

Finally, Snowdon gave her a stiff nod, "Miss Thorne. My stay in the county has been all that I could hope."

Amelia released a slow breath.

"Snowdon," a voice said at her elbow, and her heart jumped. *Edmund.*

Snowdon's demeanor shifted from annoyed displeasure to interest. "Corbyn. So, this is where you've hidden yourself. The papers have been rife with speculation, though I wondered if perhaps you weren't tucked away, perfecting some invention or other." Several of the nearby gentlemen nodded their agreement. After a small pause, Snowdon added in an undertone, "I must say, your latest patent has made me a tidy sum. I don't suppose you could give a hint—"

Edmund cut him off cleanly. "I hate to rob you of Miss Thorne's company, Snowdon, but she is promised to me for the next dance. You'll excuse us?" It was brilliantly done, and Amelia wanted to applaud his cutting tone.

Snowdon stepped back with reluctance, and Amelia allowed herself to be led away. The heat of a dozen stares followed them as they navigated the crowd to an empty place near the minstrels' gallery. Only then did she notice the dancers were organizing for a waltz. Edmund bowed, and she curtsied in reply.

"You do not have to do this," she whispered.

"No," he agreed, "but I should like to."

"That was rather spectacular," she said, referring to his neat dispatch of Snowdon.

"It was, wasn't it?"

The music began, but the evening's events remained a heavy weight. Amelia tried to allow her muscles to relax, to follow Edmund's lead as the steps of the dance spun them round the room, but she felt stiff, like a marionette dancing on knotted strings.

"You're shaking," Edmund said softly.

"I'm… angry."

"I'm pleased to hear it."

She looked up at him in surprise. He smiled again and her breath caught. His hand, large and warm through his glove, firmed on her back as he turned them.

"Shall we enjoy the dance?" he asked.

She decided then that there was time enough for anger later. She wouldn't permit anything to ruin the loveliest waltz she would ever have.

CHAPTER TWENTY-THREE

EDMUND KNEW ALL eyes were upon them, but he ignored the sensation and concentrated on the woman in his arms. She was soft and firm and *right*. When he leaned his head to hear her whispered words, Amelia's soft breath fanned his cheek.

"I'm angry," she said.

He was pleased to hear it, and he told her so. Perhaps, when her anger was behind her, she could move forward in her life. A life that would not include him, it was true, but she deserved to find peace and acceptance.

And forgiveness. Not from Society—chasing that

would always be a hopeless endeavor—but from herself.

He pressed her a bit closer as they turned, and her clean, bright scent filled his senses. Her full skirts brushed his trousers as he navigated a knot of people near the edge of the floor. The ballroom's gas lights had been turned low for the evening's revelry, and candles burned from the bronze chandeliers overhead. Their light caught on the threads of gold in Amelia's hair as she smiled up at him. He swallowed against a sharp-edged longing and focused on ignoring the future, just for this moment.

And, as he was valiantly not thinking of the future, a sudden burst of clarity brought home one solid truth: no woman but Amelia would ever do for him. None of Society's marks against her—neither the taint of her scandal nor her family's low background—none of it mattered to him, so why it should matter to others was beyond his comprehension.

Amelia was the one who touched his soul, and he thought—no, he *knew*—he touched hers. It was there in the way she gazed up at him as he turned her. In the delicate weight of her hand in his and the trust in her eyes as he'd led them away from Snowdon. He wanted to be there for her always, to protect and love and cherish her.

If there were a way… there must be a way. He would find it. Swallowing, he gathered his courage.

"Miss Thorne," he said softly. "Amelia."

She smiled in reply and he pushed on.

"You must suspect by now the depth of my feelings." He hesitated at the tiny hint of surprise that appeared on her face, then pushed on. "Do you think—"

Her surprise turned to alarm, and she gave him a tiny shake of her head. "Please, Mr. Corbyn," she whispered. "Do not ruin this waltz with talk of impossibilities."

"But—"

She swallowed and shook her head once more. He might have imagined the sadness that touched her eyes, but she went on to say, "I won't pretend ignorance to what you are about to say, but we both know you require a suitable bride, just as we both know I am not that bride."

He held her a little too closely, surprised at the intensity of his own voice when he pressed, "Would you have me believe you feel nothing for me?" He wouldn't believe it unless she told him so herself.

She looked over his shoulder at some point beyond them before bringing her gaze back to his. Her expression was apologetic as she said, "I will not lie and say I feel nothing, but neither will I give you hope where there is none. You have your family to consider. And you must see that I'm too attached to Windermere to ever leave it." She smiled again, and there was a finality to it.

He turned her automatically and felt the gentle swish of her skirts brushing against him. His heart beat a tight, thudding pulse in his ears, and his stomach churned with a miserable, twisty heat. She was right to refuse him, and a tiny, shameful part of him felt relief for it, but none of this did anything for the ache spreading through him.

"Let us simply dance," she whispered, and there was such a soft, plaintive note to her plea that he couldn't refuse her.

So, they spun and twirled and glided, their cadence much like one of her beloved poems. He was breathless by the time the music ended, as if he'd rowed the length of the Thames. He held her longer than necessary, unwilling to let the moment end, yet knowing it must.

"Thank you," she said, her color high. He lifted her hand and placed a gentle kiss on the back of her silk-covered fingers. Her eyes met his above a gentle smile, and as she turned to go, he couldn't help checking her slippers to see if they were made of glass, so fully had she enchanted him.

But as her skirts swung above the polished oak floor, he caught a glimpse of pale ivory satin. Her slippers weren't made of glass at all. It was just as well, for he'd probably have run after her begging, without another thought for the Queen or his family's legacy. Never had he felt so close to another person, and yet so distant.

"Mr. Corbyn," a voice spoke softly from his elbow, and only then did he realize he stood in the way of the dancers preparing for the next set.

"Miss Worth." Her brows lifted with expectation, and he recalled he'd secured the next dance with her. Their second of the evening. It was as good as a declaration, but he'd no wish to partner another so soon after holding Amelia in his arms. It seemed wrong, somehow, as if he could dismiss his feelings so easily, but neither could he ignore his obligation to Miss Worth. He called up a smile, but before he could offer his arm to lead her to their places, she spoke.

"I wonder if we might sit this set out together. I find myself rather fatigued from all the dancing."

If Miss Worth was fatigued, then Edmund would eat his hat. But her "fatigue" served his own inclination, so he merely dipped his head. "Of course. Shall I procure some refreshment for us?"

She agreed, and he returned with cups of punch. When she suggested a walk along the terrace, he glanced toward her mother, who was seated with several older ladies. Lady Worth gave them her nod of approval, and Edmund allowed

Miss Worth to lead the way.

The stars were out, and there was a cool crisp-ness to the air that Edmund had only felt at Winder-mere. Three other couples were also on the terrace, so they weren't quite alone, though Miss Worth found a quiet spot in the shadows of a low-burning lantern.

He handed her one of the cups and knew this was the moment he'd been looking for. He should broach the topic of matrimony. He ought to do what he could to secure Miss Worth's hand.

His heart screamed that it was wrong to do so while his stomach still churned over Amelia's re-fusal. Certainly, two marriage proposals in one night must make him a cad. And yet, the future couldn't be avoided, no matter his feelings on it. Despite his wishes to the contrary, he still required a bride.

"The punch is very good," Miss Worth said.

He took a sip and agreed. It was only then that the horrible notion occurred to him: What if he se-cured Miss Worth's hand, only to find the Queen had a more precise notion of an acceptable match for him? Then he would be honor bound to marry her without having accomplished his aim.

No. He couldn't leave such a thing to chance. He'd have some assurances from his Queen first. That such a thought hadn't occurred to him with Amelia—that he'd been prepared to weather the repercussions of making her his wife—he staunchly shoved aside.

But tonight, he need only gauge Miss Worth's interest. Nothing more. The thought sent more relief surging through him than it ought to have done.

She quirked an ironic brow at him as if she knew precisely what he was thinking. "Mr. Corbyn?"

"Miss Worth," he said, "my time at Summerfield comes to an end tomorrow."

"So it does."

"I was wondering…"

"Yes?"

He forced the words out. "I was wondering if you might be amenable to my returning at some point." There. Surely, she must know the direction of his thoughts by now, though he'd not hemmed himself in with false promises.

Miss Worth lowered her cup and studied him. He held his breath as he waited for her answer. What if she were not agreeable to his suit after all? Would he return to his grandfather in defeat, only to begin the whole wretched business all over again? Many of London's families would have left the city by now, and he'd have a devil of a time—

"I am amenable," Miss Worth finally said, though there was no period to her statement. It was the least certain he'd ever heard her, in fact.

His own breath was shallow in his chest, but

there was no going back now. He nodded and forced a smile to his face.

"Do your plans take you back to London or to Kent?" she asked.

"I return to London."

She studied him, and he searched his mind for something to say. Surely, there ought to be more said when a gentleman gave such strong hints of his intentions. Would she expect a declaration of his feelings? She would be justified in doing so.

She drained her cup and spoke again. "Mr. Corbyn, I am not one known for the seriousness of my thoughts, but I say this with the utmost sincerity: you've the appearance of a soldier with a mission to complete or a child resolved to clean his plate though he dislikes the peas."

Edmund cleared his throat. Her description of him was rather astute as he'd never been overly fond of peas. Still, he ought to offer some assurances that his intentions were sincere, if not his heart. Before he could do so, she continued.

"I hope your mission finds a successful conclusion, and I very much expect you and I will see one another again soon."

"That is my hope as well," he said. Although, he feared he was nearing the end of his mission, as she put it, only to find that success was not what he'd thought it would be.

CHAPTER TWENTY-FOUR

AMELIA FOUND THE rest of Lady Staveley's ball interminable, and she wanted nothing more than to curl up in the Vicarage's library with Lord Byron and have a good cry. But she was trapped until the carriages departed, her chest unbearably tight with unshed tears, and a horrible sensation swirling in the pit of her stomach.

Edmund had nearly proposed to her, and she'd *refused* him. What madness had taken hold of her good sense?

The journey back to Summerfield was more subdued than the one going, and conversation in the coach was all but non-existent. Even Octavia seemed uninterested in exchanging the night's *on dits*. In fact, her cousin and Edmund seemed equally determined to avoid one another's gaze, as if something had passed between them which they were loath to recall. Amelia's stomach lurched again as the carriage turned up the drive.

When everyone had retired to their rooms except Aunt Mary and Uncle George, Amelia gathered her thoughts and prepared for the coming confrontation. It couldn't be helped.

"Aunt Mary," she said tightly. "Uncle George. I would have a word in the drawing room if you please."

"Really, Amelia. It's late, and tomorrow will be very busy with my guests departing."

"Still, I would have a word," Amelia insisted. She ushered them both into the drawing room and sent the footman to seek his bed. "Please," she said, "sit." Even Uncle George peered at her more closely for the tone in her voice, but he sat. With an irritable sigh, Aunt Mary followed suit.

"What is this about?" Uncle George asked.

Amelia gripped her hands together to still their shaking and drew a breath for courage. "I wish to know if my aunt has been keeping my scandal alive all these years."

Aunt Mary flinched, one pale hand pressed to the blood-red silk of her bodice. "Gracious, Amelia, what has gotten into you? That is a ridiculous and baseless accusation."

"Ridiculous, yes. It hardly seems creditable, but then I thought back to the times before when I've considered rejoining Society. Times when *you* reminded me of the whispers and stares I stood to suffer if I so much as entertained the thought. And each time, oddly enough, the papers would revive the whole affair not long after. I never allowed myself to think too much on it—it was nothing more than the fickle whims of a bored society, after all."

"As I have always maintained," Aunt Mary said, though her gaze wouldn't hold Amelia's.

"But tonight," Amelia continued, "I witnessed the undeniable truth of it. You have been keeping the scandal alive with a word here and a whisper there, though to what purpose, I cannot fathom."

"You will not speak to me like this," Aunt Mary hissed. She stood, intent on the door, but was stopped by Uncle George's words.

"Mary," he said with a frown, "what is she talking about?"

"It's nothing, George. Nothing but the overwrought words of an ungrateful child. She's jealous of Octavia—she's always envied our daughter—and she imagines intrigues and slights where there are none."

"Mr. Daventry wished to make my acquaintance

tonight," Amelia pressed, "until you spoke with him. What did you say, I wonder? For certainly, he never approached me again after that. In fact, aside from Mr. Corbyn, no one else invited me to dance, and you can't claim *that* is my imagination."

Uncle George removed his spectacles to rub his eyes. "Mary—"

"George, you can't think to listen to her."

"I've also wondered why the scandal has hung about her for so long. Even your brother thought it would blow over in a fortnight. A month at most. The papers should have turned their pens to other, more sensational tales long before now. Tell me you've not had anything to do with that."

Aunt Mary remained stubbornly silent, her gaze intent on the wallpaper beyond Uncle George's shoulder.

"I think," Amelia said slowly, "it must have something to do with my inheritance." At the narrowing of her aunt's eyes, she knew she'd touched on the heart of the matter.

"Really, Amelia. I can't believe even you would bring such a distasteful topic into my drawing room."

"It is *my* drawing room," Amelia reminded her. "And if I rejoin Society… if I marry… my husband will gain my fortune and Summerfield. My uncle won't be needed to manage it any longer, and you'll have to return to Surrey. There will be no more funds to pay for seasons in London or your annual house parties... or new gowns from Sir Frederick."

Her uncle stood and began to pace the room. His hair stood on end where he'd run a hand through it in his agitation. "Mary," he said gruffly, "she is your blood."

Aunt Mary whirled on her husband. "Only because my brother had the stupidity to marry so far beneath him. An Irish seamstress! I made a good match and endeavored to bring our family up, but he chose to drag it down. I did what needed to be done for our daughter."

Amelia recoiled from her aunt's words. "I would never have begrudged Octavia," she said softly. "Or you, for that matter. There was no need to resort to such... such vile tactics."

Her uncle's head was bowed, one hand pressed to his forehead to grip his temples. He looked up when Amelia addressed him.

"Uncle, I don't believe my father misplaced his trust when he left my fortune in your care, but I should like to meet with you tomorrow and discuss a more suitable distribution of the quarterly funds. I'm certain we can come to agreeable terms."

Aunt Mary gasped, but Uncle George pulled in a slow breath and nodded. His misery gave Amelia some comfort—at least he'd not been complicit in her aunt's schemes. "Yes. Of course."

Only when they'd gone, when Summerfield was silent once more, did Amelia release her hands. Her fingers were stiff and her pulse continued to race as she went to find her bed.

—

"THERE YOU ARE," Octavia said as she strode into Amelia's bedchamber the next morning. "You didn't come down to breakfast to take your leave of our guests."

"No." Amelia sat in her window seat, Lord Byron curled on her lap and dutifully submitting to her distracted petting. Octavia looked as she always did, which was to say she didn't appear freshly betrothed. But then, Amelia wasn't sure a freshly betrothed Octavia would appear any less indifferent than usual.

"Mama seems rather subdued. I wonder if she's already missing the excitement of the party or if she might be coming down with something."

"I suspect your mother is coming down with a case of genteel poverty," Amelia murmured.

After a pause during which Octavia sorted Amelia's words, she said, "You finally put the brakes to her spending then? I can see how that might give her a case of the megrims, but it's no less than she deserves after what she's done."

Amelia cut a glance at her cousin. "You were listening at the drawing room?"

"One does what one must. Tell me, though…"

Amelia lifted a questioning brow.

"How do Mama's new circumstances affect me?"

"You shall not go about in rags," Amelia assured her.

"That is a comfort."

Amelia returned her attention to the window. On the drive below, two carriages were being loaded with crates and boxes and trunks of Edmund's photography equipment. Amelia's heart thumped uncomfortably in her chest, but she was unable to turn away.

Finch balanced on the cobbles on his borrowed crutches, giving William direction for the loading while Blue rested on her haunches like an aging sentry. When Finch attempted to return the crutches to William, the coachman shook his head. Even from a distance, Amelia could detect the valet's frown when William told him the crutches were to return to London with him.

Edmund stood off to one side, arms crossed over his lovely rower's chest. The sun glinted off his spectacles and lined the hard edge of his jaw. Amelia was too far away to make out the clear blue-green hue of his eyes, but she imagined it easily enough. She lifted her fingers and laid them gently on the cool glass, cursing her foolishness even as she did so. Though Octavia appeared no different today, Edmund would have spoken to her. He must have done, and they would have come to an understanding.

The fact that he'd no other choice in the matter didn't make the knowledge any more bearable, nor did it ease the horrid sensation that persisted in the region of her heart. It was an overwhelming sort of pain, distressingly similar to the grief she'd felt when news of her father's death had reached her. It was stark and raw, waiting for something that would never come—a hope defeated. She wanted to escape it, but she couldn't. Perhaps in time, it might lessen, but she didn't think it would ever go away.

"For what it's worth," Octavia said behind her, "I didn't know of Mama's scheme."

"I know," Amelia said, and she did. Not once as the whole, horrible truth of Aunt Mary's perfidy unfolded, had she questioned her cousin's heart.

To be honest, she would have preferred it if Octavia were a villainess. At least then, she might have named the ugly seething in her belly "righteous affront" rather than "undignified envy."

And there it was. She was envious of her cousin, just as Aunt Mary had accused. It was pointless, though—rather like resenting a friend for having two parents when you had none. There was nothing to be done for it, but that didn't lessen the sentiment.

"Did Mr. Temple finally come to the point?" her cousin said.

"What?"

Edmund bent to give Blue a scratch, and the dog looked up at him adoringly.

"Mr. Temple," Octavia prompted. "Did he make you an offer?"

Edmund's head angled up as if he sensed Amelia's presence, and she leaned forward, unable to remain hidden. He lifted one hand to shade his eyes, but the angle of the sun must have obscured her image behind the glass. After a last, lingering look, he lowered his hand and motioned for Blue to enter the carriage. In moments, the drivers had the vehicles turned about and rumbling down the drive toward the train in Birthwaite. Amelia feared her heart went with them.

She dropped her hand and sat back. The urge to run from the room, to chase the carriages down the drive, was strong.

She should have gone to breakfast. She should have said, "Yes, I'll marry you," though he'd not quite gotten the question out. At the very least, she should have thanked him again for his kindnesses at Lady Staveley's ball. She should not have allowed him to leave without one last exchange between them before he was truly lost to her. With an effort, she stayed where she was and drew a shuddering breath to collect herself.

Then she recalled Octavia's question. Mr. Temple.

"He did not," she said. Amelia shifted on the window seat and Lord Byron leaped to the floor.

"No? Well, why ever not?" Octavia's voice rose with a flattering degree of upset.

"I suspect that, in the end, my scandal was too much for him to overlook." Or Aunt Mary had put a bee in his ear. "It's neither here nor there. I would have declined him at any rate."

Octavia lifted one brow. *Go on.*

"It turns out, he's a rather nice man—a bit over-eager, perhaps—but he doesn't deserve a disinterested bride." *And I deserve to be more than a bank draft.* Then, because she couldn't help the words, she said, "Did Mr. Corbyn… that is—"

"No, but he intends to return to Summerfield."

Amelia had been studying a loose thread on her sleeve, but she looked up at Octavia's words. They weren't betrothed! But Edmund could only be returning for one reason. "He will make you an admirable husband," she said, though the words felt like sand in her throat.

"Hmm... Do you know, I don't think he suits me."

Octavia meant to refuse him! Amelia's heart

quickened for herself then sank for Edmund. If Octavia didn't marry him, then he must begin his search all over again. She wished for his happiness, for his success in helping his family, but she would rather he married someone—anyone—other than her cousin. She didn't think she could bear to see them making a life together, but for Octavia to allow him false hope… that was not to be borne.

"What of your mother?" Amelia said. "I can't imagine she'll be pleased if you cut Mr. Corbyn from your hook."

"She'll be disappointed, to be sure—the man will be heir to an earldom after all."

"If you know his circumstances, then you know he isn't free to marry where he wishes," Amelia said, then she bit her tongue. "Not that he doesn't *wish* to marry you, I'm sure, but—"

Octavia held up a hand. "I know what you meant," she said flatly.

"But you don't intend to accept him? This is not one of your games, Octavia. You should have been forthright and told him as much. He needs to marry well to preserve his family's legacy."

Octavia shook her head. "You, Cousin, are too noble by half. Perhaps *you* should marry him."

Amelia's heart caught at her cousin's words, but she pressed her argument anyway. "He must find a suitable bride," she repeated. "Her Majesty has mandated it as a condition of his inheritance, and he would never compromise his family's legacy. His love for them is too great. If he forsakes his family, if he marries to suit his heart, it will go against the man he is."

"I begin to believe Mama has the right of it—poetry has put ridiculous notions in your head of star-crossed lovers and ill-fated passions. You sit in your window seat and read your books, but when that rarest of love stands before you, you turn away to hide behind a scandal that's *five years old.*

"There's more against our match than simply my scandal," Amelia said.

"Your mother was a seamstress, yes, I know."

"And the daughter of a seamstress—a *Catholic* seamstress—does not become a countess."

"In whose world?"

"In *this* world!"

"It seems to me, the *world* should not have anything to say about love between two people," Octavia said airily. Amelia couldn't disagree, but neither did she make the rules. She remained silent, jaw tight.

Octavia, though, wasn't finished. "You will grow old and bitter, always wondering about a love that never was, while I shall marry a fat squire and content myself with sweets and morning calls. I wonder which of us will be the most miserable."

"You are not helping anything," said Amelia.

"And you are not helping yourself. When your Mr. Corbyn returns, I suggest you seize your happiness with both hands, Cousin."

Octavia left with an emphatic swing of her silk skirts, and Amelia, who normally enjoyed a good, rousing debate with her cousin, felt all sorts of miserable. She sank back onto the window seat, torn between dismay for Edmund, for it was clear he'd not achieved his aim, and a selfish elation that, if he must marry, at least it wouldn't be to her cousin.

CHAPTER TWENTY-FIVE

EDMUND'S FOOLISH WORDS to his mother echoed in his mind for the duration of the train ride back to London. *I can manage my heart.* What a muddle he'd made of things. He'd ridden away from the woman he loved—there was no denying his feelings for Amelia—and still he had no bride to show for it. He was perilously close to failing his family, and the notion sat heavily on his heart.

He should have made more of an effort to secure Miss Worth's hand before leaving Windermere. Spoken more directly with her or with her father, perhaps. She met all of their Queen's requirements, and there was little question that Victoria would approve her for his bride. He recognized *that* bit of nonsense now for the delaying tactic that it was, but he'd been physically unable to speak the words that would have bound them more securely to one another. Not while Amelia held his heart.

The devil take it, he *was* a bloody romantic.

Blue slept as the train rocked on the track, and Edmund realized Finch had spoken again. His valet was attempting to debate the merits of a new chemical composition they meant to try, but Edmund's thoughts were too fractured to carry his end of the discussion.

"Pardon?" he said.

Finch motioned to the book in Edmund's hand. "Is that Maxwell's thesis on color?"

Edmund lifted the leather-bound volume and turned it, his thumb running once over the embossed title. "It's Miss Thorne's book of poetry," he said. "But then, I imagine you already knew that, since you were the one who received Miss Thorne when she brought it to the Vicarage."

Finch tucked his chin in the manner that suggested he was reluctant to say what he was about to say, but it was coming anyway.

"Out with it," Edmund said to hasten him along.

"Queen Victoria will never approve the Thorne woman—"

"Miss Thorne," Edmund corrected.

"Miss Thorne." Finch studied the crutches leaning against the table—crutches Amelia had insisted he keep for the journey back to London. The edge left his valet's voice as he added, "No matter your feelings for the lady, she will never meet with the Queen's approval."

"I'm well aware of that," Edmund said through clenched teeth. Knowing the pill was bitter, though, didn't make it any easier to swallow.

"But you love her?"

Edmund frowned at his unvaletlike valet. "Remind me again, what valet training did you have?"

Finch sat back, jaw firm, and crossed his arms over his chest. A sniff was the only indication that his dignity had been wounded. Edmund scrubbed a hand over his face. He was becoming a miserable man to be around, and a poor friend and employer at that. Clearing his throat, he ran his thumb slowly over *The Prelude's* title once more.

"Apologies," he said. "I'm out of sorts." A rather monumental understatement to describe his feelings. He felt raw. Aching and ravaged, as if his heart had been shredded and left to dry in the sun. Before long, there wouldn't be anything left of it but dust.

Finch remained silent for all of two beats before saying, "You're a man of invention, accustomed to solving problems with mechanics and formulas, but the heart doesn't adhere to the rules of the natural world. Perhaps, this is one puzzle best left to the poets to sort."

Edmund crossed his arms and leaned back, turning his gaze to the window as the countryside sped past in a blur of colors and shapes. Steam power had been harnessed—heat was converted to mechanical energy every day to move men and materials across the whole of England. Edmund, Finch and others were capturing *light* with their cameras. Feats which had once seemed impossible were now becoming rather ordinary, but that was in the realm of physics. Finch was right: he had no notion how to solve problems of sentiment.

He turned away from the window. Lacking a better reply, he said simply, "Perhaps."

A note waited for Edmund when they arrived at his London residence on Curzon Street. His parents were in Town for his mother's painting exhibition, and they'd brought his grandfather to consult with a physician. Edmund was invited to call on them at Ashford House at his earliest convenience.

———

EDMUND CHOSE TO walk the short distance to Albemarle Street. Despite recent rains that had washed the cobbled streets to leave behind the scent of late summer flowers, he couldn't help but notice the differences between London and Windermere.

An ever-present haze veiled the city, hanging low over the rooftops, and the occasional whiff of cigar smoke came from the exclusive gentlemen's shops. Gone were the sounds of the lake—the gentle lapping of water against the shore and the rustle of leaves in the trees overhead. They'd been replaced with the rhythmic clatter of carriage traffic and the lively hum of Shepherd Market and its vendors on the next street. The sounds to which he'd never given any thought before now seemed harsh and overloud.

He gave a coin to the crossing sweeper then climbed the steps to Ashford House. He didn't have long to wait in the expansive drawing room before his mother arrived with a footman pushing his grandfather's wheeled chair. Edmund relieved him of the task and assisted his grandfather to a comfortable place between the hearth and tea table.

"Darling," his mother said with one of her gentle smiles. She leaned up to kiss his cheek, and he knew an overwhelming urge to cling to her as he'd done as a boy. He pressed back the impulse and straightened.

"You're looking well, Mother. I hope your exhibition goes smoothly."

"It does, but I see you've a bit of outdoor color to your cheeks. I take it you passed an enjoyable time at Windermere?"

His grandfather cleared his throat. "More importantly, was your time there productive?"

The footman returned with the tea service, and some moments passed while Edmund's mother poured out a cup for each of them. Edmund ignored the dainty chair next to her for the sturdier seating of the damask couch. He longed for the easy comfort of Captain Thorne's Vicarage.

Ashford leaned forward expectantly in his chair, and Edmund admitted to himself that he was stalling. They'd asked about his time at Summerfield. "It was both pleasant and productive," he said. "I furthered my acquaintance with Miss Octavia Worth, a lovely lady of genteel birth."

"And she is agreeable to your suit?"

Edmund swallowed. "I believe she is amenable...." He recalled the uncertainty in Miss Worth's voice when he'd inquired about returning to Summerfield, and now he wasn't so sure.

"But?"

"But it occurred to me that perhaps I ought to have our Queen's approval *before* I make the lady a formal offer."

His grandfather frowned. "Is there anything objectionable about Miss Worth's character?"

"No. As I said, she is of genteel birth. Her father is Sir George Worth of Ambervale in Surrey. I believe your acquaintance, Lord Marbury, is a relation to Sir George's stepbrother."

"Marbury, eh? And Miss Worth meets Queen Victoria's other requirements—Church of England morals, no scandals to her name, et cetera?"

Jaw tight, Edmund replied. "Yes."

His grandfather straightened and slapped his hand on his knee. His frown turned to a youthful grin as he said, "Then that's that. Edmund, my boy, well done. I can't fault your prudence, but we should arrange an audience with Her Majesty as soon as may be done. You don't want to give your lady time to change her mind."

"No."

His grandfather motioned to the footman. "To my study," he said. Then to Edmund he added, "I'll just dash something off to apprise Her Majesty's advisers of the situation." Before Edmund could think of an argument against such a sound plan, the footman was wheeling his grandfather away.

Edmund looked down at the tea in his cup and wondered what Amelia was doing at that moment. Was she walking the fells with Lord Byron? She might be reading another of her favorite poets, perhaps, or writing in her journal. Would she write about him?

"Edmund."

He looked up to find his mother watching him,

and he forced a smile to his face.

"Darling," she said softly. "Do you recall the time you took my paints to your grandmother's new plaster in the morning room?"

He nodded warily, confused by the shift in topic. "The workers had missed a spot, and I didn't wish her to be disappointed."

"And the time you rearranged your father's library?"

"*Organized,*" he stressed. He hadn't yet been able to read all the scientific titles, so he'd organized the books by size and color. His father had *not* seen the genius in the new scheme.

"And when your cravat-retrieval device brought all of Ashford's linens down on poor Cranston?"

"That was a gravity malfunction," Edmund reminded her.

She chuckled then grew serious once more. "My point is this: you are the sweetest, most helpful of all my children—a statement which I'll deny if you ever repeat it to your sisters. But sometimes, your impulse to help others is to your own detriment. If the *only* reason you're courting Miss Worth is to aid our family"—she paused and swallowed—"that is, if you don't think you can feel a genuine affection for her, you mustn't proceed." She reached a hand up to cradle his cheek, and he allowed it. "I couldn't bear it if you were unhappy."

And yet, how could he possibly be happy if he chose his own desires over his family? He leaned into her hand just a little, though what he really wished was to lay his head on her lap and allow her to stroke his hair. "I will be happy, Mother."

Perhaps, if he said it enough, it would be true.

CHAPTER TWENTY-SIX

Octavia's chickens have come home to roost.
I expect she'll make a fine broth of them.
—From the private journal of Miss Amelia Thorne

SOME DAYS LATER, Amelia found her uncle alone, reading his paper in the breakfast room. She hesitated at the threshold before striding to the sideboard.

He glanced up and greeted her with a gruff, "Good morning."

"Good morning, Uncle."

She placed toast and marmalade onto a plate then took the seat to his left. He continued reading, though Aunt Mary expressly forbade newspapers at the table. Her uncle was probably taking advantage of her aunt's absence to do as he liked, and Amelia couldn't blame him.

But Aunt Mary's absence was the reason she'd tracked her uncle to the breakfast room.

"Aunt Mary won't leave her rooms," she said.

"It's probably for the best."

"It's been nearly a week. You're not concerned for her?"

"No, but it says much for your character that you are. She'll come out when her capacity for her own company has reached its end. I imagine it will be any day now." He looked up from his paper then and removed his spectacles. "I suspect her indisposition has as much to do with learning Octavia has been transacting business with Sir Frederick as it does with your situation."

Amelia's mouth fell open in surprise. "She knows about Sir Frederick?"

He nodded. Then, replacing his spectacles, he peered at her over the rims. "I know that despite your scandal, you've a strong sense of propriety, my dear. But I also know my daughter can't be swayed when she's set her mind to something, so I can only assume Octavia was alone in her mercenary endeavor."

"Octavia has a pure heart," Amelia said, "despite what she would have others believe. She only thought to aid me with some new gowns—"

"And a few for herself as well," he said with a sigh. "I'm not blind to my daughter's cleverness. But how are *you*, my dear?"

"Me?" Amelia blinked in surprise. Uncle George had long been a fixture at Summerfield, but never in her recollection had he inquired after her welfare. "I'm… well."

He looked relieved for a moment and then resigned. "You are not well. There's something… off… about you." He waved a hand to indicate her person, and Amelia glanced down to assure her buttons were straight. They were. Was her misery over Edmund so apparent then? She fixed a smile on her face.

Uncle George flinched, so she could only assume her smile more closely resembled a grimace. He studied her a moment longer before finally returning his attention to his paper. "I won't press," he said as much to himself as to her.

Amelia turned back to her breakfast to find she'd crumbled the corner of her toast to dust. Brushing her fingers on a napkin, she considered her uncle's bowed head.

After her father's death, she'd wondered if her uncle might make up some of the space he'd left behind. No man could have filled it entirely, but she'd never really given her uncle a chance. He'd been a necessary element in her life these past years, but one whose purpose had always had an end to it. And, if she were completely truthful, she'd bore him

a little resentment for his role in managing her inheritance, though it was through no fault of his.

She considered Edmund and the lengths he was
willing to go for his family. Perhaps it wasn't too
late to forge something meaningful with her uncle,
but to do so meant clearing the air between them.

Swallowing, she spoke. "Why do you think my
father placed my funds in your care for so long?"

Uncle George's frown was gentle but immediate.
"Why?" he repeated.

Amelia traced a finger over the pattern in the
damask tablecloth. "I passed my legal majority
some years ago, so I imagine he must have been disappointed with the disaster I made of my season.
Did he"—she paused to lick her lips—"did he think
I wouldn't be able to manage my affairs on my own
once I reached my majority?"

Her uncle leaned back in his chair. From the corner of her eye, she watched as he stroked his side
whiskers in what she considered his pondering pose.
Finally, he said, "Do not think your father thought
any less of you for your scandal. He arranged for
your guardianship long before your London season.
It was just after your mother passed, in fact. You
couldn't have been more than—what?—five or six at
the time, and he worried what would become of you
if anything should ever happen to him."

Amelia looked up sharply, the tablecloth forgotten. "Truly? He wasn't disappointed?"

Her uncle shook his head. "He thought your scandal was a ridiculous bit of nonsense, fluffed about by the papers for no other reason than a shortage of more salacious tales. But as for your inheritance, he wanted to know you would be cared for always, and never abused for your fortune." He looked down and swallowed, and Amelia thought she detected a tinge of color in his cheeks. "Though, to be sure, he should have considered his own sister's ambitions. My dear, you have my apologies again that I didn't realize what Mary was doing. It's clear now that I should have."

Amelia pulled in a slow breath as she turned over her uncle's words. Her father hadn't put her fortune into Uncle George's hands because he was disappointed in her. He'd been trying to protect her. The knowledge expanded inside her until she felt buoyant with it. She allowed it to fill her corners, savoring the sensation until the silence in the breakfast room had grown lengthy. Reaching across the table, she clasped her uncle's hand.

"Thank you," she said.

———

EDMUND FINISHED DEVELOPING his plates for the day and took down the red glass shade from his lantern. Light filled his laboratory-turned-darkroom, though the lingering smell of chemicals still hung in the air. He removed his apron then lifted a photograph from where it had been propped against an empty jar.

It was his portrait of Amelia, the day he'd found her playing her violin. He'd not been able to resist developing it after all, and now, the photograph was there to torture him each time he entered his darkroom.

Oh, there were other photographs to remind him of his time at Windermere—the first, ghostly image of Amelia walking the fells, for one. And Miss Worth's portrait had come out well, as had several images he'd taken of the crags and mists above the lake, but his final portrait of Amelia trumped them all.

He laid it gently atop the others. He really ought to send it on to Summerfield. There was no need to keep it. Perhaps, if Her Majesty approved his intentions regarding Miss Worth, he might take it with him when he returned.

At the sound of approaching footsteps, Blue lifted her head from the corner where she'd been sleeping. A knock sounded—Edmund's servants knew better than to throw open the door to his darkroom without admittance.

"Enter," he called.

"Are you at home to the Earl of Ashford?" George asked. His manservant maintained a rigid adherence to social protocol, as if Edmund would ever decline to receive his grandfather.

"Of course," he said, although he could already hear the impatient wheels of Ashford's chair. His grandfather appeared, driven by a footman. Blue stood, and her tail wagged in recognition of the new arrival. His grandfather had a bit of color to him today and a sharpness to his gaze, and Edmund wondered if the news of his matrimonial prospects had had a restorative effect.

"Grandfather, you're looking well today. Should we adjourn to my study?"

"No, no. It's been some time since I've seen your laboratory. We'll talk in here." He motioned to the footman to leave them.

Edmund wheeled his grandfather into the room and answered questions about his work as Ashford examined the instruments lining his shelves.

Finally, Ashford got to the heart of things. "Victoria's advisers have agreed to an audience, Wednesday next," he said.

"So soon." At his grandfather's frown, Edmund said, "That's good, isn't it?"

"I understand Her Majesty is anxious to quit the city, but the summons is for you alone."

"I will manage it," Edmund assured him.

Ashford nodded. "I know. Now, tell me more about your Miss Worth. Were the reports of your prospects helpful to your cause?" There was a sparkle in his eye as he spoke, and Edmund tilted his head in surprise.

"The speculation in the papers—that was your doing?"

"I might have let a detail or two slip about your circumstances." At Edmund's frown, Ashford added, "It wasn't as if you could go about telling people you're my heir, but I figured it couldn't hurt your matrimonial endeavors if there was a bit of speculation roaming about. But," he said with a roll of his hand, "you were about to tell me more of Miss Worth."

Edmund swallowed. "There's not much to say beyond what you already know. She's the only daughter of Sir George Worth and Lady Mary Worth. You'll find her charming and an easy conversationalist, I believe."

"Yes, yes, but what is she *like*?"

Edmund tucked his chin, uncertain what his grandfather wished to hear. "Well… she's elegant, I suppose, and possessed of fine manners."

And then, before Edmund could think anything of it, Ashford reached for the Windermere photographs on his worktable. He lifted the portrait of Amelia and angled it toward the lantern light.

"Is this her?"

Blue, sensing a change in the atmosphere, moved closer and pressed her body against Edmund's leg.

"No. That is her cousin, Miss Thorne." Edmund tried but was unable to keep the emotion from his voice.

"A cousin, eh? This Miss Thorne has an air about her, doesn't she? A certain…"

"Light," Edmund finished. "She has a light about her." He closed his mouth firmly before he could utter any more nonsense.

His grandfather considered him for a long beat. Both his tone and his words were skeptical as he said, "So, Miss Thorne casts her light on Windermere, if I understand you correctly. And yet, you choose Miss Worth for your bride. May I ask why?"

Drawing a breath, Edmund explained that Amelia's family connections were not as illustrious as the Queen required for the future countess of Ashford.

"But she's niece to Sir George Worth," Ashford said.

"Her father was a ship captain engaged in trade, her mother, an Irish seamstress before she married. And a Catholic."

"Ah."

Edmund hesitated before adding, "And there's a bit of a cloud attached to Miss Thorne." He described the circumstances leading up to Amelia's scandal, finishing with, "The gossip rags were jubilant over the matter and took to calling her the Poisoned Thorne—you've probably come across the cartoons in the papers."

Ashford nodded slowly as he searched his memory, and then his eyes widened in recollection. "Oh, yes, I see what you mean. Of a certainty, she won't approve such a female." There was regret in his tone, but he held his gaze steady on Edmund's—whether to gauge Edmund's understanding of this incontrovertible fact or to impress upon him the importance of it, Edmund couldn't say.

He searched his photographs for the portrait of Miss Worth. Finding it, he handed the card to his grandfather. "This is the lady I mean to marry."

Ashford took the portrait of Miss Worth and held it next to Amelia's. Though there were some vague similarities between the cousins, the portraits highlighted one glaring difference. Where Amelia's spirit reached out to the camera with a bright and open energy, there was quite a bit of Miss Worth that she concealed. Edmund felt as if his soul knew Amelia's from some far-off, long-ago place, but he wondered if he'd ever know more of Octavia Worth than she wished him to.

The silence lengthened until his grandfather said, "If not for our Queen's mandate, would you still choose Miss Worth?"

Edmund busied himself arranging his trays and wondered why his grandfather wouldn't simply let the matter go. Edmund had made his choice, and Ashford ought to be pleased with it. Nothing would come of belaboring the matter. Still, he felt compelled to justify his decision, to himself perhaps, if not to his grandfather.

"Miss Worth has many admirable qualities, and she's possessed of a charm and intelligence that will serve our family. I expect she and I will get on well together."

His grandfather's cheeks puffed on a sigh. "Do you love her?"

"Love will come."

"Perhaps."

His grandfather's weak agreement was disheartening. Then Ashford asked the question Edmund had been hoping to avoid. "Do you love Miss Thorne?"

His stomach twisted with an uncomfortable heat—a reaction, no doubt, to holding the truth in so tightly. Finally, he settled for another truth. "My feelings for Miss Thorne are irrelevant."

His grandfather tapped a blunt finger on the padded arm of his chair, thinking. "So, you love Miss Thorne, but do you love her enough to defy your Queen? To forsake your family legacy?"

Edmund started as if his grandfather had struck

him. That Ashford could even think Edmund would consider such a course caused a tightness to grip his chest. He opened his mouth then stopped, as there was no answer that would serve. To say *no* was to deny the depth of feeling he had in his heart for Amelia, but to say *yes* was to cast his family and their legacy aside.

Like gravity and magnetism, the forces of his life were pushing and pulling him in opposite directions.

In the end, his grandfather answered for him. He spoke slowly, as though he were working it out for himself as he did so. "No. I can see it's not about whether you love her *enough*. But to choose your own heart over your family—that is not who you are. To act in such a manner would rend you in two."

Edmund cleared his throat and assured his grandfather once more, "I will do my duty."

"I know," Ashford said, the quiet simplicity of the words doing nothing to ease the pain in Edmund's chest. "You have always been honorable and devoted to our family. But..."

Edmund's brows dipped into a steep V. "But?"

His grandfather's gaze roamed the darkroom, taking in Edmund's notebooks and jars and instruments. "We are problem solvers, you and I. Apply a bit of logic to the matter. Perhaps you'll discover another solution we haven't considered yet."

Edmund rubbed a hand over his face wearily. "We've considered this problem from all angles, Grandfather. I can't imagine another solution exists. Queen Victoria will not approve Miss Thorne, no matter how prettily we dress her background up."

Cocking a brow at Edmund, Ashford mused, "Can you marry the one and keep the other on the — No, I can see from your expression that option holds little appeal."

"That option is not an option at all."

"Just so. Then do what you do best, Edmund. Consider the variables and challenge your assumptions, but do it quickly. Wednesday will be upon us soon."

Ashford rapped on the door and his footman appeared to wheel him out. Long after he'd gone, Edmund stared blindly at the wall of his darkroom and turned his grandfather's words over.

Night came and he missed his supper.

Challenge your assumptions.

He'd assumed Amelia would not be suitable, that Her Majesty wouldn't be able to overlook the scandal attached to her name or her background. He'd assumed that the saving of the earldom must rest solely on him. If he could overturn one of these assumptions, could he secure Amelia's hand *and* preserve his family's legacy?

Could he truly have both?

Edmund closed his eyes, considering his dilemma, and the first tiny flash of an idea came to him. He thought on it longer until the flash began to burn brighter.

He would need help, but it went against every grain of his being to ask his family for anything. It had always been that way, though they would never begrudge him.

But his mother was right. He was the son, the brother, the grandson who offered his aid, who sought ways he might improve his mother's day or ease his father's worry. It pleased him to do so. He *loved* that they relied on him.

But he loved Amelia more.

The task of saving his family's legacy needn't rest solely on him. The hope he'd barely allowed himself to feel slowly worked its way beneath his skin until, with a new, surging energy, he strode to the door and wrenched it open.

"Finch!"

"Here, sir," Finch said from where he balanced on his crutches not two paces away.

The hall was dark, save for a single sconce burning near the stairs, and Finch's jaw was shadowed with stubble. "What time is it?" Edmund asked.

"Nearly two in the morning."

His valet deserved an increase in his salary.

Edmund resolved to see to it.

"Is my sister in Town?" he asked.

Finch's brows lifted at the unexpected question. "Which one?"

"Aster. No, Helen—it doesn't matter. Are *any* of my sisters in Town?"

"I believe Eloise has removed to the country, but Aster and Helen remain for your mother's exhibition."

Edmund inhaled then gave Finch a determined nod. "Send round word in the morning that I mean to call. I've an important question to put to them. And get some sleep, Finch. You look like hell."

CHAPTER TWENTY-SEVEN

EDMUND'S SISTERS REQUIRED some convincing—or rather, a lot of it—once he told them of his plan. His grandfather required even more. There was no assurance their Queen would agree to the scheme, after all, and Edmund didn't think his plan was quite what Ashford had in mind with all that "challenge your assumptions" business.

His mother, though, offered one of her soft smiles of approval. "You've always had your father's genius," she said. But she was his mother and required by the office to say such things, so he didn't let it go to his head.

Wednesday came sooner than he would have liked, and yet, not soon enough.

The heavy curtains of his bedchamber were drawn open, and the sun cast its cheery glow about the room. Blue opened one eye to watch him from her cushion before the hearth. Edmund wished he could share her easy composure. As it was, his nerves were raw and unsettled for what he was about to do.

In the back of his mind, lay a tiny bit of uncertainty. Amelia had already refused him once before, and rather easily. He fervently hoped her affections for him were as strong as his for her. He counted on it, in fact, but deep beneath his planning and plotting, he worried. What if, after everything, she still wouldn't have him?

He swallowed and examined his freshly shaven jaw in the mirror of his shaving stand. Finch, who'd finally left off his crutches the day before, held up two waistcoats for Edmund's inspection. One was a finely tailored piece in white embroidered silk, and the other, an equally suitable choice in black velvet.

Edmund cast a discreet glance at his grandfather's valet, who nodded his approval for Finch's selections. Cranston had taken up a nearby chair to supervise the whole endeavor while Ashford watched from a warm place near the fire.

Though Edmund could well dress himself for the average social engagement, an audience with the Queen was another matter altogether. Ashford was leaving nothing to chance, and Edmund, who didn't wish anything to ruin his plan, was grateful for it. It wouldn't do to breach palace protocol before he'd even put his proposal to Her Majesty.

"The white, I should think," Edmund said.

"Very good," Finch replied. "I've also set out your coat—a silk-lined black, to be worn unbuttoned, of course, single breasted, with a stand collar and pointed pocket flaps. There's gold embroidery on the collar, cuffs and flaps, with gilt convex buttons. You'll wear trousers of a matching cloth with one row of gold lace sewn down the sides."

Edmund's brows lifted at this surprisingly detailed accounting.

"At Mr. Cranston's recommendation, I have been reading *Dress Worn by Gentlemen at Her Majesty's Court*," Finch explained, to which Edmund could only nod mutely.

"And for accessories," Finch continued, "I've set out your black beaver, unless you prefer the cockade. Sword and belt with a silk shoulder and frog of the same color as the coat. And of course, your best white gloves and a white neckcloth."

Edmund angled a glance toward the mirror to catch another approving nod from Cranston.

"Nicely done, Finch," he said.

Finch preened at the praise, or as much as a man of his size could be said to preen, and went about collecting the approved items from Edmund's dressing room.

Moments later, Edmund surveyed himself in the mirror. He'd shined his spectacles and his hair had been tamed with a bit of pomade. The crisp folds of a white neckcloth lay evenly against the silk waistcoat, and a dress sword hung at his side. If he were to fail today, it wouldn't be for a lack of dash.

He reached for the photograph on his bedside table—Amelia's portrait—and tucked it into his coat. To his surprise, Finch didn't frown his disapproval but offered him a whispered, "Good luck, sir, and Godspeed."

"You say that as if I'm riding off to do battle."

"Aren't you?"

Edmund considered the carefully plotted strategy he'd devised with his sisters and grandfather. Perhaps Finch had the right of it. "Thank you, Finch."

"Edmund," Ashford said.

Edmund strode across the room to his grandfather. He'd worried over what effect his plan might have on his grandfather's health, but Ashford seemed to sit a bit straighter in his chair. His eyes— a clear blue that shone with just a hint of moisture—

were steady on Edmund as he cleared his throat. "We are the protectors of our family's legacy," he reminded Edmund.

"Yes," Edmund began, but his grandfather held up a hand to stay his words.

"I have loved your grandmother these fifty years and more, and together, we have loved your mother and your father and now you and your sisters."

Edmund frowned, uncertain of the direction of his grandfather's speech.

"*That*," Ashford continued, "is a legacy worth preserving."

"Grandfather?" Edmund said, not comprehending.

"Don't mistake me. The title and lands are important, but they're not the only measure of wealth. They shouldn't come at the cost of denying my descendants the chance to know the love I have known. It's my most ardent wish that you receive our Queen's approval, but if you do not, I accept that."

A ponderous weight lifted from Edmund's chest—a weight he'd not even known existed until it was gone. For the first time in months, his breath came easily, as if he'd come up for air after long minutes under water. He drew a long inhale, filling his lungs, and released it slowly. Then, eyes burning, he said hoarsely, "I will honor our family."

"You already have, my boy. You already have."

———

BUCKINGHAM PALACE'S CREAMY limestone exterior gleamed in the afternoon sunlight, and flags bearing the empire's colors fluttered atop their poles. Edmund passed through the gated entrance and ascended the imposing staircase. The dress sword was an unfamiliar weight at his side.

He handed off his card to a court page in royal livery, and after some moments of consulting a large, leather-bound ledger, the page bowed and led him along a grand corridor. Edmund's shoes sank into the plush carpets as they marched toward the audience chamber.

The air was heavy with the scents of history and wood polish and the whispers of courtiers. After some twists and turns, they reached a tall set of double doors guarded by a stately Lord in Waiting. He took Edmund's card from the page, consulted another list, then acknowledged Edmund with a nod. Edmund adjusted his cuffs as the man opened the doors and announced him to their monarch.

The room was awash in the glow of three massive gaslit chandeliers, and crimson velvet drapes and full-length portraits adorned the walls. At the end of the room sat the Queen. Her smooth chestnut hair was impeccably styled, her complexion fair and radiant above a sumptuous gown of burgundy silk and lace. Courtiers in lavish garments ringed the space behind her as Edmund approached.

Only four years separated them, but it might as well have been forty for the gap in their stations. Edmund knew a sharp moment of uncertainty. Was he foolish to desire love? A simpleton to think their Queen, with her vast empire and endless responsibilities, would see matters of the heart in the same light?

Then he thought of Amelia and decided if he were a fool, he would be a happy one if all went according to his plan. His heart quickened with equal measures anticipation and resolve as he executed a deep bow.

"Your Majesty, it is an honor to come before you. May I express my family's deepest gratitude for this audience?"

Her Majesty acknowledged him with a regal nod, her expression poised but welcoming. "Mr. Corbyn, the pleasure is mine. What news have you for my court today?"

The courtiers' whispers faded as they attended their Queen's conversation with hushed interest. Queen Victoria's gaze was steady and discerning as she waited for Edmund to speak.

"I have found the lady I wish to marry."

The Queen dipped her head. "You have my congratulations. What lady has this honor?"

Drawing a steadying breath, Edmund replied, "Miss Amelia Thorne, if she'll have me."

"I'm unfamiliar with the name. Has she been presented to my drawing room?"

"I do not believe so, but her uncle is Sir George Worth of Ambervale in Surrey." He withdrew his portrait of Amelia from his coat. "With your permission, I should like to show you a photograph."

A small frown drew her brows together, but she nodded. Edmund extended the portrait, and she studied Amelia's likeness. After a long moment, she asked, "And what does your Miss Thorne have to recommend her?"

"She is intelligent and compassionate. Her virtue is unparalleled, and her spirit shines like the brightest star. I am humbled by the prospect of calling her my wife, with your esteemed approval, though I know it will not come easily."

Her Majesty's eyes narrowed at that last bit, and one of the courtiers approached to whisper in her ear. Queen Victoria straightened. "She is the one they call the Poisoned Thorne?"

"She is, though I assure you the name is unfairly earned. I've come to inquire if it might be possible for Your Majesty to overlook such a trifling scandal."

She didn't reply but posed another question. "Who are her parents?"

Edmund explained Amelia's origins, and his stomach twisted uncomfortably as Her Majesty's frown grew.

"You must know she is not a suitable countess for the Ashford earldom," she said, and Edmund swallowed. "Perhaps one of these marks against her could be overlooked, but not all of them. My requirements were very clearly stated."

"They were," Edmund agreed.

Her gaze went to the photograph again. The image was a compelling one, and despite her royal authority, the Queen did not seem immune to its pull. It was as Edmund had expected.

"You were the photographer?" she finally asked.

"I was."

She returned Amelia's portrait to him. "You are very talented, to have captured her love for you so clearly."

Edmund started. "I beg your pardon, Your Majesty. Her love?"

"It fairly… glows in her expression. I don't think another photographer would have achieved the same likeness." Edmund's heart lifted to think Amelia's love for him was so apparent. Her Majesty continued with a question. "Do you share a similar depth of feeling for her?"

"She is the beacon of my existence," Edmund said simply. "The star that illuminates my every thought. In her presence, I feel the most profound joy and purpose. Miss Thorne is not only the woman I wish to marry; she is the very essence of my happiness and the source of my deepest affections. Though I don't claim to know Your Majesty's heart, I suspect my love for Miss Thorne is not unlike your own affection for His Royal Highness."

With a barely perceptible sigh, she said, "A very pretty speech, Mr. Corbyn. So, you would marry without my approval? You would forsake centuries of the Ashford legacy?"

"I hope it does not come to that."

"I don't see how we can avoid such an outcome if you're determined to have this woman as your wife. I am not insensitive to your depth of feeling for her, or hers for you, but having made my requirements clear from the outset, I cannot approve such a match."

Her denial was no less than Edmund had expected. He steeled himself and, jaw tight, he said, "Then Your Majesty, might you consider an alternate proposal?"

CHAPTER TWENTY-EIGHT

AMELIA CLIMBED THE path that ran beneath Dragon's Breath Crag, and then she climbed some more. It was only when Lord Byron cast her a look of dubious concern that she relented and turned them toward home.

Her heart was lighter for having taken a stand with Aunt Mary and for her uncle's revelations. To know that her father's decision around her guardianship had come *before* the disappointment of her scandal caused no shortage of relief to swell within her. It was unexpected but not unwelcome.

So yes, her heart was lighter, but… wobbly as well. As if it couldn't quite find its footing. It awaited only Edmund's return for his doomed proposal to

Octavia. When Octavia declined his offer, he would leave to find a suitable bride somewhere else, and Amelia would mourn his loss all over again.

And she would regret—again—that she'd refused him.

Octavia would never have done such a pea-brained thing, and Amelia lamented that she wasn't as bold as her cousin. That she'd not seized her happiness with both hands while she had the chance.

Whenever her thoughts traveled this path, her better sense reminded her that the reality of Edmund's situation couldn't be ignored. She'd done the right thing to refuse him—for them to marry would mean the loss of his family's legacy, and she'd not have that on her conscience.

A ground mole crossed the path ahead of them and dashed into a nearby thicket. Lord Byron gave a short, delighted bark as he dove after it, and she envied his easy satisfaction.

Why could she not be content with all the blessings laid before her?

Summerfield and the Vicarage were hers, their sunny reading spots ready to claim at will. She had Windermere, with its sparkling surface and enigmatic mists and unpredictable rains. Wordsworth and Keats and Shelley. Emerson's bookshop and Octavia's company, for now at least. Any of these should have been enough, but to have all of them… there was no reason she could not be content in her life.

She would fill her days with reading and writing in her journal and walking about the lake. She would take baskets to the poor, and perhaps she might teach at the school in Bowness. Yes, she thought she could do that very easily. Why, she might even try her hand at writing her own poetry. She had no illusions she'd be as brilliant at it as Mr. Wordsworth, but there was no reason she couldn't attempt a few verses of her own.

And she would make calls. Not so many to limit her time at the Vicarage, of course, but she would add a bit more human interaction to her days. She would not allow one mistake five years before to dictate her future.

Lord Byron emerged from the thicket with brown leaves and bits of twig dotting his white coat. His quarry had eluded him, but he panted his pleasure with the chase as he rejoined her on the path. When they returned to the Vicarage, he would curl up before the fire, pleased with today and unconcerned with tomorrow.

She could do as much. She *would* do as much. Her heart would not shatter. It might feel pinched or bruised. It would certainly skip a beat at seeing Edmund again, but it would survive. *She* would survive. But why did survival have to feel so… weepy?

——

EDMUND LEFT BLUE and Finch in London and re-traced his journey back to Windermere. The trains were slow and his impatience was high, but he used the time to read. And when he finished *The Prelude*—all fourteen books of it—he began again.

He smiled as he ran a finger over one of Amelia's notes. Her enthusiastic script covered the margins of nearly every page. She'd not exaggerated when she told him she'd found many favorite places to mark.

He also used the journey for another purpose; drawing a folded bit of paper from his pocket, he studied what he'd written. The page was something of a mess, with words hastily scratched across it then marked out, and creases where he'd nervously folded and unfolded the paper. The business of poetry was not as easy as it appeared.

The train's whistle sounded as it pulled into the station at Birthwaite. He folded the paper once more and tucked it back into his coat. He hired a carriage, and the same driver from his last journey recognized him.

"Aye! You're back again, then."

Despite the nerves writhing in Edmund's belly, he smiled. "I am."

The driver looked behind Edmund. "You came without all your fancy boxes this time. You'll just be needing t'one carriage?"

"Just the one."

"To Summerfield then?"

Edmund drew a long breath and nodded. "To Summerfield."

The Westmoreland scenery must have passed beyond the carriage window, but Edmund didn't notice any of it until the glimmer of Windermere caught his eye just before Bowness. He pushed the curtain aside for a wider view, hoping to see Amelia but knowing it was unlikely. If she were out walking, she'd be hidden somewhere along the narrow paths above the lake.

He had the driver stop at the Crown in Bowness, where he arranged for a room at the inn before returning to the carriage. Soon, the driver pulled onto Summerfield's gravel drive and stopped below the steps. Edmund climbed down, his palms damp despite a chill breeze that blew in from the west.

The carriage rolled away and he knew a moment's uncertainty. What if Amelia and her family were away from home? Perhaps they'd gone visiting. What if—

His thoughts were cut short as the double doors opened and one of Summerfield's servants appeared at the top step. And then, directly behind him, came Miss Worth. She dismissed the man, and Edmund smiled up at her.

The last time he'd seen Miss Worth, he'd asked her if he might return. His implication then had been clear, and he'd known this moment would be awkward. He'd even spent some time on the train preparing a pretty speech in his head.

"Miss Worth," he began.

"Have you come for your favor at last, Mr. Corbyn?"

Edmund faltered—he'd all but forgotten about her favor.

Miss Worth gave him a dismissive laugh as she came fully onto the portico and closed the doors behind her. "Oh, do say you've come for my cousin."

Edmund tucked his hands behind his back and cleared his throat as relief coursed through him. "Yes."

"Thank the heavens you're not the dolt I feared you were," she said, which was hardly flattering.

"Thank... you...?"

She came down the steps, looped her arm through his and began walking. "As you might have guessed, my cousin is out there somewhere." She waved a hand vaguely toward the fells. "Her habit is to go directly to the Vicarage after one of her rambles. You might wish to await her there."

Edmund looked up to see she'd led them some distance down the path toward the hunting lodge. Its familiar entry was a comforting sight, but his manners had him hesitating. "I should make my presence known to your mother and father first."

"I advise against it," she said. "*That* is my favor to you. Speak with Amelia and then, when the matter is a *fait accompli*, present yourself at the house. My mother will be distraught over my failure to land you, of course, but I believe my father will be pleased with this turn."

"I don't want to cause you any trouble—"

"Pish." Then, peering more closely at him, she added, "You *have* come to secure my cousin's hand in marriage, have you not?"

"It is my most fervent wish, if she'll have me." He wondered if Miss Worth would take offense at his words. It wasn't that long since he'd given her every indication he meant to make *her* his wife, but she merely tossed another question at him.

"And regarding the matter of your family legacy and whatnot—Amelia satisfies your requirements?"

"In every way."

Miss Worth's gaze, which had been rather intent up to this point, softened and a slow smile came to her lips. "Mr. Corbyn," she whispered, "you make me almost wish you'd come for me." Then, with a brisk wave toward the Vicarage, she added, "Well, then. In you go."

———

AMELIA DESCENDED THE path that ran behind the Vicarage and turned her feet toward the hunting lodge. An afternoon curled on the library's chaise with her books was just what she needed to set her heart aright. Or, if not *aright*, at least it might smooth the rough edges of her emotions.

She opened the door and Lord Byron bowled ahead as though he feared she might steal his favorite spot. Shaking her head, she closed the door behind her then frowned as Lord Byron gave an excited yip. Had a field mouse found its way into the library? She groaned. She'd have the devil of a time removing the thing and calming Lord Byron.

She strode down the corridor and stopped short at the library. Her heart skipped ahead and she blinked, uncertain if her eyes deceived her. But no, Edmund was truly here. He crouched before the window, lit from behind by the afternoon sun as he gave Lord Byron's belly a scratch.

Amelia's breathing increased its pace, as did her pulse. Had he come for Octavia already? But why was he at the Vicarage?

He looked up at her entrance. "Miss Thorne," he said, standing to his full height. There was an endearing formality to his tone, and the rich quality of his voice puddled in her stomach like warm chocolate. With a steadying breath, she took in his strong jaw and the dimple in his chin, the blue-green hue of his eyes beneath his dark brows.

"Mr. Corbyn. You've returned. Did you leave something behind?" *Stupid, stupid.* Of course, he'd meant to return. For Octavia.

"I did. Something I fear I cannot live without."

Amelia's pulse leapt. He wasn't speaking of Octavia. She knew it, though if pressed, she wouldn't have been able to explain *how* she knew it. "I'm certain my aunt would have been happy to send… whatever it was… on to London," she said. Then she cursed her tongue.

"I would not trust this matter to anyone else. It's far too valuable."

"Mr. Corbyn, please stop speaking in riddles." Amelia folded her hands before her and waited, breath tight in her chest, for him to say what he meant to say.

He crossed the carpet, Lord Byron at his heels, and took her hands in his. He'd removed his gloves, and the delicious warmth of his skin on hers was a welcome comfort after the brisk air from her walk. His large hands engulfed her smaller ones, and she allowed herself a moment to indulge the feeling. Peace and joy and comfort all fought for a place alongside the thrilling anticipation his touch brought. She reminded herself to breathe.

"I've left my heart, Amelia." Her own heart turned a somersault to hear her name on his lips again. "It's *you* I cannot live without."

"Oh," she breathed.

"I know you refused me once, but I mean to plead my case more earnestly, if you'll but give me the chance to get it all out this time."

Amelia pulled her hands from his. The loss of his warmth was knife-sharp as she reminded him, "I would make a horrid countess, and you require someone more suitable—"

"There you go… interrupting a perfectly sound proposal again. But to address your point, *you* suit me very well."

Amelia's eyes widened. She wanted desperately to believe him, but though her scandal might fade in time, nothing could change her parentage. She'd never be a suitable bride for the heir to an earldom.

He kept his gaze fixed on hers as he reached into his coat and withdrew a worn piece of paper. He opened it, and she could see marks where it had been folded and unfolded many times.

"I finished *The Prelude*," he said, "and though I cannot ever hope to match Mr. Wordsworth in verse… well. Perhaps it's best if I just read. This is titled, *The Bright Thorn*."

Amelia pulled in a sharp breath. He'd written her a poem! Her heart thumped a frantic drummer's beat. "What—?"

He placed a gentle finger over her lips to silence her. She inhaled once more to collect herself then gave him a short nod. He cleared his throat and began to read.

"Though winds may blow and storms may rage,
The thorn stands firm, its strength engaged.
Defiant 'gainst the tempest's tides,
In noble love, its heart resides.

Through misty dawn and twilight's gloom,
Amidst the field where colors bloom,
With vibrant light and beauty shown,
My bright thorn, alone, is known."

Amelia opened her eyes, unaware that she'd closed them. Edmund looked sheepish as he refolded his paper and put it away.

"It's a bit rough around the edges," he began, "and all the bits in between," he finished with an endearing grin.

She couldn't disagree. On the whole, it was rather… well… dreadful. But that final line was absolute perfection. *My bright thorn, alone, is known.* How perfectly he'd captured her. Oh, how perfectly he *knew* her. How perfectly he'd claimed her for his own.

"It's beautiful," she breathed, her voice catching. "But your grandfather… your family's legacy—"

"Is no longer an impediment."

She considered his words for a moment then gasped. "What have you done?" she asked as dread settled in the pit of her stomach. No matter how noble the sentiment, if he'd forsaken his family, he would surely grow to resent her for it. But he only grinned, unrepentant, and Amelia pressed shaking fingers to her mouth.

"I have done the only thing I could," he said simply. "I have relinquished the earldom—"

"Oh, Edmund!"

"—to my sister."

Amelia pulled her head back, frowning. "What? What do you mean?"

"My eldest sister, Aster, is married to a former army captain who served admirably in India. Aster is amenable to becoming a countess in her own right, and Queen Victoria approves the scheme. Aster and Andrew have two sons, ready-made heirs, so to speak. Her Majesty has already amended the letters patent and put her seal to them. It is done." His smile grew, and it lit his eyes.

Amelia pulled in a long breath. "You would give up your future as the earl? What of your children and their future?"

"*Our* children, if we're so blessed, will have riches aplenty. They'll have our love." Amelia swallowed around the lump in her throat. "Does it concern you that I won't be titled?" he said. "That we'll live a quiet life as a scientist and his wife?"

"No, of course not. It's only a bit of a shock that you would do such a thing. What—what if I were to refuse you?"

Edmund took her hands in his again. "That is a gamble well worth the risk because I love you, Amelia. I love everything about you—your spirit and your intelligence and the fact that *you* love poetry so much that you named your dog Lord Byron. Do you think—that is… do you feel the same?"

There was a long pause as Amelia considered him and all that he'd told her. She was certain her heart had ceased its beating sometime during his speech. *Seize your happiness with both hands.*

Edmund might be a fool to give up his future for her, but she wasn't. She'd not let another chance at happiness escape her. Tears stung her eyes as she said, "I do, Edmund. I do love you."

His grin grew as he pulled her toward him. He wrapped his arms about her then, lowering his head with delicious intent, he kissed her.

EPILOGUE

I gazed—and gazed—but little thought
What wealth the show to me had brought.
— William Wordsworth, Daffodils

SEVEN MONTHS LATER, SPRING

THE SLOW GLIDE of the oars propelled the little rowboat through Windermere's moonlit waters. Edmund leaned back in a familiar, easy rhythm, pulling the oars with smooth strokes as they neared their destination. Across from him, Amelia carried a thick wool blanket on her lap, and a lantern and hamper of food sat at her feet. The lantern was turned low as moonlight spread over the lake's surface like an ink spill to light their way.

Edmund admired his wife, seated demurely on her bench. Her hair was uncovered—at this hour, there was no one about to see them—and her hands rested atop the blanket, fingers plaited together. Her neck was long and elegant above the lace edging her bodice, and her eyes caught and held the moonlight as she watched him row.

He still thought she would have made a fine countess, but to take her to Kent—to separate her from Windermere—would have been to separate the stars from the sky.

"Why do you look at me so?" she asked.

"Why would I not?" Marriage, it seemed, had turned him into a puddle of warm sap.

His wife's lips curved into an easy smile. "I had a letter from Octavia today," she said, neatly turning his thoughts.

"Oh? Does she enjoy her season in London?"

"I think the more apt question is, does London enjoy Octavia?"

He laughed. "Do you think she'll make a match this year?"

Amelia arched a brow in near-perfect imitation of her cousin. He interpreted it to say, *Octavia will marry when it amuses her to do so.*

"Just so," he said. "And your aunt and uncle? Do they get on well?"

"Octavia writes that we may expect a petition for an increase in my aunt's allowance, unless Uncle George catches it in the post first."

Lady Worth, whose hopes for her daughter's future as Countess of Ashford had been hard to dislodge, had initially opposed Edmund's marriage to Amelia. Sir George's approval, though, was easily won. Recognizing defeat was at hand, her aunt finally came around. Octavia reported back that her mother was now fond of boasting to new acquaintances of her connection to "my niece, Amelia Corbyn—she's wed to the Earl of Ashford's grandson, you know."

Following Edmund and Amelia's marriage, the Worths had removed to their home in Surrey. Though Edmund had come to like Sir George, he'd never been so pleased to see the back of anyone before. He and Amelia spent the first week of their marriage ensconced at the Vicarage, opening the door only to admit servants bearing food and coal from Summerfield.

Since then, they'd roamed the fells together with Blue and Lord Byron. And, given Amelia's new family connection with the Earl of Ashford, the local ladies had begun to pay more calls.

Amelia balanced her at-homes with regular trips to Emerson's bookshop and Edmund, with his wife's help, had established the old gardener's shed as his permanent laboratory and darkroom. He and Finch progressed bit by bit in their experiments for capturing color. Advancements were made in the field of photography every day, and color couldn't elude them forever. Perhaps one day, they might even find a way to capture motion. The thought was a heady one, and Edmund's oars faltered briefly.

They glided past St. Mary Holme with its chapel ruins. Amelia sat straighter on her bench as they neared the twin islands to the west. "You're taking us to see the lilies? That is your surprise?"

"That is my surprise."

"You remembered," she said in wonder as she gazed at him down the short length of the boat.

"I remember everything you've ever told me," he said in mock affront.

"You didn't recall that we'd accepted Lady Staveley's invitation to dine at Stonecroft last week," she said teasingly.

"That wasn't poor memory but a bit of strategic ignorance," he clarified. "I'd much rather dine alone with my wife."

"Hmm… and perhaps work on your new formulas with Finch."

"Perhaps," he agreed.

"I think Windermere suits you," she said. "But are you certain you don't miss London?"

"Not a minute of it." Blue was content, and though she was slowing with age, she'd roused herself to swim in the lake a few times. He missed his family on occasion, but each of his sisters had paid them a visit, and shortly after their marriage, Edmund had taken his new bride to meet his grandparents in Kent. They'd been easily charmed by Amelia and she by them, and they'd left with promises to return again in the summer.

He guided the boat toward a bit of open beach, where the night air carried the warm scent of woodland blooms. Edmund stepped out and secured the craft on the sand before reaching for Amelia. He lifted her easily with both hands and settled her on dry ground. She held him a little longer than necessary to gain her footing, and he took the opportunity to press his lips to hers. She was warm and firm in his arms, and she tasted delightful. It was some moments before he lifted his head again.

He retrieved the hamper of food, and Amelia turned up the lantern to guide their steps. She tucked her free hand in his and together, they wound through the sand and beach grasses and up a narrow path. Somewhere, a night bird called to its mate.

Soon, they emerged at the top of a small woodland of oak and ash, and Amelia gasped at the sight before them. Edmund grinned at her obvious pleasure. A sea of tiny white blossoms carpeted the ground beneath the trees, silver and luminescent in the moon's beams, heads nodding gently in the breeze. The grass was heavy with dew, and here and there a firefly flickered.

"Edmund," Amelia breathed as she dimmed her lantern, "isn't it the loveliest thing you've ever seen?"

"Not by half," he said softly, looking at his wife.

She tapped his forearm reprovingly. "Look," she commanded, and he did. "It's even better than I imagined it would be. It's…"

"Poetry?"

"Precisely. It's poetry without words."

Edmund couldn't think of a better description for the view that stretched before them. He set the hamper down, and they spread Amelia's blanket at the edge of the woodland, careful not to disturb the flowers.

With the lilies' radiance lighting the ground and their sweet fragrance perfuming the air, Edmund gathered his wife in his arms. Together, they stared out at the night.

THE END

THANK YOU!

Subscribe for updates at klynsmithauthor.com/sotf (or scan the QR code below) and receive exclusive access to the online album featuring some of Edmund's Windermere portraits.

Other subscriber benefits include early sneak peeks of upcoming releases and the sweet Regency novella, *Discovering Wynne*, where a lady innkeeper gets a second chance at love with the smuggler who's always held her heart.

AUTHOR'S NOTE

I create a mood board of the visual references I use when writing. If you would like to see my inspiration for Edmund, Amelia, Blue and their environs, please check out my Pinterest board.

Stars of Twilight Fair is a book of fiction based on events, attitudes and practices of the period. Below are some of the themes that influenced this story, as well as a few Easter eggs for those of you fond of hunting them.

*** SPOILERS AHEAD ***

Letters Patent. Fans of Jane Austen-era fiction may recognize the Earl of Ashford's dilemma. Like Mr. Bennet and Sir Walter Elliot, Ashford had a daughter but no sons to inherit. Unfortunately (or fortunately, for purposes of this story), he didn't have any living male cousins, nephews or siblings, either. His problem became readily apparent to me, if not to readers, with *The Astronomer's Obsession*, and I wondered how it all might eventually play out. And thus, the seeds for *Stars* were sown.

Enter the letters patent. In the context of the British peerage, these are the legal documents, generally issued by the monarch, that grant and define noble titles and privileges and outline the terms of inheritance and succession. Unless the patent allows the title and estates to pass through the female line (which is uncommon), an amendment is required to modify the terms.

The 18th-century Marlborough dukedom is one example from real life. The patent originally provided that the dukedom could be inherited by the heirs male of the body of the first duke, Captain-General Sir John Churchill. After both of the general's sons died, though, the patent was amended, and Marlborough's daughter, Lady Godolphin, became *suo jure* Duchess of Marlborough in 1722. A peeress "in her own right" or *"suo jure"* holds her title independently of her husband with all the associated rights and privileges.

Edmund's Light Perception. Edmund's "affliction" may be a form of synesthesia, a neurological condition in which stimulation of one sense activates another, unrelated sense. A person may hear colors, see sounds, taste numbers and so on. Emotional synesthesia manifests as visual experiences in response to different emotions. It's estimated that about four percent of people have some form of synesthesia.

Not surprisingly, many synesthetes have found their calling in the arts—Vincent Van Gogh, Duke Ellington, and Billy Joel, to name a few. And yes, Franz Liszt.

Color Photography. Experiments in color photography began as soon as the first photographs were taken. Early color images were achieved primarily through hand coloring or taking multiple exposures with different filters, but these were complex and time-consuming processes with limited success.

It wasn't until the Lumière brothers shared their autochrome process in the early 1900s that color photography took off on a commercial scale. The autochrome combined the filter screen and photographic emulsion on the same plate, and the rest was history. Edmund was certainly onto something.

If you're interested in knowing more, the UK's Science and Media Museum has an excellent brief history of color photography.

Cambridge Connection. There are some very subtle connections between the characters and Cambridge University. Edmund attended Cambridge, which was his father's alma mater in *The Astronomer's Obsession*. Cambridge was also the alma mater of

William Wordsworth. He was an undistinguished student who felt he was "not for that hour, nor for that place" (*The Prelude, Book II*). Further connection can be found in the annual boat race between Cambridge and Oxford, in which Edmund and Temple competed during their time at university. The annual tradition was started in 1829 by William Wordsworth's nephew, Charles Wordsworth, while *he* was at Cambridge.

The Word "Photograph." Etymonline.com reports the word used to describe a picture obtained through the process of photography was first coined in 1839 by photography pioneer Sir John Herschel, son of astronomer William Herschel. Yes, the same William Herschel who inspired Ashford and Harry Corbyn's very large telescope in *The Astronomer's Obsession*.

Victorian Tourism & Windermere. The Lake District became wildly popular as the Romantic poets and artists of the early 19th century found inspiration in its serene waters and rolling hills. Later, when the advent of the railway made travel more accessible, tourists began flocking to the Lakes in greater numbers.

I've tried to depict Lake Windermere and its surroundings as they would have appeared at the time of this story. Despite Amelia's disdain for guide-books of the area, a number of them were invaluable in providing a glimpse of the lake's tree-fringed shores and pebbly bottom as well as the eighteen-ish islands or *holmes*. (Holme is the Norse word for "island.") The Lilies, a pair of islands decorated with wild lilies of the valley, were favorite destinations of tourists, who used to row out to pick the flowers.

By the way, don't go looking for Dragon's Breath Crag, as it exists only in my head. If you *do* find it, please send pictures.

And… More Easter Eggs. A couple more for readers of *The Astronomer's Obsession*: In addition to his synesthesia, Edmund also gets his blue-green eyes and his liking for sweet buns from his mother. Lady Celeste's depriving Ashford of his breakfast sausage at the start of this story is reminiscent of a similar scene in TAO when *her* mother did the same with a glass of wine. And, yes, Edmund's lament that Finch can't tie a proper knot is a sneaky little nod to his father's struggles with his own cravat in TAO.

Did you catch others I may have forgotten?

BOOKS BY K. LYN SMITH

Something Wonderful
The Astronomer's Obsession*
The Artist's Redemption
The Physician's Dilemma

Hearts of Cornwall
Discovering Wynne (Prequel Novella)
Jilting Jory
Matching Miss Moon
Driving Miss Darling
Kissing Kate
Saving Miss Swan
Charming the Captain
Engaging Miss Enderby
Regarding Rebecca

Love's Journey
Star of Wonder*
Light of a Nile Moon*
Stars of Twilight Fair
Beneath a Brighton Sun*

* These stories feature other members of the Corbyn family, including Edmund's parents Harry and Celeste (The Astronomer's Obsession) & sisters Aster (Star of Wonder), Helen (Light of a Nile Moon) and Eloise (Beneath a Brighton Sun).

STAR *of* WONDER

A HOLT MEDALLION FINALIST

Enjoy the following excerpt from Aster Corbyn's story, *Star of Wonder*. Here's how readers have described this Victorian holiday novella, in which a soldier returns to claim the lady of his heart before she marries another :

"Sweet and deep characters you can't help falling for. Excellent read." —Books You Can Feel Good About

"Everything I want in a historical Christmas story" —@kindlesallthewaydown

"Such vivid characters… a truly delightful read." —Goodreads reviewer

"Pairs well with a crackling fire, cozy blanket, and warm beverage" —BookSirens reviewer

Letter from Andrew Grey to Miss Aster Corbyn, crumpled and dashed upon Miss Corbyn's hearth then hastily retrieved and smoothed upon her desk:

8th January 1839
Cavalry Barracks, Hounslow, London

Dear Aster,

I realize not more than forty-eight hours have passed since I left you in Kent, but I write to fulfill my promise to keep you apprised of my situation (insomuch as my post allows). My post. The words make me smile, and I can hardly believe I've been so "utterly beef-witted" (as you succinctly put it) to cast my lot with Her Majesty's finest, although you have to admit, the scarlet coat does lend a certain dash.

My incredulity is matched only by yours, I suspect. And possibly that of my parents.

At any rate, my company remains in England until the end of February, so you see, we're not so distant from one another yet. Keep watch on our star and I shall do the same.

Yours,
A

REPLY FROM MISS ASTER CORBYN to Andrew Grey, tear-stained:

10th January 1839
Redstone Hall, Kent

Dear Andrew,

I stand by my earlier assessment: you are an utter beef-wit to leave me so unexpectedly (although I reluctantly thank you for your diligence in keeping me apprised of your situation). Your mother's eyes grew suspiciously damp when I mentioned your name at tea, and I harbor only the tiniest bit of guilt in bringing it to your attention.

Not so fondly,
A

LETTER FROM ANDREW GREY to Miss Aster Corbyn, also crumpled and flung upon Miss Corbyn's hearth before being tucked into her writing desk:

29th January 1839
Cavalry Barracks, Hounslow, London

Dear Aster,

I write with exciting news: our departure has

been accelerated. By the time you receive this, I will have sailed for India.

I've had occasion to speak with a number of fellow soldiers who have returned from that exotic land, and my enthusiasm only grows for the adventure that awaits. Worry not; I shall write and share all the details.

Have you returned to London yet for the new term? I'm certain your teaching post will keep you so thoroughly occupied you'll hardly know I've gone.

Indeed, the months will fly and before you know it, we shall see one another again.

Yours,

A

PS: Never say you're still put out with me. I couldn't bear the loss of my Faster Aster's affection.

REPLY FROM MISS ASTER CORBYN to Andrew Grey, also tear-stained:

31st January 1839
Mrs. Ivy's School for Girls, London
Dear Andrew,

You've truly gone then? I am still put out with

you, but as you say, my teaching post does keep me quite busy. So much so that I hardly have time to think of you at all. Despite this (and in case you're unable to decipher the true nature of my feelings), I miss you dreadfully. Your smile and your laughter make my heart sing. Ironically, England is greyer with one less Grey. Please return safely, and soon.

Your friend,
A

LETTER FROM ANDREW GREY to Miss Aster Corbyn, stained a questionable shade of brown:

30th June 1840
Custom-House, Calcutta, India

Dear Aster,

We depart Calcutta soon and journey to Cawn-pore, which is seven hundred and fifty miles distant. I'm told that's more than the entire distance from the northern tip of Scotland to the southern coast of our fair country, although it spans but a mere frac-tion of this land. We're to travel by way of the Hooghly and Ganges rivers over the course of four-teen days. I believe that equates to a rate of fifty-four miles per day. (You may confirm and correct my calculation if need be. I suspect you will have already done so by this point.)

Thank you for sending the chart, so I might find our star in this unfamiliar sky. I continue to watch it and am comforted to think of you doing the same.

Yours,
A

PS: Please excuse the coffee stains. My companion, Lieutenant Monty Doyle, is not the tidiest of bunk mates.

LETTER FROM MISS ASTER CORBYN to Captain Andrew Grey:

5th December 1841
Redstone Hall, Kent

Dear Andrew,

I can hardly fathom you've been gone for nearly two years. I write from Redstone Hall, where I've returned to spend Christmastide with my family. My parents and sisters arrived two days ago, and my brother Edmund came down from school only this afternoon. I know you would be amazed at how much he's grown!

Today, of course, is the eve of St. Nicholas, and as always, there is an air of excitement about the Hall that is unique to this time of year. (Never mind that all of us are too old to believe any longer in the "magic" that brings sweets and coins to our shoes while we sleep. My father must persist in perpetuating the myth and we persist in indulging him.)

You have my congratulations on your well-deserved promotion to the rank of Captain. Although, if you've gained it in the same manner in which you achieved your supposed victories in our childhood games... Well, I shall say no more on *that* subject.

It relieves me to know you're safely arrived in Bombay; your account of the perils along your journey lifted the hairs on the back of my neck. I continue to watch our star and pray for your safety, if no longer your swift return.

BOMBAY, MAY 1844

ANDREW STIFLED A GROAN AS the doctor left his bedside to tend the rest of his patients. The stench of blood was sickening and inescapable, and he feared he might embarrass himself once again. He swallowed back the bile in his throat.

A man moaned to his left. He imagined most of the fellows to either side of him had been attacked by tigers (in the plural) or run through with the tip of an enemy's blade. Certainly, none had been so beef-witted to mangle themselves on a *tree*. Sweat beaded his lip and fever burned his brow, but none of that was anything to the lance stabbing his leg.

Dr. Heyworth couldn't have any more years than Andrew's own two and twenty. The fellow seemed tolerably well versed in general anatomy, but he certainly couldn't boast the expertise or experience of Andrew's physician father or his surgeon mother. Certainly, he inspired neither trust nor confidence. Why, the man's hand had *trembled* as he'd inspected the torn flesh of Andrew's thigh, and Andrew had found only marginal comfort in the presence of an older gentleman at Heyworth's elbow, a mentor of sorts.

"Be sure to leave enough skin to cover the stump," the mentor had said. Heyworth nodded uncertainly at this counsel before leaving Andrew to his rampaging thoughts.

He squeezed his eyes shut. When he opened them again, the shadow of Montgomery Doyle darkened his narrow cot. Monty removed the cheroot from between his lips and frowned.

"Ye have to be the most fortunate man I've ever had the, er, misfortune to meet, Captain. We all thought ye were done for when the cliff fell away."

"King?" Andrew's voice was a rough croak that

sounded nothing like him.

"Your horse is fine," Monty said, his Irish brogue making *horse* sound like *arse*. "It took some doin', but with ropes and patience, he was fished up."

Andrew nodded. That was some small comfort. Their company had traveled a good distance from their planned route so they might cross the rain-swollen Godavari. King had confidently picked his way along the edge of a precipice until the sodden ground gave way beneath his hind legs.

His mount had made several honorable attempts with his fore feet before falling backwards, and Andrew had awakened some thirty feet below, wedged in a thorny tree without any recollection of how he'd gotten there. His horse, to his relieved surprise, had been stopped by another tree some fifteen paces further below.

Monty snuffed his cheroot on the floor before adding, "Ye were not so easy to fetch up. Of the two of ye, I'd say your horse was the more agreeable to our noble efforts on your behalf."

Andrew scowled at his friend and tried to call up a suitably sarcastic retort, but the effort died beneath the agony-tinged haze fogging his brain.

Monty reached into his coat and extracted a stack of letters. "I retrieved your post, by the by," he said. "Ye've received a few letters from England. These" — he squinted — "are difficult to decipher, but the frank is from London."

His mother. Her penmanship had always been abysmal.

"But this one has promise. The script is neat and precise. It's definitely in a lady's hand." Monty lifted the missive to his nose and sniffed. "'Tis a pity the crossin' is so long. I imagine it must've smelled nice once."

Aster. Andrew closed his eyes again. Even without the scent on the letter he could still recall her soft, lemony fragrance.

She'd written him faithfully for five years. He'd considered cashing out and returning to her—many, many times—but he wasn't ready. He wasn't the man she deserved yet. And now, with his leg wrapped in blood-soaked linens, he was even further from his aim.

"Would ye like me to read it to ye?" Monty asked with an eager waggle of his woolly brows.

"No," Andrew grumbled as a rivulet of sweat slicked down his cheek. His whole body was afire, heat radiating from his leg to his fingertips. Even his eyelashes felt hot. He reached within himself for the devil-may-care attitude he was known for, but it eluded him.

His insouciance had seen him safely through his twenty-two years—up to this point, at any rate. As a boy, it had poked and teased at Aster until she held her sides with laughter. And then, it had made the years of separation from her bearable.

But now, that character was so distant from him as to be another person entirely. In his delirium, he saw himself shriveling into an embittered and humorless man with naught more than a stump for a leg. *That* was not the man for Aster.

And that was enough of a rallying cry to bring him back to himself. "Monty," he grunted. "Don't let them take my leg."

His friend's thick brows lifted before collapsing across the bridge of his nose. Monty lowered his voice to say, "The sawbones says there's nothin' to be done. If they don't take the leg, it'll fester and ye'll probably die."

"Probably?" Probably was not certainly.

"Ye'll die, Grey."

"Don't let them take the leg, Monty. If you allow it, I'll retrieve it from the rubbish bin and beat you about the head with it."

**You can find *Star of Wonder*
in paperback and eBook formats.**

ABOUT THE AUTHOR

K. Lyn Smith's heart resides in Birmingham, Alabama, where she writes sweet historical romance about ordinary people finding extraordinary love. Her debut novel, *The Astronomer's Obsession*, was a finalist for the National Excellence in Romantic Fiction Award, and many of her other titles have been shortlisted for honors such as the American Writing Award, the Carolyn Reader's Choice Award, the HOLT Medallion and the Maggie Award.

When she's not lost in the pages of a book, you can find her with family, traveling to far-off places and binging period dramas. And space documentaries. Weird, right?

Visit www.klynsmithauthor.com, where you can subscribe for new release updates and access to exclusive bonus content.

9 781737 657996